"I never

He stood before the o[...]
his dark hair, brighte[...]
shadow. "I took one look at you and I bolted."

"You ran?"

"I'd ventured halfway down the street this morning before I realized my foolishness. I invited you out here, and yet I am terrified of you. You're young and pretty. From your letters, I expected someone different. Older."

"I'm not all that pretty." Libby spoke up, touched by his words. "I just want a home. A real one."

Jacob Stone remained silent, staring out the window, still and motionless. "I can't give you what you want." He didn't turn to look at her. "We've spent over six months corresponding. That amount of time should tell you right there how unsure I am of making a marriage again."

Grief haunted his words, and the echoes of that grief hung in the air like the thick Montana dust. Libby wanted to reach out and comfort him, but how could she?

It was not her right.

Dear Reader,

March is the time of spring, of growth, and the budding of things to come. Like these four never-before-published authors that we selected for our annual March Madness Promotion. These fresh new voices in historical romance are bound to be tomorrow's stars!

Among this year's choices for the month is *The Maiden and the Warrior* by Jacqueline Navin, a heartrending medieval tale about a fierce warrior who is saved from the demons that haunt him when he marries the widow of the man who sold him into slavery. Goodness also prevails in *Gabriel's Heart* by Madeline George. In this flirty Western, an ex-sheriff uses a feisty socialite to exact revenge, but ends up falling in love with her first!

Last Chance Bride by Jillian Hart is a touching portrayal of a lonely spinster-turned-mail-order-bride who shows an embittered widower the true meaning of love on the rugged Montana frontier. And don't miss *A Duke Deceived* by Cheryl Bolen, a Regency story about a handsome duke whose hasty marriage to a penniless noblewoman is tested by her secret deeds.

Whatever your tastes in reading, you'll be sure to find a romantic journey back to the past between the covers of a Harlequin Historical.

Sincerely,

Tracy Farrell, Senior Editor

Please address questions and book requests to:
Silhouette Reader Service
U.S.: 3010 Walden Ave., P.O. Box 1325, Buffalo, NY 14269
Canadian: P.O. Box 609, Fort Erie, Ont. L2A 5X3

LAST CHANCE BRIDE

JILLIAN HART

Harlequin Books

TORONTO • NEW YORK • LONDON
AMSTERDAM • PARIS • SYDNEY • HAMBURG
STOCKHOLM • ATHENS • TOKYO • MILAN
MADRID • WARSAW • BUDAPEST • AUCKLAND

ISBN 0-373-29004-7

LAST CHANCE BRIDE

Copyright © 1998 by Jill Strickler

JILLIAN HART

currently lives near Phoenix, Arizona, but as a Washington State native feels very much out of her element. The desert is beautiful, but she misses the rain. She feels the value of a good rainy day is the opportunity to curl up in a comfortable chair with her twenty-pound cat on her lap and read the day away. Now she's learned to read in the sunshine.

When she isn't reading the day away, Jillian likes to spend time with her husband, whom she met on a blind date set up by a mutual friend nine years ago. It was love at first sight, and she's been living happily ever after since.

To my husband,
who did the dishes so I could
write this book.

Thanks.

Chapter One

Montana Territory, 1866

Where was Jacob Stone?

Her heart tight, Libby searched the knot of the small crowd. Strangers surrounded her, but she saw no sign of Jacob and his child in the hustle of this busy post. Surely they had not given up on her. Surely they remembered she was arriving today.

Disappointed, Libby stepped away from the stagecoach, patting at her wilting hair. She must look a fright. The ride overland had been dusty and dirty, not at all kind. Her best dress was wrinkled and dust stained, her wheat blond hair sliding into her eyes. She felt like a rag used to scrub a particularly filthy floor, all wadded up in the bottom of a sodden bucket. Hardly an attractive appearance for a prospective bride.

Perhaps Mr. Stone had taken one look through the confusion of the crowd and run for the hills at the sight of her. She feared he could see beyond her new dress, soiled as it was, to the real woman inside, to the very reason why she had to answer a man's advertisement for a wife instead of finding a husband on her own.

She felt a rush weaken her knees, and heat crept up her face. Surely he would not run off without a word. He couldn't. She needed to meet him, to know if he would be a good man to marry. From his thoughtfully penned letters, he seemed so gentle. A man who would make a good husband and father, a man worth traveling so far to meet. That is, if he decided to show up.

Placing a hand to her stomach, Libby eased through the excited crowd, past those greeting newly arrived loved ones, and walked quietly to a lone bench fronting the station. Her hopes began to wane. The blistering heat of the late August sun bore down on her, even on the partly shaded bench, and she sat baking like an egg on a frying pan.

"There she is, Pa!"

Libby turned toward the child's excited voice. The spindly girl skipping across the dusty road had to be Emma. Libby's heart twisted hard at the sight of the beautiful child. The child who could become her daughter.

Her hand to her heart, Libby stood through the long seconds it took for the girl to dash across the street.

"It *is* her! I knew it!" Emma skipped to a hoppity-stop, her twin braids bobbing too, and tipped up her face. Bright blue eyes shone like the sky overhead and her sweet smile stretched twice as wide. "You *have* to be Miss Hodges!"

"Yes, I am. I'm so pleased to meet you, Emma." Libby managed a wobbly smile. She could only stare at the little girl dressed in a crisp red calico dress. Twin brown braids pointed stiffly over her shoulders, adorned with matching red ribbon.

"We've been waiting for *hours* for the stage to come."

Libby laughed, delighted. Already she adored this small girl, not more than six years old, whom she read about so hungrily in Jacob Stone's letters. She wanted a home and a family, but had not imagined having such a wonderful stepdaughter.

"I saw so many interesting things on the stagecoach here," she said now. "I saved up all the memories to tell you about."

"Did you see any Indian ponies?" the girl asked.

"Yes, and even the Indians sitting on them." Matching Emma's smile, Libby's mouth stretched painfully. She'd been so worried traveling so far from civilization—and feared she was making the worst mistake of her life. Anything could happen. Jacob Stone could be a drunk or a brutal man. But seeing this child reassured her. Anyone could see how well cared for she was—and what a good father Jacob Stone must be.

"Miss Hodges?"

The sound of a man's voice—of his voice—sliced through her joy, making her nervous all over again. Libby turned, feeling so small and inadequate as she looked up into the gray eyes of a tall man, into eyes as deep as a winter sky. A gentleness lived there, and she knew him at once.

"You're Jacob."

He bowed his chin, and his firm mouth lifted in the corner; an attempt at a smile. Her heart thudded against her breastbone. Her knees trembled. This handsome man, so powerfully built and confident, was more than her dreams. Her gaze roamed over his wide shoulders—over nice, dependable shoulders.

He cleared his throat. "You arrived safely, I see. Heard there was Indian trouble."

"Nothing serious at all." Libby shrugged. She'd been so ill during the journey, she'd hardly noticed the danger. "I was afraid you weren't coming."

The smile slid from his firm mouth. "I'm a man of honor, Miss Hodges. I said I would be here, and I am."

He was kind and strong and honorable. Anyone could see it. Libby's throat filled. She had not been wrong in traveling so far. He was so much more than she expected, than she deserved.

"I like your hat," the girl said.

"Thank you." Libby murmured the words, placing a hand to the brim of her straw poke bonnet. The nervousness in her stomach eased. It was going to be all right. "Maybe I can make you a hat just like this."

"Could you? Please?"

Emma clasped both hands, and Libby melted. "I'd be happy to."

"Emma, go with Jane. Now. She'll take care of you while I speak with Miss Hodges alone."

The stern words made Libby wince.

"But—"

"Do as I say, now."

The brightness slipped right out of Emma's blue eyes and she trotted away, glancing back wistfully before joining up with an elderly woman who waited beneath a green-striped awning. The two walked away together, young and old, and Libby watched as some emotion tugged to life inside her. The child and woman entered one of the many storefronts and disappeared inside, out of the glaring heat of the brutal sun.

"I don't want you making promises to my daughter."

"I didn't mean to. I just thought—"

"Emma lost her mother. I don't intend to allow her to be hurt like that again."

"Of course not." Libby stood, pulse racing and speechless. A hot breeze tugged at her skirt. She'd angered him without meaning to. Did he have a quick temper? Without the gentleness shining in his eyes, he looked formidable, almost frightening. "I would never want to hurt Emma."

His gaze skirted over her. "You seem sincere. You seem everything I had hoped you would be."

"Everything?" He hardly knew her, but surely that was a good sign. She needed a home and a husband. Her hand strayed to her stomach.

He shrugged one powerful shoulder. "I suppose I'm leaping ahead of myself. I should fetch your bags and get you settled. You look exhausted, and we have much to discuss."

Libby watched, breath held, as he turned, his navy blue shirt and his black trousers casting him as if in shadow. He walked out onto the boardwalk and snatched up two lone carpet bags. "I assume these are yours?"

"Yes." Libby quietly followed the strong-shouldered back of Jacob Stone down the dusty street to the neatly painted hotel.

It was going to work out. It had to.

She'd never told a lie in her life, and she wasn't sure if she could do it now. Guilt weighed down her step as she slipped through the glass door Jacob held open for her. Her elbow brushed his arm, and she caught a pleasant scent of wood smoke.

Jacob Stone was a good man, polite enough to hold the

door and treat her like a lady. Anyone could see it. Her stomach tightened. He didn't deserve being deceived.

It took her a moment to adjust to the change of light inside the hotel. Her eyes saw only momentary dimness, but she still detected the sound of men's voices and the solid scent of tobacco. Libby followed Jacob Stone into a front lobby where a large glass window gazed pleasantly out at the dirt street.

Could she live with a lie? Could she look this good and honorable man in the eyes—and she knew this about him from his thoughtful letters and these first few minutes in his presence—and make him live a lie too?

"I brought you here so we could talk quietly," he began, his voice rumbling low. He settled his large frame into a flowery wing back chair, so big and powerful he looked out of place in the dainty furniture.

She could see him better in this soft light. Heavens, he was a handsome man. Thick jet-black hair peeked out from beneath the narrow brim of his modest hat and cascaded over a tall, square forehead. Equally dark brows arched over his cool gray eyes. His straight nose slanted down a chiseled face that had been weathered by time and sun and cold. The face of the man she wanted to marry.

It had to work. It just had to. Libby clung to that belief, choosing a chair opposite him. The loud men's talk rising from the bar, the ring of the bell at the front desk, and the drum of her nervous heart faded as his gray gaze snared hers.

Time stopped and Libby saw only her future. He simply had to like her.

"I suppose we need to get right to the point," he began, his voice quietly controlled. "We've corresponded. Now we have met. Are you comfortable with the idea of marrying me?''

''Yes.'' Libby bit her lip, catching it between her teeth. It took all her willpower to keep her voice low. She feared her whole heart showed in her words. ''I—I will do my best to make you and Emma happy. You have my word.''

''Good.'' His smile, slow and endearing, revealing the tender man she'd known through his letters. ''This is awkward, speaking with you in person. We are still strangers in many ways.''

Her heart twisted. ''Yes. But you don't feel like a stranger to me.''

''Or to me, either.'' His smile deepened, carving handsome lines into his face and reaching his eyes. ''I want to be honest. There were many things I couldn't say to you in a letter. Although I tried.''

''What things?''

Jacob Stone watched her pale face grow paler beneath the straw brim of her plain bonnet. Her soft blue eyes widened with alarm.

Damn, he knew this wouldn't be easy. Jacob tore his gaze from her pretty face and stared hard at his big hands. ''I don't know how to begin. I should just say it.''

''You've changed your mind?'' A hint of panic vibrated in her soft voice.

He shook his head. He wanted to change his mind, Lord knew. He didn't want to involve his heart with another woman. And he wouldn't. ''No, my mind is set. I want to marry again. Emma needs a mother to care for her, not a hired woman, but someone who will love her.''

''Yes, I know. I read your letters, Jacob—''

''You don't know,'' he corrected, holding himself rigid

in the uncomfortable chair. Her eyes glimmered with hope; he could see her heart shining there. It wasn't right and it wasn't fair. "I asked you to marry me for my daughter's sake."

"Yes, I—"

"Not for mine." His heart broke as understanding struck her like a slap to the face. Her jaw slackened, and she looked lost.

"You don't want me." Her blue gaze met his without accusation, but puzzlement. "You proposed to me."

"I offered an arrangement."

"You said your Emma needed a mother. I thought—" She stopped. "I don't understand."

Jacob closed his heart against memories sharp enough to tear him apart. "I want you to know this right from the start. I want there to be no misunderstandings between us, only honesty. You will be my wife in name only. Not in my heart and not in my bed."

Elizabeth Hodges glanced up at him, white as snow. Guilt tore through him. How did he tell her what Mary's death did to him? Every day had been a battle, from morning until late at night, living without her. He would never give his heart again. Not even to a pretty, slender woman with eyes as blue as morning glories.

"But what about children?" A tiny wrinkle frowned across her forehead, half hidden by the scatters of wheat blond curls escaping from beneath her bonnet.

"I have one child too many." Tiny, helpless dependent creatures who could steal a man's heart. He couldn't bear that. "I wanted you to know how it is with me right up front. I never meant to deceive you."

"You could have told me." She stared hard at the old

reticule clutched in her lap. "I know you are widowed. I understand it might take time to finish grieving, even to build a relationship between us."

"That isn't what I want."

Beneath the starkness in those gray eyes, Libby caught sight of a kindness, a decency that gave her pause.

Jacob Stone possessed the integrity she had so hoped he might have. She imagined he failed to speak of the death of his wife in his letters because of deep personal pain, but he did so now for the sake of honesty. She respected him for that, even if it left her alone and ashamed. Hadn't she considered deceiving him?

Then he stood, the starkness gone from his eyes and a gentle softness shaping his mouth. He held out one big hand, strong and callused from honest work, and she gave him hers. Her belly twisted, low and pleasant.

"Let's see about getting you a room."

Jacob helped her to her feet, and Libby could not stop the awareness trickling through her. Her fingertips tingled long after he'd released her hand.

She needed to marry and she wanted him for her husband. But when she looked into his eyes, she saw a good and decent man still hurting from his wife's death. How could she deceive him? How could she tell him the truth?

Chapter Two

Libby waited patiently while Jacob checked her into the hotel, surprising her by paying ahead for the entire week. He stood solemnly, counting out bills.

Every worried knot inside her unraveled. He was an admirable man. Strong. Dependable. *He was a man strong enough to be tender.*

Last winter she had nearly dropped her newspaper at the sight of the advertisement. "Lonely widower seeks kind-hearted woman for mother to six-year-old daughter." Just the sight of those words gave her hope; a hope she needed so desperately. *Kind. Wife. Mother.* Images of a family fell into her mind like the snow from the sky outside the boarding house window.

She had hoped he would never have to know. *Honesty.* He wanted honesty between them.

"I'll take her bags," Jacob said in his low, rumbling voice that skidded down her spine like warm water.

Libby watched him thank the desk clerk. He was well-spoken and polite; she liked that. He ambled toward her, sure and powerful, and the sight of him made her stomach twist.

She followed him up the stairs and into the first room on the second floor. With every step she took, Libby knew she had to be honest with Jacob Stone. He deserved the truth.

He set the bags on the foot of the bed, and she closed the door. A question lit his gray eyes.

"You were honest with me," she said, clenching her hands together. She didn't want him to see how she trembled. "It's the least I can do for you."

"I see." He straightened, a wariness creeping into his face. "So, I'm not the only one with secrets."

"No." Libby squared her shoulders and met his unflinching gaze. What she had to say would not be easy. "As you suspect I am not an innocent."

He neither grimaced nor judged her. Jacob Stone merely dipped his head slightly as he answered. "That does not matter to me."

"Good, because there's more." She would tell him the truth, and he would leave. Libby stared hard at the plank floor. "I don't know, I mean, I'm not certain."

It's too early to tell.

"You don't want to marry me?" he asked.

She looked up into eyes filled with concern. His concern for her. She didn't want to say what followed. Best to just blurt it out. "I could be pregnant."

"Pregnant?"

"I'm not certain," Libby hedged. *He's going to leave me.*

But Jacob Stone said nothing. He stared down at his large, empty hands. Libby stood motionless, her heart thudding painfully in her chest. She thought of Emma and that big sparkle of hope in the girl's blue eyes.

"This is unexpected news." He spoke slowly, as if carefully weighing his words. "After all, we have been corresponding."

She could hear his condemnation. "I did not come here thinking I could pawn off another man's child on you." Although she had considered not telling him during the overland trip.

"I didn't think you would." Jacob Stone faced her, his gaze no longer averted but leveled powerfully on hers. At that moment Libby could not deny the physical strength in the man nor the emotional power she felt with the blast of that gaze. He spoke. "In your letters you led me to understand you had no other prospects for marriage."

"I have none now," Libby admitted sadly, feeling her heart drum ever harder in her chest.

"Not even with the man who may have fathered a child with you?" Jacob stepped closer, so close she could see the black flecks of color in his gray eyes and smell the leather and smoke scent of him.

"No."

"You could have written me about this."

"I didn't know what to say," Libby answered honestly. He looked both sad and angry at once with his thick fingers gripping the brim of his hat and his jaw set like stone. He would never understand. "You had the same problem, letting me believe you wanted a real wife."

He bowed his head. "Yes, I guess that's true. We're even then."

Silence fell between them like sunlight through the windowpanes.

Libby braced herself. "If you decide you no longer have any interest in me, I thoroughly understand, Mr. Stone."

There, she had said it. Those words had taken more courage than she knew she had.

Jacob Stone cleared his throat and didn't speak. After a quick glance around the room, he lowered his eyes. Libby watched him, clearly a proper, hardworking and decent man, who had no doubt caught sight of the wide bed in the exact center of the room. A bed she was also aware of.

What must he think of her? She looked at the plain quilted coverlet, once white and already yellowing. Did Jacob Stone look at that bed and wonder what kind of woman she was?

He strode across the small room and tugged open the window. A hot, dry breeze tumbled inside, but it was far from refreshing. The street noise from below blew in with the wind. Libby knew she would never be good enough for him, not now when he knew she had considered deceiving him.

"I never wanted a wife." He stood before the opened window, sunlight glinting on his dark hair, brightening it, and cast his face in shadow. "I took one look at you and I bolted."

"You ran?"

"I'd ventured halfway down the street this morning before I realized my foolishness. I invited you out here, and yet I am terrified of you. You're young and pretty. From your letters, I expected someone different. Older."

"I'm not all that pretty," Libby spoke up, touched at once by his words. "I just want a home. A real one."

Jacob Stone remained silent, staring out the window still and motionless, outlined by the distant blue-white peaks of the Bitterroot mountains. What was he thinking?

"I can't give you what you want." He didn't turn to look at her. He stood broad-shouldered, his muscled legs parted, his booted feet planted on the bare plank boards. "We've spent over six months corresponding. That amount of time should tell you right there how unsure I am of making a marriage again."

Grief haunted his words, and the echoes of that grief hung in the air like the thick Montana dust. She hated seeing him hurt. Libby wanted to reach out and comfort him, but how could she? It was not her right.

He turned, approaching, his jaw set, his gaze intense, a decision clear in his eyes. "Tell me something. Will he follow you here?"

"No."

"Then it is none of my concern." Jacob pinned her with his hard, assessing gaze. "You say you are not certain."

Libby blanched. "No. It is too early yet to know for sure either way."

"When will you know?"

It was such a private question, and while Libby wanted to say so, she also knew he was affected by the answer. "Soon enough, maybe this week."

"Fine." He frowned. Libby watched his gaze stray to her bags that were still on the bed where he'd left them. "You'll stay here until you know the answer to my question. We will make the appropriate arrangements then."

He hadn't sent her away outright. Libby's breath caught. "If I'm not...will you still wish to marry me?"

"I don't know." Jacob Stone pinned her with the full weight of his cool gaze. "I counted on this match working. Emma needs a mother. We've spent time exchanging let-

ters, and you've traveled all this way. I don't want to go
through that again.''

In those eyes Libby didn't see hatred or condemnation,
and it surprised her. Standing before him, aware of his
height and his breadth and his strength, she saw not his
handsomeness but the sadness in his eyes. And an understanding that touched her inside, in her heart where nothing
had touched her for years.

''Then there's hope?'' she asked.

''I have no promises to give you.'' Jacob shook his
head. ''You put me in an awkward situation. I don't know
how Emma will take this if you have to leave.''

He didn't want her now. Libby closed her eyes, tears
hot beneath her lids. *It was over.*

She heard the sounds of the door opening, of Jacob
Stone's boots striding out into the hall, of the door closing
and latching. But when she opened her eyes, Libby still
hoped to see him standing there at the window, a man with
honesty and compassion ringing in his voice.

Who was she fooling, Libby asked herself. Anyone
could see she'd ruined her chances of marrying Jacob
Stone. She brought up her unvirtuous situation. She caused
him to be angry and forced him to walk out on her.

Anyone could see he wasn't coming back.

Jacob pounded down the stairs and through the lobby,
out into the glaring summer heat, inwardly cussing himself
for what he'd done. But any way he looked at it—whether
Elizabeth Hodges was pregnant or not—she was not the
woman he wanted to raise his daughter.

He marched down the long boardwalk, dodging Mrs.
Holt carrying packages out of the mercantile, hardly aware

of the traffic on the street and the ever present buzz of the sawmill at the end of town.

He didn't know her well enough to expect her to show up pregnant. No, *possibly pregnant.* She didn't even know for sure.

Then why the hell did she have to tell him?

Because she was an honest woman.

"Pa!" Emma hopped out onto the boardwalk in a swirl of red calico. "Where's Miss Hodges?"

Jacob's heart wrenched at the sight of hope so bright in his daughter's blue eyes. "She's in her hotel room."

Better Emma know nothing of the type of woman who stepped off that stage.

"Doing what?"

"Unpacking. Resting from her long trip."

Emma sighed, sounding disappointed. "She's still comin' to supper, right?"

Jacob felt the weight of the little girl's hope settle on his shoulders. His heart wrenched. "I'm not sure, Emma."

"But you promised." Her quietly spoken words struck him like an ax.

"Yes, I guess I did." He had so little to give her. How could he go back on his promise?

Emma's sweet smile stretched across her small face. "Pa, I want just one more thing."

"One more thing?" He rolled his eyes, teasing. "I'm afraid to ask. What is it?"

She giggled. "I just want some new hair ribbons for tonight."

"Whew. I think we can do that. Have Jane help you."

"Oh, Pa. *Thank you.* I have to look my best for Miss

Hodges.'' Her entire heart shone in those words. She spun away, dashing back into the store, braids flying.

He couldn't disappoint Emma. Yet he couldn't allow her to be hurt, either.

Jacob stepped out into the street and gazed back at the hotel. How could Elizabeth go and ruin everything?

Libby sank onto the soft mattress. She did the right thing, she knew it. Whatever lay ahead, she had faced her greatest fear. Now she could face herself. A lightness settled across her shoulders, and she felt calm for the first time in weeks. *She'd done the right thing.*

When Jacob had written, asking her to marry him, she sat and cried over what she'd done. She feared she could never face him, nor tell him the truth about what happened. But as the long hours passed and the night deepened, Libby began to hope. Maybe it could still be. Maybe Jacob need never know. Perhaps she wasn't pregnant.

Libby had clung to that belief during the trying journey west, but as the nausea hit, she feared it was more than travel sickness. And she told herself it would be all right.

Except now he didn't want a wife in the real sense.

Libby closed her eyes. She never meant to deceive him. She just wanted to love this man, the Jacob she'd created in her mind. She so wanted him to love her. Even now, she could not let go of hope.

She could not bear to think she had lost him.

Late that afternoon, washed and changed and nervous, Jacob took a step closer to the door and hesitated, standing like a fool in the middle of the narrow hotel corridor. Emma was home with Jane. A meal would be waiting.

What would he say? He didn't want to talk about it. He didn't want to face the pretty and fragile woman he'd come to know through her letters. The woman he'd made up in his mind, so gentle and quietly humorous, would not have slept with another man.

Anger thudded in his chest and he almost turned away. But he'd promised Emma. The remembered hope in her blue eyes kept him from running out of the hotel. He lifted his fist and knocked.

"Who is it?" asked a quiet voice through the wood door. Elizabeth's voice.

"It's Jacob."

The door swung open to reveal her thin, pale face. Kind blue eyes met his and he felt the impact straight to his gut. He caught a whiff of rose water, sweet and light, saw the careful coronet of tightly plaited braids crowning her head, heard the gasp of her breath telling him he'd surprised her.

Hell, he surprised himself.

"Can I come in? I want to talk with you."

"Yes." Slim, graceful fingers gripped the edge of the door, pulling it open, allowing him room.

He wanted to hate her for her duplicity. It would be easier if he could. Jacob slipped past her and stood in the middle of the room, the bed between them.

Elizabeth carefully pushed the door to, but not shut. Silence settled between them. He fingered the hat he gripped in both hands.

"Jacob," she began. She looked breakable. "I'm sorry about this. I need you to believe that."

Sincerity burned in her eyes. He looked away. "I gave you a surprise, too. I'm sorry about that. I should have told you, I should have prepared you. You came all this way with expectations about a marriage and a family I can't meet.''

She blinked, embarrassment pinkening her pleasant face. ''I'm the one who is wrong.''

He couldn't answer her. It took all his will to hold back the burning edge of rage—rage at her for being less than he had hoped, less than the mother Emma needed.

''I received over fifty letters.'' Hell, he shouldn't have told her that.

Surprise flickered in her eyes. ''Fifty women wrote you?''

''Emma and I read through every letter.''

''I never imagined so many women would write you.''

''Neither did I.'' His breath caught. ''Yours was the one she liked the most. So I wrote you.''

She smiled, a softness crept across her plain oval face, changing her from pretty to beautiful.

''I can't tell you what your letters meant to me,'' she said. ''I was so alone, and suddenly I had someone to talk to, even if it was in writing.''

His throat constricted. ''Your letters meant a lot to Emma, too.''

''I'm so glad.''

Their gazes met. He saw sadness large enough to touch him.

''Yours was the only advertisement I have ever answered,'' she confessed. ''Or that I ever wanted to.''

She seemed so innocent, a touch shy. Beneath it all, she had to be a good woman. Jacob's anger and disappointment tangled inside his chest, twisting painfully. He wanted to vent the rending confusion of his emotions. Hell if he knew what to say, and how to say it without hurting her. He'd never felt so helpless in his life.

Maybe he should call this whole thing off. He could walk out the door and never look back.

But he didn't want to start looking for another woman. Elizabeth met every one of his requirements. She was kind, honest and gentle. And Emma wanted her. It was too late to go back, too soon to go forward.

She ambled away from him with a swishing of her simple skirts. She wore a blue calico, he noticed now, nothing fancy or pretty, just a serviceable dress. This was the woman he'd imagined during those long months of correspondence.

"I've brought a gift for Emma. May I give it to you? I want her to have it."

Jacob said nothing.

Libby took that as an agreement as she crossed to the small bureau near the door. "I didn't want to show up empty-handed. Now that things between us have changed..." Her throat closed. "I know I won't be seeing her again, but this still belongs to her."

"You shouldn't have gone to any trouble."

"Oh, it was no trouble, only pleasure." She tugged out the drawer, risking a glance at him.

He stood with hat in hand, his black hair neatly combed. He wore a crisp red flannel shirt and dark trousers and his boots shone, despite the thin light in the room.

If only. Libby held back her heart as she extracted a wrapped bundle from the top bureau drawer and folded back the paper. She wanted Jacob's friendship and his respect. How could she earn it now?

Her hands trembled as she laid the doll on the dresser.

"That is a lovely gift," Jacob said, stepping forward to join her.

Libby glanced up into the mirror's reflection. With his head bent, she could see the cowlick at the back of his scalp. He seemed vulnerable somehow, despite his obvious strength and height and breadth. He lifted one thick-knuckled hand and brushed a finger across the doll's happy cloth face and brown yarn braids.

"You wrote me and said Emma had brown hair."

"Yes, I did." He towered above her with emotion shining in his eyes. "This is an expensive doll."

"I purchased the fabric, but I made the doll," Libby explained, pleased with her work. "I wanted something special to give Emma, something a mother might make for her daughter."

Jacob's throat worked, and he turned away.

She'd said the wrong thing. "I know I can't expect anything from you, anything we agreed to months ago, but I made this doll for Emma, from my heart. It would mean everything to me if she could have it, no strings attached."

"Why?"

Because losing dreams hurt. Libby carefully covered the doll with the brown paper. "I put my heart into making this for Emma. It belongs to her."

His jaw firmed, and he looked away without speaking. He wouldn't accept the gift. Libby stared hard at her hands. She was alone now. Without Jacob, without a home. Perhaps she'd been foolish to tell him the truth when she wasn't even certain. But in her heart Libby knew, she could never hurt Jacob.

"I have dinner waiting for us at home," he said quietly.

Did he mean…? Hope beat in her heart. *Home.* It had been a lifetime since that word meant anything to her. She had been a small girl. Libby remembered the little trundle bed tucked in the corner of the shanty where she slept at night, safe from the rain and the wind and the harshness of the world. Now she caressed the word over and over in her mind, as if home could mean that again.

"Do you mean—" she didn't dare hope "—you haven't changed your mind?"

"You have come only to meet us, nothing more." Jacob turned toward the door. His boots rang on the floorboards. "You and I may decide not to marry for many reasons. I'm willing to see what happens."

He was such a fair man. Libby's chest ached. *Please, let it work out.*

"I just don't want Emma hurt." His cool gaze trapped hers with the weight of his heart.

"Then we are in agreement. I don't want her hurt, either."

Jacob smiled. Truly smiled. Libby watched his face soften and the tension in his shoulders ease. This man, with his gentle smile warming the stark gray of his eyes, was the man she'd dreamed of.

"Emma can talk the ears off a mule, if she sets her mind to it," he said, leading the way out into the hall. "I thought I'd better warn you."

A lightness burst in Libby's chest. "She's a lively child."

"And too much for me to raise all alone." He waited while she closed and locked her door. "I'm outnumbered."

"And I suspect Emma knows it."

"Yes, she uses it to her advantage constantly." Jacob's smile sparkled.

Libby felt dazzled all the way to her toes. Somehow she managed to walk down the stairs and through the hotel's busy lobby without tripping. *He was willing to see what happens.* She wanted him so much. She'd never met a man like him before.

The sun threw long-fingered rays across the sky and slanted into her eyes when she stepped out onto the boardwalk. She blinked against the light as Jacob halted beside a small, well-kept buckboard.

"Are you ready?" His gray eyes swept hers.

"I think so."

He offered his hand.

Big fingers closed over hers and, palm to palm, he helped her up into the wagon. Her heart did crazy flipflops. She settled on the buckboard's comfortable seat, waiting for Jacob to circle around the vehicle and join her.

It was going to work out. *It had to.* She had never wanted anything so much.

"Emma named the horses." He hopped up and settled into the seat beside her. The buckboard swayed slightly, adjusting to his weight. "She insisted."

"Life must be like sunshine sharing it with her."

Jacob gripped the thick leather reins. "Yes. That little girl is everything to me."

"I can see why." Libby looked at the package she

clutched safely in her lap. Would Emma like the doll? It was homemade, not bought at a fancy store. The sleek, perfectly matched bays drawing this handsome buckboard told her something new about Jacob: He wasn't poor the way she was.

"The near one is Pete," he said with an easy grin. "The other is Repeat."

Libby laughed.

Smile lines crinkled around Jacob's sparkling eyes.

He didn't need to tell her which house was his. She knew without words when it came into view, tucked between the thick boughs of cedar and pine. Neat and tidy, with precisely cut logs and thick stripes of chinking, the log cabin sat in a small clearing. Two large windows watched them from either side of a solid wood door. The house looked sturdy and cozy and built to withstand an eternity of winters.

Home. The one word buzzed through her mind, rendering her incapable of speech. She felt warm down to her toes.

Jacob reined in the horses with the jangle of the harness, and Libby stared at the house, trying not to let her hopes grow.

The door flew open and Emma's red-dressed figure hurled into view, braids flying, black-shoed feet pounding the hard-packed earth. "You're here! I've been waiting *forever.*"

Libby laughed. Happiness welled in her heart, spilling over with joy. With the sun slanting through the thick-boughed pines and the sight of the little girl bouncing to a stop before her, Libby's throat filled with happy tears. She knew every hardship in her life had brought her here, to this shining, singular moment.

She'd come home.

Chapter Three

Nothing in Libby's life had ever prepared her for this heart-aching hope smoldering inside her chest. Like embers, she could feel that hope burn.

"We're having a treat for dessert." Emma's voice rang like a merry bell in the hot air. "I'm not supposed to tell what it is because it's a secret."

"A secret dessert?" Libby repeated, enchanted.

Emma nodded. Excitement pinkened her cheeks. "We worked on it this morning to pass the time. Your stage didn't come in until noon, and I couldn't wait."

"Neither could I."

Emma clasped her hands together. "Jane and me made pie...ah, the dessert and then it was time to go meet you."

Libby's throat felt too full to speak.

"It's even a secret from Pa," the little girl confessed.

"That's enough now, Emma," Jacob circled around the wagon, his voice gently amused. "Don't wear out Miss Hodges' ear before we even get her inside the house."

"Ah, Pa. How can I wear out her ear? Ears don't wear out."

"Yes they do. You know Grandpa can't hear well."

Emma laughed wholeheartedly. "That's because he's old."

"It's because you talked too much."

They could be a family. Libby's chest hurt just thinking of it.

"May I help you down?" Jacob offered his hand.

She slipped her bare fingers into his broad palm. Male-hot skin scorched hers. Libby swallowed at the sensation. He overwhelmed her like a dream, a hero, a fairy-tale prince come true. Her stomach twisted with a knot of need. She hadn't been sick all day. Maybe it was all right. Maybe she could have her own happy ending.

Libby hopped to the ground, skirts swishing. She kicked up a small puff of dust with the impact of her worn shoes against the solid earth.

"I like your doll."

At the sight of Emma's shy, wistful face, Libby had no doubts. She had chosen her gift to the girl well. "This isn't my doll."

"She isn't?" Hope shivered in those words.

"No. I made her."

"You *made* her?" Her mouth opened into a round O.

"Yes. I chose everything carefully. The big blue button eyes. The brown yarn braids. The calico dress."

"It's red too. We match."

"Yes. It's a coincidence, isn't it?"

Emma nodded solemnly, the puff of wind teasing her skirt. "Did you make her for me?"

"Yes."

Emma didn't move, didn't blink, didn't even breathe.

"She doesn't have a name yet. I thought you might have

a few ideas." Libby stepped closer and pressed the gift against the girl's chest. Immediately those reed thin arms embraced the rag doll, hugging her hard.

"Oh, *thank you!*" Now that Emma had found her voice, it vibrated with the deepest joy. "Pa, look! I have a real doll! Not just a wooden carving, but a real doll!"

"I see that, Emma." Jacob's eyes twinkled.

Emma squeezed her doll tightly. "Oh, I do hope you can stay with us."

Silence.

Libby stared hard at the ruffle hemming her skirts. She could feel Jacob's gaze on her, feel his silence.

"Well, now, Emma, you know we'll just have to wait and see how things work out." His words came gently, like a loving touch.

Libby's eyes smarted. Maybe she wasn't pregnant.

"Pa, Miss Hodges has to stay. Everything is going to be perfect. I just know it."

Libby glanced up. Jacob pinned her with his hard, assessing gaze. Her heart kicked in her chest. If only he could understand.

"Dinner's ready!" a woman's voice called from the door, fracturing the tension strung as tight as a clothesline.

"Thanks, Jane." Jacob snagged hold of the harness, turning his back to Libby. "I've got to take care of these horses. Emma, take Miss Hodges into the cabin."

"Can I show her my room?"

Libby closed her eyes. She could feel dreams slipping between her fingers, impossible to grasp.

"Just don't keep Jane waiting." Jacob led the horses off, the buckboard rattling over the rocks and ruts in the yard.

"Jane made chicken pie." Emma slipped her small hand inside Libby's. "I helped her. I got to make the dough and everything."

Libby stared down at the hand within hers, so small and trusting. "I bet it will be the best chicken pie I've ever had."

"Jane put carrots and peas in it." Emma led the way across the dusty front yard toward the snug cabin.

Heavens. Libby paused in the threshold, glancing about the pleasant room with its puncheon floors and log walls and simple furnishings. Emma bounced through the front room as if there were nothing special about the solid walls so carefully made and sealed tight against the winds. But to her...this cabin came right out of her dreams.

Libby belonged here. She could feel it. A tremble of joy shivered through her.

"It isn't much." Jacob's voice startled her, and she spun around.

He could read the surprise on her face. She hadn't heard him approach.

"Oh." She placed a slender hand to her chest. "This is the most beautiful home. Did you build it yourself?"

"Yes. Felled the trees. Chinked the walls. It's snug and it's sturdy." Pride simmered in his chest. No matter what she was, Elizabeth Hodges was a woman of simple tastes. He liked that.

"It's so roomy and bright." Her eyes shone not with greed or want, but with something deeper. "Why, with curtains at the windows and a rug on the floor, this would look like a picture in a book."

He smiled. "I'm glad you think so."

She confused him. He didn't know if he wanted to marry

a woman with a questionable reputation. Yet he liked her. She was soft and pretty. He suspected life had not been easy for her, a woman alone in the world.

"Pa, come *on.*" Emma crowded next to Elizabeth, grabbing hold of the woman's capable hands. "Jane's puttin' supper on the table. I want to show Miss Hodges where to sit."

Alone on the front step, Jacob watched his little girl drag Elizabeth away. It was best not to think of the future.

But as he glanced about his simple, adequate home, he noticed the polished furniture and the glistening window-panes. Jane and Emma must have scrubbed the room from floor to ceiling hoping to make a good impression.

Now she stood at the table, patiently listening while Emma set her doll down in the chair by the window, as if to make the rag doll a part of the family. Elizabeth leaned down and meant to brush a strand of hair from Emma's eyes but snatched back her hand, uncertain.

Jacob's stomach tightened. He could see the goodness in her. He didn't want to like her.

"Come sit down while it's still hot," Jane said, barreling around the corner with the potatoes steaming in a glass bowl.

He clomped across the room and pulled back his chair. Elizabeth looked so uncertain. She certainly wasn't a bad woman. He had to give her the benefit of the doubt. "Go ahead and sit down. I'm wagering Emma has a chair all picked out for you."

"She's sittin' beside me." The girl beamed.

"I could have guessed that." Jacob sat down in his chair.

Emma grabbed Elizabeth's hand and showed her to the

chair between them. The woman looked overwhelmed. She lifted her chin and happiness filled her eyes.

"This is all so wonderful," she said in a voice as gentle as morning. "I'm just so grateful to be here."

"I'm glad, too," Emma chimed.

Guilt kicked Jacob like an ill-tempered mule. He'd not been fair to Elizabeth Hodges from the start. Promising her marriage when he never intended to love her. He'd dreaded her arrival, and if it hadn't been for Emma, Elizabeth wouldn't be sitting at his table right now, pregnant or not.

"I picked the beans fresh today." Emma clutched the cut-glass bowl in both small hands. "You like beans, don't you Miss Hodges?"

"I love them." Delight shimmered in her eyes like sunlight playing in the creek.

He'd harbored so many worries. Would she be a decent woman? Would she be a loyal wife? A loving mother? They evaporated now like fog before sun.

"Pa bought these hair ribbons just for tonight," Emma chattered. "They're velvet. For a special occasion, Jane said."

"Very fancy. The color makes you look very pretty."

Emma beamed. "Tell me about the Indians. They ride their ponies bareback."

"Yes, they do."

Jacob could hardly swallow, and he stared down at his empty plate. He hadn't dished up. Now, he wasn't hungry. He reached for the bowl of beans Elizabeth passed to him. His fingers brushed hers, and in that instant of contact he raised his gaze. Their eyes met and held.

He had to start risking again, for Emma's sake. His gut clenched. If only it wasn't so hard. If only...

"I want to ride a pony wild in the meadows," Emma's voice broke between them. "Would you let me, Pa?"

"Not a chance."

"I knew you were gonna say that."

Unable to move, Libby sat perfectly still, her heart beating wildly like the wings of a grounded bird. Happiness threatened to fill her up so full she couldn't breathe. The normal sounds of the meal—Emma's fork scraping against her tin plate, the clink of the pan as Jacob dished up generous pieces of succulent chicken pie, the tinkle of water in the glasses amazed her. She'd never known a home like this, safe and cozy, so happy.

Emma asked questions about riding in the stage. Between mouthfuls of the good food, Libby answered the best she could. No, they didn't meet any road agents on the trail. No, they didn't get robbed. Yes, the teams of horses were pretty.

"You can see why my father went deaf," Jacob mumbled.

"Pa!" Emma protested, laughing at the same time.

Happiness skidded down Libby's spine like cool water, refreshing and sustaining. "I think I'm losing hearing in this one ear."

Emma giggled.

"I told you, you talk too much," Jacob teased.

Oh, no. Libby placed a hand on her stomach. The laughter slid from her mouth and she stood, fighting the abrupt twist of nausea rising in her stomach.

It couldn't be. She knocked over her chair and bolted for the door. Tears blurred her vision as she pounded down the front steps, holding her skirts out of the way as she raced blindly around the house. A second twist of nausea roiled in her belly, and she tasted the acidic burn of bile.

She *would not* leave a mess in the yard.

The outhouse was a tidy, sturdy building just behind the cabin. Libby raced past the elderly woman's surprised face, and flung open the privy's simple door. She fell to her knees on the clean floorboards and leaned over the carved hole.

The contents of her stomach hurled violently up her throat, and Libby didn't hold back her hot tears or her choking sobs. After three violent retches, her stomach was empty.

Exhausted and hopeless, Libby leaned against the wall and buried her face in her hands. There was no blaming this on travel sickness. She was pregnant.

"Are you all right, dear?"

Libby raised her face from her hands and turned to gaze up at the spry, time-weathered woman. A gentle understanding shone in Jane's eyes.

"I will be fine," Libby insisted, firming her chin. She climbed to her feet and dusted off her skirt.

"I only hope it wasn't my cookin'," Jane said lightly, although no humor shone in her eyes. "My Albert always used to say my cookin' could rot a man's gut."

"No, it wasn't your cooking, trust me." Libby summoned up a polite smile.

"I see." Sober eyes looked up into her own. "Well, now, Jacob's here. I suppose you'll be wantin' to talk to him. Emma, come with me into the house and show me that new doll of yours."

As the woman and small girl ambled off, Libby could feel the weight of Jacob's gaze. The pain of what she had just lost speared through her like an Indian's arrowhead. *This couldn't be happening.*

He said nothing, and the silence stood between them as the weight of the night began to drain the webby light from the sky.

"I thought you said you weren't sure."

Holding the pieces of her heart, she managed an answer. "I wasn't."

The wind tugged at her skirts. An owl hooted from the high boughs of a nearby pine.

Pregnant. Jacob fisted his hands, wanting to will the truth away. He studied her pale face. His gaze swept downward. Her stomach looked so flat. She looked so fragile.

He glanced up to read the pain in her eyes and saw the broken pieces of her heart. He twisted away, marching out toward the stable, then stopped. Frustrated. Angry. He didn't know what to do. "You lied to me. You came here tonight knowing your condition."

"No, I wouldn't do that to you. To Emma."

"You had to know. Were you going to use me? Did you accept my offer to cover your own mistakes? To come here and pretend the bastard was mine?"

"Not exactly. I wasn't sure—"

Anger flashed through him. "I'm not about to let you use me. Or Emma. She's the reason you are here in the first place."

"I never meant—"

"She needs a mother, not a lying woman of questionable reputation." Jacob closed his eyes. It wasn't fair. He was angry with himself. Angry for agreeing to find a mother for Emma. Angry for thinking such a plan would ever work.

"I'm sorry." The words squeaked, broken by emotion.

He looked at Elizabeth. He remembered the look of affection on her pretty oval face when she'd shown him the rag doll, remembered the way she'd almost brushed the curls from Emma's eyes, and her loving manner as she joked with the girl.

Damn it. The loss was Emma's. Elizabeth would have been the right mother. *If only she hadn't...* He didn't know what she'd done. If she was an innocent forced or went willingly with a lover. He didn't know anything about the woman except she was going to break his little girl's heart.

Damn her for doing this to Emma.

Elizabeth surprised him by bursting into tears and without another word, she simply walked away.

He watched her go.

"Where's Miss Hodges?" Emma tugged at his shirtsleeve. Dust cast a blue-gray light over the world and shadowed her button face. "Is she all right? Jane is afraid her cooking made her sick."

"Miss Hodges left." An odd roaring echoed in his head.

"If she's feelin' better tomorrow, maybe she can come have some of that pie we made." Emma's face wrinkled with worry. "You like Miss Hodges, don't you, Pa?"

Hope and adoration lit his daughter's face. How did he disappoint her? Damn it, how could Elizabeth Hodges disappoint her? Jacob felt ready to explode. He forced the breath from his lungs in a long hiss. "No, Emma, I don't like Miss Hodges."

"You don't?"

Jacob forced the hot rage from his chest. "No. She's

not going to stay. We'll have to go about finding you another mother.''

"But she made me a doll!" Pain rang high in the girl's voice.

"I know she did. But it's not your decision." Night was falling, in his heart and in the forest. "Go inside and finish your meal. Jane will put you to bed."

The girl knew better than to cry. It wouldn't get her what she wanted. Emma hung her head, a single sob escaping as she dashed toward the cabin.

Disappointment battered him. He couldn't change Elizabeth's situation. He couldn't allow her to be Emma's mother.

Relief slid through his chest, and Jacob sat down on the front stone steps. Truth be told, he was glad. He didn't want another woman in his house to remind him of Mary. He didn't want the sweet scent of a woman, her touches of softness and care anywhere in his life.

The coming night fell silently, and Jacob didn't move. He watched the skies darken, stealing the last bit of light from the day. Owls screeched, bugs chirruped and bats circled harmlessly overhead, but nothing could penetrate the sadness in his heart.

For a moment, he let himself remember the dark, soul-devouring despair that consumed him after Mary died in childbirth. He could not risk going through that again.

Chapter Four

Her heart empty, Libby stepped to the window and gazed out on the main street below. Even this early in the morning, the thriving town, perched on the side of a rugged mountain, buzzed with activity. The sawmill upriver whined, wagons rattled, busy voices rose from the boardwalk below.

She'd learned from the other passengers on the stagecoach yesterday that Cedar Rock was a boomtown. Men came from all parts of the country to work the gold mines or prospect on their own. Montana Territory was filled with stories of men striking it rich on gold and quartz and silver.

There had to be something for her here, Libby reasoned. She did not have the money to return home, if she could call Omaha home. Perhaps she could make her own opportunities, just as she had always done before. She could cook and sew. Libby had never been afraid of hard work.

It wasn't the end of the world, although it felt like it. There was no going back. She had her chance—and lost it. Now she would do what she must.

With trembling hands, Libby tugged her reticule from its place in the bureau drawer and sorted through its contents. Her fingers brushed upon the smooth, heavy parchment folded in neat, even creases. Her hands shook, rattling the paper, as she unfolded the outmost letter.

"Dear Elizabeth," she read. "I am pleased you have agreed to come visit and see if a marriage between us will work. Emma pesters me daily as to when you shall arrive. I fear she does not understand the great distance involved...."

She tore her gaze from the page. Squeezing the tears from her eyes, she removed all of Jacob's letters from her reticule and bundled them in her satchel. Happily-ever-afters don't happen to you, Elizabeth Charlotte Hodges.

After carefully locking her door, she approached the kind man behind the front counter. He politely referred her to a woman's boardinghouse off Clinton Avenue.

Armed with determination, Libby stepped out into the already hot morning sun. One thing was certain, she would not be beholden to any man, not even Jacob, for her survival. She could find her own lodging, and pay for it, too.

"Good morning, miss." A man balanced a barrel of flour on his shoulder. "Nice day."

She dropped her gaze. "Good morning, sir."

Strangers unsettled her, and she kept walking. Jacob had never felt like a stranger, not from the first moment she opened his letter.

The town bustled with activity. Libby kept her gaze low, hearing the wagons rattling by, the clop of horses, the jingle of harnesses. Men's voices rose discussing the weather and the business of the day. She dodged them the best she could.

The Faded Bloom was a bright blue, three-story structure gracing the wide alley behind a row of saloons and gaming houses. A painted sign swung from the eaves of the front porch. Rooms Let, it said. Women only.

Well, it looked homey. That was a start. Libby climbed the few steps to the porch and knocked on the door.

A window slammed opened, startling her.

"Can I help you?" A plump, wise-eyed woman pulled the pane higher and popped her head out. A wild tangle of rich black curls framed a friendly face.

"I'm looking for a room. Something not too expensive."

The woman frowned sternly, eyeing her up. "I ain't seen you before. Are you new in town?"

"Yes. I just arrived on the stage yesterday." Libby stared down at her fingers. "I'm staying over at the Cedar Rock Hotel for now, but I need something more affordable."

"Are you here for a few days or longer?"

It wouldn't be easy living in the same town as Jacob, seeing him and being reminded of what she'd lost. "Longer. I plan to find work in town. What might a room cost?"

"Ten dollars a week. Breakfast is fifty cents and dinner is a dollar."

Libby wilted at the price, but the boarding house appeared clean and respectable, the owner friendly. She glanced about, noting a ring of sturdy yellow flowers marching around the house. She couldn't do much better, and she knew it. She'd seen most of the town on her walk here. "I'd like to see what rooms you have available, please."

"Sure thing, deary. Wait by the door and I'll let you in."

Libby hadn't considered how hard it would be to stay. Now she realized how awkward she might feel bumping into Jacob in the mercantile or seeing Emma buying hair ribbons. If she had the money, she would leave.

The door opened into a dim, narrow foyer. The woman appeared, her hair tied back neatly and her plain green calico dress serviceable and pretty. "Call me Maude. Everyone around these parts does. Come on inside out of that sun."

Libby introduced herself as she stepped inside and glanced around. She noticed a door at her elbow and realized it led to Maude's apartment. Across the hall she could see a pleasant parlor for receiving guests and ahead of her the narrow staircase leading into the dim second story.

"The girls who usually live here work over at the dance hall," the woman explained, her keys jingling in her hand as she climbed the stairs with a heavy, confident gait. "They get in late, most of 'em, and sleep late. I try to be quiet so as not to wake 'em. We got other gals too, one works in the diner across from the livery."

Jacob. The thought of him hurt. Jacob owned the livery.

"What kind of work do you do?" Maude asked over her shoulder.

Libby followed the woman up to the hotter third floor. "I—I came here to meet s-someone, but I'm on my own now. I'm normally employed as a seamstress."

"A seamstress?" Humming thoughtfully, Maude marched down the narrow door-lined hallway. "Old Harv over at the dry goods has been talkin' about gettin' a woman to alter some of the ready-made clothes. You just might want to talk with him. Tell him I sent you.''

''Thank you.'' Libby brightened. Perhaps she might find a suitable position right away.

Maude stopped at the end of the hall. ''Whew, this heat would melt the core of hell, that's for sure. I'm afraid it don't get much cooler, just hotter right through the summer until autumn comes.''

Libby's problems were more serious than the heat. ''As long as the room's clean.''

''Oh, it's clean. Don't tolerate filth in my place.'' Maude swung open the door and stepped into the corner room.

Libby peered inside, almost afraid to enter. She'd learned to expect the worst, but her outlook brightened as she studied the little room.

A bare straw-tick mattress sat on a small wooden frame. A simple, scarred bureau was tucked into the corner beside a battered, but newly painted wardrobe. Maude crossed the polished wood floor and tugged open first one window and then the other. Crisp white curtains fluttered back in the hot breeze.

''It'll be uncomfortable hot for the rest of the summer.'' Maude turned to glance at the unmade bed. ''I've got linen downstairs I'll let you use.''

''This will be perfect.'' So much more than she deserved. Libby managed a wobbly smile.

''Good.'' Maude offered her hand, and they shook. ''Since you're such a nice young gal, I'll knock off two bucks due to the heat.''

Eight dollars a week. It was too good to be true.

* * *

Maude had invited Libby into the dining room and offered her a free cup of coffee. While she turned down the offer of breakfast, placing a hand over her queasy stomach, the cup of strong, bitter coffee knocked some of the lightness out of her head.

Things were going to be fine. As she ventured out into the hot morning, Libby felt hopeful with her new keys tucked safely in her pocket and two week's lodging paid ahead. Only $21.21 remaining. While it wasn't a fortune, it was much more than she'd had at some points in her life.

Maude's friend, old Harv, turned out to be the proprietor of Ellington's Dry Goods. Libby hesitated in the doorway. The fine establishment was empty of shoppers, but stuffed with a variety of goods. Ready-made garments sat in neatly folded stacks on tables. Trousers and canvas, shirts and skirts, and a few bolts of colorful fabric. She spotted a row of fancy ribbons.

Emma. Libby tripped, and caught herself. Sadness tore at her heart.

A tall, thin man wearing spectacles appeared from a doorway in the back. "Can I help you find something, miss?"

Libby gathered her courage. It wasn't easy. "Are you Mr. Ellington?"

"That I am."

"I heard from Maude Baker you might be interested in hiring a seamstress. I sew tight and even seams, and I do excellent buttonholes."

Mr. Ellington folded his arms across his chest. He was well dressed in a gray silk vest and a tailored white shirt. He looked like a man able to afford help in his store.

"I can't say if I plan to take on someone full-time."
Ellington shook his head. "As you can plainly see, I sell
ready-made. Too many bachelors up here, or married men
who left their womenfolk behind. It takes only a few
minutes to find them what they need."

No work. Libby hid her disappointment. "Well, perhaps
you would keep me in mind if circumstances change," she
said cordially.

"I will at that." But he didn't sound promising.

"I'm rooming at Mrs. Baker's. Good day."

No work for a seamstress. Well, she'd see about that.
Libby vowed to try the other shops as she stepped out on
the boardwalk. The pummeling heat of the sun slammed
into her as she walked out of the building's shade. Already
the burning disc of the sun climbed toward the zenith,
marking the passage of the morning.

She had little time to look for work before she ran out
of money. This was a busy town. Someone would hire her.
Someone had to. Her remaining funds would not last her
long.

The tentative knock on the hotel room's door startled
Libby from her packing. Her morning had been an exhausting string of rejections. Expecting it to be the Indian
woman she'd seen cleaning rooms down the hall, Libby
tugged open the door without thought.

"Surprise!"

Emma stood in the dimly lit hallway, a covered pie plate
balanced carefully in both hands. Jane shadowed the girl,
standing back against the far wall.

"You left before dessert," Emma explained, "so Jane
and I brought ya some."

"That's very thoughtful of you, but—" Libby's throat tightened. "Does your pa know you're here?"

Excitement slipped from Emma's round blue eyes. "Pa's busy at the livery. We brought fried chicken and everything."

How could she say no? Libby held open the door. "You are the best thing to happen to me all day. Come in. You too, Jane."

Emma walked past, careful to keep the pie balanced. Jane, bone thin and slightly stooped at the shoulders, carried a basket on one arm. Wise eyes met hers.

"Oh!" Emma stood stock-still, gazing about the room in fascination. "Look at the pretty quilt!"

Libby remembered the sparse interior of the Stone's snug log cabin.

"Some would think that there quilt has seen better days." Jane chuckled, meeting Libby's gaze. "Emma, don't touch."

"I want a quilt of my own," the girl said wistfully.

Libby's heart went out to her. Emma needed a mother's touch. Is that why she'd come, to try to fix what Jacob couldn't?

Jane's voice broke through her thoughts. "Are you still feelin' poorly?"

"I'm a bit better today." She felt heat creep up her face. *Jane knows,* she thought. "I'm embarrassed about last night. I just left without even thanking you for the wonderful meal. You went to all that trouble."

"Didn't look to me as if you had the chance to enjoy it. If your belly's feeling settled, maybe you'd like some of my tasty chicken."

"I want to have a picnic. We can eat right here." Emma

knelt to set the pie plate on the varnished bare floorboards and looked up expectantly. Hope shone bold in her blue eyes.

Today Emma wore a sunshine yellow calico cut in a princess style with a small yoke and rounded collar. Her sleeves were rolled up to her forearms, giving her growing room, and her skirt sported a sassy ruffle edged with yellow satin ribbon.

"Maybe Miss Hodges doesn't want to sit on the floor, Emma," Jane said gently.

"I don't mind." Bittersweetness tugged at her heart. She might never get another chance to see Emma. "It's too hot for a picnic outside."

"And too dusty. I don't like town." The girl wrinkled her nose.

"I don't like town, either. The forest is so beautiful." Libby settled onto the floor and tried not to sound wistful for the log cabin home in the woods.

"Sometimes we get trouble with bears. They wanna eat our horses."

Jane began unpacking the basket. "But your pa built the stable doors solid, so the bears can't get in."

Libby helped with setting out the food. Jane brought tin plates and flatware knives and forks, and crisp blue cotton napkins. Libby fetched fresh water from the hotel's kitchen to go along with the corn bread, fried chicken and fresh, raw green beans.

They talked of Jane's upcoming trip, of the town and the people in it. Libby managed to keep the conversation light until Emma burst out, "Don't you like my Pa?"

Jacob. Libby felt her heart twist. "I think your pa is a fine man," she hedged.

"But do you like him enough to marry him?"

Libby stared hard at her plate. She knew what the girl wanted to hear. "That question goes two ways, Emma. Your pa has to like me well enough, too."

"He's awful lonesome." Emma's blue eyes widened, an obvious show of her not-so-innocent intentions.

The little matchmaker. Libby hid her smile. "I'm awful lonesome, too. But I don't think your pa will marry me."

"That's not fair. He likes you. I know he does."

"Sometimes liking someone isn't enough reason to marry them." Libby studied the pain pinching Emma's deep blue eyes. "I'm sure glad you came to visit me. I wondered what kind of surprise you and Jane made for dessert."

"Huckleberry pie!" Emma announced. "Jane and I spent all morning picking berries. It took forever to get enough."

"That's because you kept eatin' 'em." Jane teased.

Libby's stomach tolerated the meal. She ate slowly, because Emma would leave when the meal was over. Libby didn't want her to go.

"I tried to invite Pa, but he was busy with a customer." Emma finished her piece of chicken and caught Jane's gaze. "I cleaned my plate. Can we have dessert now?"

"Yes, little one."

While Jane cut thick wedges of juicy pie, Libby cleared the dishes and stacked them neatly in the basket.

"I think Pa would have come if I asked him. He hardly saw you at all yesterday," Emma commented, her eyes sincere, her face pink with hope.

Libby's heart sank. Now she knew Emma's and Jane's

true purpose—to convince her to stay, then talk Jacob into wanting her. "I thought we already talked about this."

"I want you to be my mother."

"I'd like that, too, Emma. Very much. But wanting doesn't make it so." Libby felt the words cut like a razor blade against the back of her too dry throat.

"Pa *has* to like you. I know he will if I ask him to."

So much pain rose in those heartfelt words. Libby winced. *I don't want to hurt you, Emma.* "It's not that simple. I'm sorry. I wish things could be different."

The little girl bowed her head, hiding what shimmered in her eyes.

Tears. Libby ached with them. "I hope you'll keep the doll I made for you and always remember me."

"I'll never forget you." A depth of feeling resonated in her small voice, sad like the dying ring of a church bell.

"Have you decided on a name for her?"

"I'm going to call her Beth."

Even Libby knew why Emma had chosen it. Jacob called her by her given name, Elizabeth.

Heavy boots thudded to a stop outside her open door. Libby twisted around to gaze up at the darkly dressed man framed in the threshold.

Jacob.

At the dark wrath in his eyes, Libby braced herself. He didn't want her. And he didn't want her near his daughter.

Libby stood. "We were just saying goodbye."

The tight slash of Jacob's mouth told her the depth of his disbelief. "It didn't sound like it to me."

"Pa, this is the pie I helped Jane make." Emma hopped to her feet, excitement shining in her eyes. "Come have a piece with us. *Please.*"

"No, Emma. This isn't going to work. I'm not changing my mind."

"But—"

"Help Jane pick up the dishes." His hands fisted tightly at his sides, an effort at control.

Libby's heart skidded in her chest. He didn't understand. She tore her gaze from the sight of him, so strong and heart-drawing, framed by the threshold, and began stacking the huckleberry-juice-stained plates into the bottom of the basket.

"Pa's got a temper," Emma whispered. "But don't go away because of that. Nobody's perfect."

She certainly wasn't. Libby closed her eyes. Awareness tingled down her spine. She turned around to find him watching her.

"Don't get angry with Emma because of me," she pleaded.

Tall and formidable, he said nothing, stepping into the room. "Say goodbye, Emma."

He thought the worst of her. Libby slipped the last plate into the basket. The packing was done.

Emma obediently stood. "I know I already thanked you for making me the doll, but I really love her."

All those hours spent late into the night pushing a threaded needle through muslin now felt like too little. "You take good care of Beth for me."

"I will." With sadness in her eyes, Emma ambled past her father, into the hallway and out of Libby's sight.

Jane placed a hand on her arm. "I live in the little white house on the trail north out of town. I won't be leaving for another few weeks yet. Remember me, if you need anything. Even someone to talk to."

Jane's kindness warmed her like nothing she'd known
in so long. "Thank you," she managed to reply.

Jacob waited until Jane closed the door before he turned
to her, his gray eyes as harsh and as cold as a winter's
storm. "Just what game are you playing with my daughter?"

Chapter Five

The color drained from her face, her slender hand clenched rigidly at her sides. She looked ready to break apart.

"Jacob..." Elizabeth's lower lip trembled. "I'm so sorry about the way this looks. I didn't invite her, although I'm glad she came."

"You had no right to keep her here."

"You have no right to think I would use her." Embarrassment might flicker in her eyes, but pride lifted her chin. "I promised you I would never hurt Emma, and I mean it."

"Why was she here in your room?"

"Why do you think?" Her eyes filled. "She thinks she can still get us together."

"She's wrong."

"I know that."

Silence.

Jacob watched the fight slide from the rigid line of her shoulders. Fragile. She was so fine-boned, so small. He suspected most women were fragile, tenderhearted and easily hurt.

"Jacob, I've hurt her, haven't I? By coming here, letting her think we would marry and I would be her mother." Tears stood in her eyes. She tucked her bottom lip between her teeth.

His breath caught. "No, she understood all along this might not work out. I prepared her. I wanted to make sure she wouldn't end up with a broken heart."

"She's just a child. She doesn't understand...."

Their gazes met. He saw anguish in her morning-sky gaze, remorse, and guilt. But her heart was there, too, pure and good.

She wasn't a bad, deceitful woman. Deep down, he knew it. Jacob's heart twisted in his chest. "Emma will be disappointed," he said at last. "I will make sure she understands. She won't show up here trying to matchmake again."

It wasn't Elizabeth's fault. He knew Emma had motives of her own and needed a talking to.

"Jane left the basket of food." Elizabeth's voice quavered as she turned away, her pink dress shivering around her slender form. "Here. You should take it home with you."

The sight of her hands curling around the woven handle—red and rough from years of work—stabbed him with a sad knowledge. Life for her had been hard. She'd never said it, never hinted at it, but he sensed it now.

"No." He said, too gruff. "Jane left it here, she meant for you to keep it."

"The basket is mighty fine. And there are plates inside."

"Then return the plates and basket. Keep the food."

She stared hard at the basket. "So much good food. Thank you."

More silence. They continued to stand there. Questions and the explanations he owed her knotted in his throat. He wanted to tell her why. He wanted to make her understand it had nothing to do with her. And everything to do with the fragile hold he had on survival.

Mary had been pretty and kind, gentle and honest. And those qualities hadn't spared her from a painful, frightening death. He was fortunate Emma had been spared.

"Cedar Rock isn't so small a town, I suppose we will probably see one another now and then." She spoke softly, as if she trusted him enough with her confidences.

Jacob leaned closer. The scent of her rose water tickled his nose, made his stomach twist. Sunlight filtered through the window, casting gold shimmers in her light hair.

"Are you staying?" The idea neither frightened nor pleased him.

"I've let a room in Maude Baker's boarding house. That's not too far away from your livery stable." Uncertainty flickered in her eyes. "I didn't plan it that way. The man at the hotel's desk said it was the only respectable place for women."

"He told you correctly. Baker's is the best place. I'm glad you're there. It's safe. Maude boards her gelding at my stable."

"Then you're not angry I'm staying in town?"

He wanted to be. "What I think doesn't matter." He watched regret shape her mouth. "You insisted on paying your passage here, so I have little to say."

"I wanted to come."

"Do you want to leave? I'm guessing you can't afford

your way home." He felt like a jackass. At the time he hadn't argued over the money. "I always intended to re-imburse you for the journey."

"I don't want your money, Jacob."

Just my name and my home. Bitterness soured his mouth, then shame. He knew those accusations weren't true. Elizabeth could have lied to him. Chances were, he would have married her without knowledge of her preg-nancy—and it would have forced him to relive fears and memories of Mary he couldn't face.

"It isn't right, you coming all this way for no reason after all." Jacob tugged his billfold from his shirt pocket.

"I had every reason to come." Shyly averting her eyes, Elizabeth brushed at her plain cotton skirts.

The truth hit him. She'd wanted to love him. She came because he'd unintentionally led her to believe... He couldn't think about it. Angry at himself, Jacob counted out the crisp bills.

"Let me do this for you." He looked up. "Please. You gave up your job and left your home to come here."

"But I owe you money."

"That can't be right, Elizabeth."

She withdrew a thin collection of bills and coins from her skirt pocket and pressed it into his shirt pocket. "I won't be staying here in the hotel any longer. I feel as if I should reimburse you for last night, too."

Jacob's stomach twisted. He stared down at the money in his hands, not so much at that, and realized what Eliz-abeth was giving him. She was letting him know this wasn't about money, but about respect.

He wouldn't argue. He would find a way to give her what he owed her. "You don't need to be so fair."

"I have to. Your letters changed my life." She smiled in memory. "I can't tell you how nervous I was when I held your first envelope in my hand. You could have been any kind of man, but I had to meet you. I had to know if I could have what I saw in your advertisement."

"What did you see?"

"Everything missing from my life." She looked hard at the window. "From your first sentence, I wanted to love you. You seemed so gallant and educated. And with each letter, you made me want to believe men could be good to their wives, good to their children. You seemed to care so much for your Emma. How I wanted you."

He heard what she did not say. The loneliness that prompted a single woman without family to answer a newspaper advertisement. The pain behind the man who'd made her pregnant.

Tears brimmed her eyes. "Coming here to meet you felt like a dream come true. I haven't had many dreams."

He would have married her. She would have been so right for Emma—for him. "You knew you were pregnant when you left Omaha."

"No. I honestly didn't." She clasped her hands. "I'm so sorry, Jacob. I never m-meant...I n-never w-wanted t-to hurt you."

Sobs tore through her, strong enough to break her in two. He reached out, and before he knew it she was in his arms, crying against his chest. He wanted to comfort her. He wanted to push her away.

"I've hurt Emma," she sobbed. "I don't know how I can live with that."

Perhaps it was the luminous depth of her eyes or the attraction he'd felt buzz through him the first moment he'd seen her in the street. Jacob didn't know. He didn't care. Acting on impulse, he touched a callused finger to her gently rounded chin and tilted her face upward.

Her mouth looked soft and ripe. Jacob brushed her lips delicately, tenderly. She tasted of sweet berries. She felt like fine velvet. At the explosion of feeling, his pulse leaped.

What was he doing? He would not give his heart a second time. And not to a woman who could die the way Mary did.

Jacob stepped back, his hand falling away from her chin. She gazed up at him with startled eyes, her goodness shining there like a constant light.

She needed him. She wanted him.

Tenderness for her welled in his heart. A useless tenderness. He couldn't marry her. He could not even bear to look at her, knowing and remembering his Mary. Jacob closed his eyes before he turned away. He did not want to remember Elizabeth's face as he walked out of her life.

Libby settled in her new room that afternoon. Even with the windows open, the hot breeze offered no relief from the baking heat. She didn't mind. This was a new start in a new town. She wanted to think optimistically.

It didn't take too long to unpack. She hung her dresses in the tidy wardrobe and folded her underwear and winter things into the small bureau. After she'd made the bed with Maude's clean, white sheets, Libby opened her second satchel and withdrew the precious quilt.

The blues and pinks in the double wedding ring design were set against the background of snowy white. Her mother had sewn the careful stitches and the sturdy ties long ago before her own marriage, well before Libby was born. It was the only item she had of her mother's, and she cherished it. The memories of the gentle-voiced woman who liked to sing had blurred with time.

Unpacking had helped her block all the unpleasant thoughts from her mind...and the pleasant sensation of Jacob's remembered kiss.

Now that the bed was made, her unpacking was done, Libby could not hide. She had no idea what she would do next. She had no husband. No marriage. But she did have a baby on the way.

She sank down into the lone wooden chair. She needed to keep her hands busy so she wouldn't long for the man she could not have.

Determined to forget the amazing sensation of being in his strong arms, of being kissed by him, Libby grabbed her scrap bag from the bureau drawer and began sorting through it.

She withdrew a tiny piece of pink calico, cut into pieces to be sewn into a doll's dress. A terrible longing stole over her. She planned to make a whole wardrobe of clothes fitted with tiny ruffles and lace and ribbons, scraps from her own sewing and from the shop she'd worked at in Virginia long ago. The owner had allowed her to take the smaller scraps since they were simply thrown away.

Now, years and a lifetime later, she'd found a good use for those scraps. It broke her heart that she couldn't finish the dress for Emma's sake.

Jacob wanted her to stay away from his girl. She understood why. It just hurt.

But the good fabric would go to waste, she reminded herself.

Libby fingered the darling dress pieces. She hated waste; she had so little all her life that wastefulness felt like a sin. Perhaps Jacob wouldn't mind if she finished up the bits of fabric she'd already cut. She didn't have the right to try to see him again, but she felt happier. As if doll's dresses made from scraps could make up for the hurt she'd caused.

Jacob set down his pitchfork and wiped the sweat from his brow. The August sun beat with an inferno's fury, heating the inside of his stable until it felt like an oven.

Weeks had passed since he'd last spoken with Elizabeth. He thought of her often, usually when he was alone with his work or in the silence of night when sleep eluded him.

He couldn't get her out of his mind, damn it.

Long distance proposals didn't work out all the time. Elizabeth had come here without a promise of marriage. Neither one of them had made promises in their numerous letters, as if equally afraid of the future. But as Jacob unbuttoned his shirt, then tossed it off, he didn't feel comforted. No, he felt empty, troubled. He pitched the soiled straw from the box stall as hard as he could, trying to purge his feelings. Sweat ran off his brow like water. He ignored it.

Already he was thinking of her. He'd asked Maude Baker how Elizabeth was doing, and he learned she worked at a hotel near the blacksmith's shop, cooking in the kitchen.

Before Jane left for her trip south, she'd let him know the gossip concerning Elizabeth Hodges. As the new woman, she was the talk of town. Single. Pretty. Young. Scores of bachelors lined up to ask her to supper, but she declined every offer.

Jacob suspected he was the only man in town who knew the most popular woman was pregnant.

He stopped pitching and closed his eyes. Guilt battered him. Couldn't he go to her and ask her back? He wanted to. He truly wanted to look past her pregnancy—past the shadows of his own fears—and try again.

She was the right woman for them.

But he didn't want a real marriage. He didn't want more children. He never wanted to sit in the parlor waiting for another woman to give birth, knowing the risks. Life is too short. Love doesn't last forever. Death intervenes and leaves you with nothing but suffocating grief.

Jacob learned these lessons the hard way. He was a fool to consider, even for a second, he could march up to Mrs. Baker's boardinghouse and ask Elizabeth to be his wife.

"Deary, I'm sorry but I can't accept your money."

Libby took a step back in Maude's crowded apartment. Knickknacks crammed the surface of the many tables, low shelves and whatnots in the corners, making maneuvering difficult. "I don't understand. I owe you next week's rent."

"You don't owe me a thing." Maude smiled.

It only confused Libby more. "I owe you money if I want to live here come Monday."

Mischief twinkled in Maude's wise eyes. "Oh, you'll be here on Monday, all right. Someone paid your rent for you."

What? The moon could tumble from the sky and it wouldn't shock her as much. "Who would do such a thing? Eight dollars is a lot of money."

"Not to some people." Maude turned with a rustle of

homemade petticoats and marched into the small kitchen. "I was just gonna have me some refreshment. Come join me for lemonade and cookies."

Refreshment? Her stomach felt too troubled. "It was Jacob, wasn't it?"

"He told me not to tell you. He wanted to keep it a secret."

"Well, you didn't try very hard, Maude."

"True." The kitchen echoed with her jolly laughter. "You're paid up for the entire month of August."

"That can't be. He wouldn't do that. He doesn't even like me." *But he kissed me.* The remembered tingle of his lips caressing hers heated her face.

Maude set a plate of sugar cookies on the small round oak table. "A man doesn't gotta like you in order to love you."

Libby stepped over to the table, the kitchen as crammed with breakable knickknacks as the front room. "I want you to refund Jacob his money."

"Can't do it." Maude grabbed a pitcher tinkling with ice. She poured two cups. "This came over from Trace's diner. The best in town."

Not even the sight of the luxurious lemonade soothed the ache in her chest. "Maude, it's simple. You find Jacob at his livery and give him his money."

"He won't take it. Besides, after he gave me thirty-two dollars for this month, he and I made an arrangement. He's giving me free care of the horse I've got over at his livery, and I give you free room and board. It's a fair deal for me."

"You can't do that. I won't be obligated to him." She'd

caused him enough trouble. Thinking of the baby growing in her belly, Libby blushed.

"Pish posh. You listen to me. This world is tough on a woman alone. If a well-off gentleman wants to help you out—with no expectations—then I would let him. A girl needs all the help she can get."

Not this one. Libby sank into the offered chair. "You don't understand, Maude. I owe Jacob more than I can pay him."

He'd given her beautiful dreams—for as long as they lasted. She'd wasted all his time corresponding when he could have spent the time finding another woman who would be good enough for Emma. Not that Libby blamed him. Oh, no. She blamed herself for making promises she could not honor, for letting Jacob down.

Maude's hand covered hers. "It's a matter you must take up with him. He and I have an arrangement I like. And he's good to my horse. Have a cookie, now. They're fresh from the diner, too."

Jacob secured the Baker's palomino in his stall, trying not to remember.

"Jacob?" Her voice. Elizabeth's.

He didn't realize she wasn't a dream until he turned. The wide front doors of the barn framed her slim shape, allowing glimpses of Main Street with its dusty boardwalk and painted shop fronts. The hot, early September wind breezed the green fabric of her plain calico dress.

She looked beautiful to him with wisps of honey blond hair whipping around her oval face.

She self-consciously dipped her chin. "I hope I'm not bothering you."

"Not at all." He stepped forward.

"I need to speak to you about my rent." She tucked her lush bottom lip between her teeth, looking uncertain.

He grabbed hold of the worn-smooth handle of his favorite pitchfork. "Seems to me your rent is a matter you should talk about with Mrs. Baker."

Her eyes searched his. "I know you are the one, and it has to stop. Not that I don't appreciate it."

He wished so much could be different between them. "I'm glad to help out, Elizabeth. You refused my money, if you remember."

She remembered the heat of his mouth over hers, burning a blessed sensation straight through her belly. In the dim interior of the barn, she could see only Jacob's shadow. She moved closer. *Make him understand how important this is to her.*

The comforting scent of wood smoke and new hay filled her nose. The same scent clung to Jacob's clothes the few times she'd been close to him.

"I want to pay my own way, Jacob. I need to do it."

Jacob moved toward her with a slow, hesitant gait, gripping his pitchfork. "Maybe I need to help you."

"But you should be trying to find Emma a mother, not worrying over me." Although she wanted him to.

"Somebody has to care about you. Have you given a thought to what you will do when that baby comes?"

He eased into the spill of sunshine through the wide stable door. He wore trousers and no shirt. Sweat glistened across the mesmerizing expanse of his muscled chest, touched by the sun.

She had never seen such a chest. She had never seen such a man. *He isn't yours to touch, Libby.* Her face hot, she dipped her chin. "I'm getting along considerably well at the boardinghouse, and I've found a job."

"Not as a seamstress," he corrected, as if he knew all about her position serving men their meals.

"It was the only job I could find. Mr. Oleson offered to hire me as a dancing girl in his saloon, but I had to decline. Apart from my...condition I don't know how to dance."

Jacob's rich chuckle vibrated across her skin. "I know a few dances. My mother taught me."

"My aunt thought dancing was sinful." Libby fingered the soft bundle she held. "I suppose the sort of dancing in Mr. Oleson's parlor might be considered that."

"The new minister in town thinks so. He's started to picket some of those establishments."

"Sometimes the women joining him spill over onto Leah's front steps and keep away the hotel's business. It makes her furious." Libby's smile faded. "Will you stop giving Maude free board for her horse?"

"No." His eyes turned somber, pinching thoughtfully in the corners. "You need my help, Elizabeth."

What kind of woman did he think she was?

"No, I don't need you," she said, chin lifted. "I've never depended on a man's generosity, and I'm not about to do it now. I have always managed just fine on my own, no matter what you think of me."

Face flaming, Libby turned, the bundle in her hands forgotten as she walked as fast as she could toward the street.

"Don't leave. Please." His voice echoed in the loft overhead. "Do you have a moment?"

Libby considered his words, then stopped. She couldn't look back at him. "I was on my way to the hotel."

"Let me buy you a glass of lemonade over at the diner so we can talk."

Talk. Libby's stomach flipped over. Looking at him made her want him. He wasn't hers to have. "I—I start work soon."

Jacob nodded, as if that suited him fine, and held up one finger indicating she should wait.

Wait? She should hightail it out of here and put as much distance between them as humanly possible. He didn't want her, would never love her. But she wanted him to.

Jacob appeared from the back of the stable, now wearing a plain blue muslin shirt, open at the collar. It had been tucked hastily into his trousers and looked sadly wrinkled.

"Has Jane left?"

"What gave you that idea?" He smiled ruefully. "I never learned how to iron. Without Jane, I use the laundry in town, but by the time I get the clothes home, they look like this."

"What does Emma say about it?"

"She says I ought to get myself a wife. That there's a nice lady living in town I could ask." His joke failed. The light left his eyes. "I'm sorry. I wasn't thinking."

"It's all right." But it wasn't. As they walked the half block together, she felt his gaze stray to her stomach.

He held open the door of the diner and smiled as if... Libby tried not to complete that thought. He was just being polite.

"We'll have two glasses of lemonade," Jacob informed the young woman who wandered into sight. "Let's sit near the window," he said to Libby.

Libby sat down while Jacob folded himself into a too

small chair. The opened window gave her something to look at besides Jacob.

"I guess I really just wanted to know how you are doing. If you need anything." Concern rumbled in his voice.

And brought tears to her eyes. She blinked hard. "How is Emma doing?"

"She misses Jane. I haven't found anyone to replace her yet."

Would he find someone to replace me? Libby laid the cloth bundle she carried on the clean table. She waited as the young woman placed two ice-filled glasses between them. Fresh, sour-sweet lemonade scented the air.

"What do you have there?" he asked.

"Something for Emma. If you will let her have them." Waiting for his rejection, she unwrapped the small bundle of clothes. Folds of happy calico and gingham peeked out from the soft flannel. Aprons. Bonnets. Dresses. Nightgowns. Shoes.

"Elizabeth, I don't think—" He fisted his hands. "Emma will get her hopes up."

"Then don't tell her they are from me. Say you bought them. It's important to me she has these for her doll."

"Why?"

Libby rubbed the condensation from the glass. "I had planned to finish the clothes before I arrived, but time got the best of me. It isn't Emma's fault I didn't sew them before I arrived."

Jacob's face twisted. "Emma will know they came from you."

"I see." All these pretty things. Libby folded the flannel back over the clothes. "The fabric was already cut and would only go to waste. I couldn't bear that. I didn't think it would make you angry.''

Jacob raised his gaze to hers. "I'm not angry.''

"Then you'll give them to her?''

"Yes.'' Jacob reached for the bundle. "Emma will be thrilled with these pretty things.''

Thank you. Libby's throat tightened, and she did not say the words. It was enough to know she would make Emma happy.

"You have a talent.'' His gray gaze caught hers. Held.

Libby longed for his touch. Unable to look away, her heart hammered. "I'm just an ordinary seamstress.''

"Seems with this skill you could find work in town.''

"I just started doing piecework for Mr. Ellington. Mostly altering and mending and hemming. It isn't much, but enough to fill my Sundays.''

"That's good.'' Jacob wrapped his able fingers around the thick, cold glass and drank deeply.

She sipped the ice-cold lemonade, too. "My time is up. I don't want to keep Leah waiting. The hotel has been so busy lately.''

"Is she treating you right? Kitchen work can't be easy.''

She could hear his thoughts. *For a pregnant woman like you.* Libby looked down. "Leah is a generous boss. I'm lucky to be working for her.''

A flicker built in her heart—the beginnings of hope. Maybe he would look past her pregnancy. Maybe he wanted to marry her for *her*—the woman with whom he'd exchanged hopes, stories and words from his heart.

Libby stood, fishing for coins in her skirt pocket. "Goodbye, Jacob.''

And it was goodbye.

"It's my treat." His firm voice stilled her hand, and he laid an array of small coins on the table.

He cared about her. And it hurt more than his hatred.

"Take care of yourself, Elizabeth." He stood, his unreadable gaze trapping hers, causing a tingling warmth through every nerve in her body.

He was never going to kiss her again. Libby turned away, not looking back, fighting the weakness for him in her heart.

She'd never ached for a man's touch. She'd never felt this way about anyone.

Chapter Six

"Miss Hodges! Miss Hodges!" The child's voice rang like a merry bell above the din of the dusty streets.

Libby turned, her errand forgotten at the sight of Emma Stone, dressed in a white calico dress, trimmed with lace and velvet, racing down the boardwalk, braids flying.

She glanced around for Jacob and relaxed when she saw he was nowhere near. She wanted to see him; she *didn't* want to see him.

Emma bounced to a noisy halt on the boardwalk, her brown braids slamming against her back. "I saw you and I just had to come over. I like your dress."

"And I like yours."

Emma's grin flashed.

Libby smiled back. "Don't tell me your pa is letting you run all over town by yourself."

"No." Emma laughed. "I ran away."

"From your pa?" Confused, Libby glanced down the street. Shoppers traveled from one shop to another, men hauled freight through the busy town.

"I would never run away from Pa." Emma's dark bangs

lifted in the cool mountain winds. "But I would leave school."

"School?" She knew there wasn't a schoolhouse in town; she'd heard a woman in the dry goods store complaining about it.

"Mrs. Holt is a lady who used to be a teacher." Emma rolled her eyes. "Now she's got kids and thinks she ought to teach 'em."

"Oh." Libby could well imagine Jacob, who seemed so educated, would want his girl to get schooling. "Then I suppose you're taking lessons in Mrs. Holt's home."

"Yes." Emma sighed, sounding greatly pained. "She makes us sit in her hot parlor that smells like mice because one got stuck in her wall and died."

Libby's laughter faded when she spied a fashionably plump blond woman glancing up and down the street. "Is that your teacher? She looks mad."

"She's always mad, so I don't care." Emma leaned closer. "I saw you through the window and I know I'm not supposed to see you 'cuz you aren't gonna marry us, but I have to thank you for the new dresses."

The doll clothes. A warm pleasure sliced through her. "I'm glad you liked them."

Emma smiled wide enough to light up the sky. "I love them. Did you know Pa made Beth a cradle? Now she has a place to sleep during the day when I'm at school." Emma wrinkled her nose.

"Emma! Emma Mary!" The angry-looking woman marched closer, barreling up the street like a teamster ready for a fight.

"Looks like I'm in trouble. Gotta go." Emma's eyes

sparkled as she spun around, running hard. Her stiff braids flew with each pounding step.

"Don't you dare run away from me like that!" Mrs. Holt's voice carried above the sounds of the busy town.

"Sorry." But the girl didn't sound apologetic.

Libby clutched the package of eggs against her belly. Maybe, if she were lucky, she would have a daughter of her own.

Jacob bolted awake. He'd been dreaming of Elizabeth. Sitting up in bed in the darkness of his room, he could hear himself breathe.

You have to get the woman out of your mind.

It wasn't easy.

Jacob threw off the covers and limped through the dark. The silent house echoed around him. He opened his bedroom door and waited by Emma's closed one. Inside she slept soundly. But without a mother's love.

He'd put off placing another advertisement. He didn't want another woman. He wanted Elizabeth. Finding a friend in her through their letters and knowing the goodness shining in her eyes told him one thing. He could come to care for her.

Troubled, Jacob sat down at the table, the early autumn air cool at his feet.

He hadn't dreamed of Elizabeth in a sexual way. Instead, he'd dreamed of her sitting at the diner, the gentle sunshine sloping through the window and brushing golden highlights in her carefully braided hair, her blue eyes luminous, her presence more captivating than a thousand rainbows.

Stop thinking of her. Jacob covered his face with his

hands, then remembered kissing her, warm and sweet, her eyes flashing confusion...and desire.

He couldn't love her. Anger knotted in his gut. No, it wasn't anger, but fear. Fear because Elizabeth could sneak past the carefully erected defenses around his heart and leave him vulnerable.

A door whispered on its leather hinges.

"Pa?"

He lowered his hands, listening to Emma's bare feet padding on the varnished floor. He twisted around in his chair to face her.

In the faintest silver moonlight, he saw her grab the back of his chair, her white muslin gown glowing like a ghost.

"What is it, Emma?"

"I can't sleep." She rubbed her eyes with her free hand, and he knew she'd been crying.

"Did you have another bad dream?"

"Uh-huh."

Jacob felt helpless against the weight of his daughter's nightmares. He tugged out the nearest chair. "Come sit down with me."

"I miss Jane." Emma padded over to the chair. "I saw Miss Hodges in town today."

He heard the want in her voice. "Yes, Mrs. Holt told me you ran out on your lessons."

Emma's chin dipped. "I didn't want to be rude. I had to thank Miss Hodges for Beth's dresses."

"I don't want you running off like that again, do you hear?" Jacob waited for Emma's solemn nod. She was a pretty little thing, dear to his heart, despite his fears of loving her.

"Mrs. Holt was angry I talked with Miss Hodges."

Emma tugged off her cap and tossed it on the table. "She said I shouldn't talk to a woman like that."

"A woman like what?" he demanded.

Emma bowed her head. "A woman who works in a hotel. Is that a bad thing?"

"No. It's honest work. There's no shame in that."

What kind of woman was Elizabeth? The same woman he'd corresponded with, sharing stories of his life in Cedar Rock, of working at the livery and trying to raise Emma. The same woman who'd stepped off the stage, so breathtaking he couldn't force himself to speak to her.

There was no denying it. Afraid or not, he dreamed of her tonight because he ached to hold her again, to taste the heat of her mouth.

"Pa?"

"What?" He turned toward his daughter.

"If I had a mother, I wouldn't have no more nightmares."

He saw through her like glass. "Don't try matchmaking, missy. Come on, I'll tuck you in."

Emma's chair scraped as she hopped to the floor. She tucked her small, trusting hand within his.

It wasn't easy being alone. For either him or Emma. Not easy at all.

Jacob tucked his daughter into bed, his heart wooden, his movements stiff. As he handed Emma her rag doll, he thought of Elizabeth. Of the care she'd put into making such a gift.

What a wonderful mother she would have been to Emma. Isn't that what mattered? Certainly not his fears, not his heart. It was the living again that frightened him.

Afraid to step forward, to change his life, Jacob sat a long while in the dark.

"Those men are standing out there like a herd of mindless cattle." Leah released the curtain at the hotel's kitchen window.

"It's becoming a nightly event." Libby offered her employer a weary shrug.

"That's what happens when a pretty single woman lands in this town. Every lonely loser thinks he can find a woman to cook for him."

Libby smiled. "I'd hate to put you out of business, Leah."

"One skinny woman isn't about to do that. Are you sure you don't want another helping? This pot roast is mighty good."

"That's because I baked it," Libby teased, then stood from the small table, intending to rinse her plate.

Deciding to stay in Cedar Rock was the best decision she'd made yet. Why, it was only fortune she'd landed a job here at Leah's hotel. The free meals were a great bonus, and Leah's friendship was a blessing. Leah was the only person in town, aside from Jacob, who knew of her condition.

"Do you suppose any of the men out there would make good husbands?"

Libby scrubbed her plate in the basin of soapy water. "I'm not looking for a husband."

Leah snatched the wet plate out of Libby's hands. "Your shift is over. No more washing dishes. A woman in your position might be able to find a tolerable husband. There's Matthew Cain, sitting on the bench across the street. He owns the feed store, you know. He does well for himself, and he looks like a good sort.''

Libby glanced across the wide dusty street. A blond-haired, handsome man sat with his feet crossed at the ankles, his black hat sitting beside him on the bench.

Her heart twisted. She hadn't wanted *any* man—that wasn't why she'd answered an advertisement, why she'd left everything behind to travel here. She wanted Jacob.

''Don't worry about me, Leah.'' Libby lifted her sunbonnet from the peg by the back door.

''Honey, I have to worry about a woman with all those single men on the loose.'' With a rustle of navy skirts, the hotel proprietor opened the door. ''Look. Those darn pickets are back, protesting the dance hall.''

''Maybe all that picketing will distract the men and I can escape,'' Libby joked. Soon enough, her belly would grow so not even her full apron could hide it. Then she'd lay money on the table that every eligible bachelor in town offering to walk her home now would be running for the high hills.

There was only one man she wanted. He ran, too. No, not ran. He had to keep Emma's interest foremost. And the grief bruising his heart touched her from the first moment they'd spoken. He didn't want a family, he didn't want love.

She said goodbye to Leah and wove through the hotel. With the reverend's protesting outside, she could slip unnoticed down the front steps and weave among the picketers, maybe avoiding the overly interested bachelors waiting for her.

There were so few single women in town, besides the dancing girls, even she had become popular.

"Miss Hodges?" A freshly shaven man stepped out of the chanting crowd. "I would like the honor of walking you home."

A cooling autumn breeze shivered down from the mountains, dissipating the day's heat, catching the ruffled hem of her apron. The feed store man. He looked kind, substantial. *But he wasn't Jacob.*

"No, thank you." She dipped her chin, shy in front of the stranger.

"Excuse me, but seeing Miss Hodges home will be my honor." A different voice, a rumbling baritone familiar and beloved, brushed over her like sunshine.

Libby's heart lifted. "Jacob."

He smiled at her, his eyes smiling, too. The milling crowd looked small behind his solid frame. He wore his work clothes, simple black trousers and a plain blue shirt, yet a shiver started low in her belly. *He looks like heaven.*

"May I see you home?" He held out his hand, dependable, sturdy.

Libby placed her hand in his, accepting what little he offered her. She had to face it—dreams didn't come true, not in this life. "Why are you here, Jacob?"

"I have my buckboard." His eyes shadowed, hiding an emotion she feared. His gaze had slipped to her belly. "I'll drive you home, if you don't mind."

She lifted her chin. *Remember he isn't yours to have.* "That would be fine. This is about Emma, isn't it?"

They skirted the edges of the crowd. Jacob kept her hand wrapped firmly within his. "Emma?"

"She ran up to me one morning last week. I wasn't sure if you would approve." Libby looked down at her dusty shoes.

He halted beside the polished buckboard. "Why wouldn't I?"

"You know. Pretty soon a lot of people are going to know."

"I suppose." Jacob glanced down the street. "Maybe a lot of those fellows trying to court you will decide to leave you alone."

He didn't mean it unkindly, but the words hurt.

"I suppose you're right." Libby lifted her chin. "You aren't angry with me?"

"About speaking to Emma? Of course not." He helped her up. "She adores you. I wouldn't want to take that away from her."

The strength in his arms, the closeness of his chest, the rugged scent of wood smoke filled her head, igniting a sweet need inside her. A need for him.

Blushing, she straightened her skirts and waited for him to climb up beside her. Thank heavens she'd worn her apron home. The folds of soft muslin hid the small roundness her skirts did not.

Jacob remained silent as he gathered the reins in his strong hands, the thick-knuckled and capable hands of a man who worked at an honest living. Libby remembered the sight of his bare chest in the barn. She tingled at the memory.

Now he kept his gaze trained on the street ahead of them, as if ashamed of looking directly at her.

During the ride to the Faded Bloom, neither of them spoke. Libby could feel unspoken tension stretched between them, like a lull in the storm. Had he come to ask her to leave town? Would her condition be an embarrassment to him in the future?

No. Jacob wouldn't think like that. Her throat filled. He was a man of integrity. Something she admired so much, had known so little of.

Affection flooded her like a rising river. She let the breeze brush her face and fan the tendrils that escaped her pinned braids.

Jacob halted the horses outside the boardinghouse. His gaze swept over her, measuring, thoughtful.

"I appreciate the ride," she managed to say. Her feelings filled her words.

"Don't go." His free hand snared her wrist. "Please."

Libby studied his face. As the day's light faded from the sky, it was hard to read what brewed in his storm gray eyes. "You said you wanted to talk with me."

"Yes." Jacob cleared his throat. "I never should have let you come here without knowing what I expected."

"I understand." She did. A terrible longing swept though her. She wanted to help him, to heal the pain in his heart.

"How can you understand?" His voice sounded thick, and he looked away. "I don't think I could have married anyone, even for Emma's sake, even though I'm tired of being lonely. I thought I could, until I met you."

The cool breeze puffed over her, scattering the hem of her apron and skirts.

"Will you forgive me?"

"Oh, Jacob." Her whole heart twisted. "I never blamed you. For what it's worth, I wanted to be your wife."

He clenched his jaw; she saw a muscle jump along his temple.

She stared down at her hands. She wasn't good enough for him, to replace the wife he still loved so much.

"I need a favor," he said.

"A favor?" She looked up into eyes so troubled, so bleak, she almost cried in sympathy. "What can I do for you, Jacob? I would do anything, if I can."

Without speaking he reached down and tugged a brown-paper-wrapped bundle from beneath the seat.

"Ellington doesn't carry little girl's ready-made dresses." He spoke quietly as the fading light of the sky silhouetted him, hiding his face. "Jane used to make Emma's clothes, but she needs something for winter. I could pay you to sew the dress for me. I've already purchased the fabric."

He unwrapped the bundle. Fine flannel, Libby could tell even in the dark without touching it. She'd heard from Maude that Mrs. Holt often sewed for the more respectable people in town.

But he'd asked her.

Foolish hope beat in her heart. *Be sensible,* she scolded herself. He doesn't want you. He feels sorry for you.

Yet she would help him all the same, just to be near him.

"I—I would have to measure Emma."

Jacob's voice smiled. "I'm sure she won't mind."

"It might take a while," she hedged. "I only have time to sew in the evenings."

"We'll wait." His hand caught hers as the last of the gray light faded from the wide-open sky. She could hear the sincerity in his voice.

She could hold on to him forever. Emotions twisted through her, and she felt too full to speak. "I have Sundays free. Perhaps I could measure Emma then."

"Sounds fine to me." Jacob moved, just a shadow in the night, to slip his hand from hers.

"Should I come out to your cabin?"

"I'll ride out to get you," he said, sounding distant. "Say, tomorrow at nine o'clock?"

"Yes." Libby nodded to hide her disappointment. She had to keep her heart from caring. Jacob Stone wasn't hers to love. She would do best remembering that.

"Elizabeth?" His arm brushed her shoulder.

"Yes?" Libby tried to ignore the fluttering wing-beat of her heart.

In answer, his fingertips brushed her chin, lifting her face to his. No moon shone to illuminate him so she did not know what burned in his eyes, but she could sense it. *He is going to kiss me.* Libby held her breath, her heart hammering wildly as his lips covered hers.

Chapter Seven

The tentative brush of his lips captivated her. Gentle. Touching. Her eyes teared at the tenderness.

Then his kiss deepened, becoming possessive, passionate. His broad hand slipped down her throat, trailing over the rise of her breast, hesitating there to cup her wonderingly before his palm spanned the bulge of her belly.

She broke away breathless, shame heating her face.

"Tell me what happened," he whispered, his mouth so close his lips brushed hers when he spoke.

Libby pressed her face against his throat, smelling the salty scent of his skin and the wood smoke and sweet hay clinging to his shirt. Good, comforting scents. Unshed tears burned in her eyes.

How could she tell him the truth?

Jacob gazed out into the night. "Could we go inside?"

"Maude doesn't allow gentlemen into the house after eight o'clock."

"Oh." He looked down at his right hand. His fingers tingled from touching her small wrist, his mouth buzzed from kissing her, his heart hammered like a tightly wound clock. "I know where we can go."

Nerves twisted in his stomach as he gathered up the leather reins. His palms felt clammy. His heart thundered. What did he think he was doing? Getting in over his head, that's what. And that was some place he didn't belong. Hell, before Elizabeth he hadn't really kissed a woman in nearly seven years—and she had been his wife.

But he chirruped to the horses and guided them down Clinton and across Main. Darkness hugged the street where closed shops stood silent for the night, upstairs lamps burned behind curtained windows.

When he was near Elizabeth, the numbing pain in his heart eased. Looking at Emma, talking to her, made him remember the woman who birthed her, but Elizabeth...she made heat burn in his veins and his nerve endings crackle. She stirred up his feelings. She made him act impulsively. *Just like that kiss.*

Jacob held his breath. He wanted to kiss her again.

With gentle pressure on the reins, he brought the bays to a halt behind the stable. The horses snorted, knowing oats were waiting. He didn't meet Elizabeth's eyes as he helped her down.

Her skirts rustled. Her hand felt small in his. She smelled faintly of rose water.

Like a kick to his gut, he reacted. The way a man reacts to a woman. Old, sweet feelings filtered through his heart. He wanted to run. He wanted to stay.

Jacob held open the stable door for her and closed it behind them. The comforting barn smells of sweet hay and heated horseflesh lifted some of the fear from his heart.

"Oh!" Elizabeth gasped in the dimness.

Jacob caught her by the elbow, then spotted the familiar nose, chuckled. "She's a wily one."

"She's got my apron ruffle in her teeth," Libby said quietly, a little nervous, a little amused.

"She doesn't normally like strangers." Jacob knelt down and ran his hand along the mare's jaw. The teeth relaxed, the ruffle slipped free unharmed, and the horse rolled her head upward for a good scratching.

"You have a gentle way with animals."

"I've been around horses all my life." He closed his mind against the remembrances of his father's farm in Kentucky and the horses he raised there. Some things hurt too much to think about.

"I've never been around them." She sounded wistful. "I think horses are beautiful."

Jacob stood. "I bought this mare from a miner who'd beaten her near to death because she was too exhausted to pull his cart up the last hill into town."

Elizabeth's face pinched in sorrow. "She looks recovered. It must be due to your gentle ways."

"The secret is fine oats." He shrugged off her compliment like water. He grabbed up the lantern from its nail in the wall. "I always have a supply of horses to sell, but I'm keeping this mare for someone special. I didn't put so much work into her just to have some rough miner abuse her again."

Jacob watched the nameless mare nudge Elizabeth's hand. That horse was no fool. She knew a kind heart at first sight.

As he lit the lamp, snuffing out the match carefully and dropping it in water, he didn't tell her his real feelings. How long could he live like a hermit? Going through the motions, working, providing for Emma and keeping his heart buried? As lantern light danced across the doe-eyed mare and Elizabeth, who was tentatively stroking the horse's nose, his gut clenched with a dead-on certainty.

Just being near her made him feel alive. To ache for joy and the silken touch of her hair and the heat of her kiss. Maybe he could do it. Move past his fear.

It was time to start living again.

"I have a place out back," he said finally, starting toward the back door. "It's private and quiet. We can be alone there."

A place out back. Memories beat in her heart—ones of shame and humiliation. Her knees turned wobbly, but she managed to follow Jacob through the barn and outside to the small shanty. Just as his cabin had been, this structure was well-built and battened against the most fierce winds.

He isn't going to understand. Her heart beat with the certainty. A man wouldn't understand. Men weren't as vulnerable, as powerless.

He unlocked the door, and the doorknob squeaked, the noise grating along her spine. The lantern's glow revealed a single room with a stove along one wall. One curtained window graced the wall next to the door.

Libby noted the layer of dust coating the bare wood floors to the black stove and emphasizing the tiny house's lack of use. Cobwebs shivered on the wooden table and chairs in the corner and on the carved bed frame tucked against the farthest wall.

Jacob unfolded the clean cloth he'd grabbed from the stable and began dusting the small table. "I bring in supplies toward the beginning of next month. Blizzards come as early as October around here, and I like to be stocked up. Last winter I spent three days holed up in here, unable to get back home. I was grateful for a supply of food. I doubt I would have been able to make it across the street to the diner.''

He stared at her, and Libby's insides coiled.

"We can talk here, Elizabeth. No one can hear us." He held out his hand. "Come sit with me."

Such gentle hands. Gentle enough never to hurt her.

She slipped her palm against his. His big fingers caught hers, easing her toward him. She settled down on the nearby chair, so close her thigh brushed his.

Fire. Desire like flames raged through her, obliterating her common sense. She'd never known the power of such feelings. In the webby light she could see the need in his eyes. The need for a woman and the need to forget, for just a moment, the pain of life.

She knew what he wanted. Love. Physical comfort. Her hand trembled as she reached out to touch his cheek. His jaw felt slightly rough, a wonderful man's texture against her fingertips.

"I'm sorry I rejected you the way I have, at how I've been treating you." Jacob tensed his jaw, gazing at her hair. "I didn't mean to hurt you."

Libby looked into gray eyes filled with pain and immeasurable sorrow. She felt it as surely as heat from a red-hot stove. But how to comfort him? She longed to hold him, to find a way to heal his pain. Would he let her? "You didn't hurt me, Jacob."

"Yes, I did." He leaned both elbows on the table and covered his face with his hands. "I swore I'd never care about a woman again. I couldn't survive that happening to me twice."

"I understand. It's an honorable man who can love someone so deeply."

He didn't answer.

If only he would love her like that, Libby wished. She knew better than to hold her breath.

"I thought marriage would solve my problems with Emma. I thought I might be able to find someone to exist with, share the same house but not the same bed."

Jacob knew it would be wiser to keep silent, to keep from sharing so much. But when he looked up, Elizabeth's eyes glistened with need, and he felt driven to protect her, to make amends for what he'd done.

"One look at you, wearing that green-striped dress and straw bonnet, and I knew I'd made a mistake. You were so much more than I expected, than what I wanted. I knew you'd come to find a real home and a family."

She stared down at her hands folded in her lap. Jacob couldn't tell if the frown on her face meant how she felt about him, but he suspected he knew. She didn't understand. She'd never lost every piece of her heart.

"Tell me what happened," he invited. "I need to know."

The lantern light brushed her face in gentle strokes, and the warmth drained from her eyes. "I can't. I just can't."

Shame shivered in her words.

Jacob's conscience squeezed. "You are safe here, Elizabeth. Before I make any decisions, we need to talk about your baby."

Silence filled the small shanty except for her strangled sigh.

She won't tell me, Jacob thought angrily, then stopped.

Maybe it was his fault. Maybe she couldn't trust him enough to tell him the truth. He'd certainly given her little reason to.

Lantern light cascaded over her, caressing her honeyed hair the way his fingers ached to. *She's a fine woman,* he reminded himself. He wanted to believe in her, to accept her. For Emma's sake. For his own.

"Can you feel the baby move?" he asked to counter her silence.

"No, it's too soon." Her voice sounded so fragile.

His gaze fell to her belly. She wasn't so large yet or cumbersome, the life inside still small so her stomach curved like a soup bowl beneath the gathered waistband of her pleated apron.

"You can trust me, Elizabeth."

Her bottom lip quivered. She tucked it between her teeth. The sight teased him. Made him want to lean closer and kiss her hard, with all his need.

But tears filled her eyes, stopping him.

He shouldn't be thinking about her like that. He looked away, even as her voice tugged at him.

"I was born in a shanty like this. Not much bigger." Her voice whispered soft, low, remembering, drawing Jacob around in his chair. "My father worked for a plantation owner in Virginia before the war. He was gone often, working long and hard. When my mother died, I watched him wither inside a little more each day that passed. He couldn't live without her."

She lifted her right hand and traced a pattern on the smooth oak table. "That's why I understand, Jacob. I've seen what losing a wife can do to a man."

Like a blow to his breastbone, he gasped for breath. Sharp images pierced his heart, leaving him raw. He opened his mouth. No words came.

"I don't blame you, Jacob. My father couldn't take care of me. He couldn't bear to. He said I had my mother's eyes. That looking into my face was like being reminded of his loss anew.

"He asked my aunt to take care of me. It was hard for a little girl, losing her mother, then her father, her home, everything she knew. I went from a loving home to a house filled with anger and coldness. My aunt had several children, and I was only another mouth to feed."

Jacob didn't know what to say. He was no different. He'd been no better to his Emma.

"My uncle was a strict man. He made certain I earned my keep in their home, both on the farm and in the house. You see, my aunt thought my mother had ruined my father's life. They feared I was just as selfish."

Jacob realized the coldness, the harshness Elizabeth had endured. Her finger kept tracing patterns in the wood.

"Growing up, I was very restricted in what I could do. I was lucky enough to attend school for a while, but as my aunt had more children, I was needed to help make a living. When the war broke out, my uncle enlisted and they could not afford to keep me."

Jacob closed his eyes. The war ruined many lives, took men who deserved to live when he had only wanted to die. "Where did you go?"

"I let a room in a boardinghouse and kept my job, sewing coats in a local factory. The long hours left me exhausted, but I didn't have to walk back to the farm and put in a long evening of work. It was an improvement. Until the factory closed.''

Jacob watched fear flash over her face, reflecting the difficulty of a young woman alone in an uncertain world without family, without protection.

"I had to find work." Her voice was so hollow, it haunted him. "I walked to the nearest city and secured work as a seamstress. Over the next two years I worked long hard hours to support myself, to keep a safe roof over my head and warm food in my stomach.''

She looked so vulnerable in her plain calico dress, sewn skillfully, but he could see the garment had been worn and washed and worn again across many years. There was much hardship Elizabeth wasn't telling him.

"I answered an advertisement for work in Omaha. They needed skilled seamstresses, and they were paying so much money. I ended up traveling west, only to find too few jobs. I was lucky to secure a good-paying position in a tailor shop, basting and doing the finishing work. Arthur, the shop owner, he was a kind man and always smiling. I just thought…''

Elizabeth's pain sliced through him. She sat so straight, he feared her spine might snap. Her jaw locked tight, her chin set straight. Pride. He could see how desperately she struggled to hold on to it. Jacob sensed pride meant a lot to her.

"I know I was wrong now." Her finger stopped. "Oh, Jacob." Tears filled her eyes, spilling down her face. Her thin shoulders bobbed. "I should have known a successful man would want nothing with a woman like me. He was so charming, so sincere. I was his only employee; we spent ten hours a day, six days a week together in his shop, sewing side by side as the winter winds blew through the board walls and the red-hot stove puffed out smoke.''

She took a deep breath. ''We talked to fill the hours. I didn't feel comfortable with him, the way I did with your letters. I felt woefully inadequate. I am so inexperienced around men, and I believed him when he said he cared more for me than anyone.''

A black rage roared through Jacob. He could see the situation. An innocent young girl, unaware of the way things were between men and women, and how the older, wiser man took advantage. Elizabeth was so damn innocent, it would have been no trick at all to deceive her.

''I never imagined he would feel that way. I didn't love him—I wasn't in love with him. But you were so far away and nothing but a fantasy, and he was a flesh-and-blood man who told me I was pretty, that he wanted to marry me.''

Tears streamed down her cheeks, glimmering like diamonds in the lantern's glow. ''I wanted to know what it was like to have a man love me, in the emotional sense. I didn't know about the physical part. I didn't know...''

Her lower lip trembled. ''I didn't know, and then I didn't know how to stop him. He said if I loved him, I would let him, and I...I never said yes, but I didn't say no. I didn't say no, Jacob.''

She folded her hands, falling silent. He studied her slender fingers, work-reddened and rough. He remembered how she'd hesitated from touching Emma that day in the cabin. She'd grown up without affection, was so hungry for it she believed the first man who came along. Damn, but he was angry with her for being so innocent. And so very lonely.

"Then your letter came asking me to come visit you, to marry you. How could I say no to a dream, to a man I'd made fantasies about, to a man I wanted more than anything?"

"You slept with a man after I proposed to you?" He bit out the question.

"No, Jacob. But it didn't matter. He'd grown tired of me anyway. His wife was coming out from back east. I didn't know about the wife."

"The wife?" A hard knot twisted in his chest. "You gave yourself to the first man who showed any interest in you—and he was *married?*"

"Jacob, I'm so sorry." A sob tore through her. "I never thought...I didn't know...I thought he...I-loved me."

He didn't want to understand. His heart felt raw, his entire body felt numb. Elizabeth covered her face with her hands and never made another sound.

He craved the feel of her against his chest, in his arms, tucked beneath his chin. Another part of him hurt at how easily tempted she'd been. How she betrayed him in her letters by never mentioning this part of her life, of her job, of the man who made promises he never intended to keep.

Not since Mary's death had he been at such a loss. When he could have reached out, he stepped away.

Living again hurt like hell. He wanted to live again. Fear—of loss, of risk, of losing—held him back.

Jacob reached for the lantern. "Come. I'll see you home."

He held his heart tight as she followed him soundlessly, never saying another word.

The big moon spilled silver-white light on the quiet streets as Libby sat beside Jacob in his buckboard, heading home. She didn't want to talk any more on what lay between them. Apparently neither did he.

He guided the horses with gentle sureness. "Pleasant night," he said.

"It's a beautiful night." The stars, white as cotton and twinkling, never looked as big and close as in Montana. The spiraling pink of the Milky Way dusted the inky black sky and shimmered.

"Look. Northern lights." Jacob eased the horses to a stop after turning off Main.

Libby lifted her face to the sky. Along the horizon's north rim of trees and high mountain foothills snapped ribbons of luminous pink, streaking across the endless black sky.

It was wondrous. Libby held her breath. "I've never seen such a thing."

"It's caused by the earth's magnetic poles," Jacob said quietly. "I can see them from my cabin. Some nights I sit up late just to watch them."

He knew so much. What would he want with an uneducated, unsophisticated woman like her? Maybe it was pity that drove him. She didn't want his pity.

"I never had much time to watch stars," Libby said. "I always had work to do."

"The stars always give me hope."

"Hope?"

He nodded. "There is so much strife on this earth, injustice and war. Everything in life changes, but these stars keep shining."

It was strange, Libby thought, they shared much in common. Loss and hardship and the need to find hope. Jacob gripped the reins, and the bays responded instantly, drawing the buckboard down the dark street. An owl hooted, sweeping low on wide wings, hunting for mice.

The silence felt companionable. *Don't let it end,* she wished even as the Faded Bloom eased into sight. He halted the horses. When she moved to hop down, he laid his hand over hers, stopping her.

His gaze caressed her face. "Let me help you."

Her heart fluttered. She wanted his touch the way a prospector wanted gold. Some treasures were too precious to let go.

He circled around the buckboard and offered his hand.

Moonlight dusted over him, illuminating the handsome angles of his face, his high forehead, strong nose, solid cheekbones. And the smile soft on his firm mouth.

Libby placed her hand in his, and he swept her to the ground. Her head spun. She felt intoxicated by his nearness.

"I guess I'll see you in the morning," he said, walking her to the door.

"Yes, tomorrow morning." She'd forgotten her agreement to measure Emma. That's how much Jacob unsettled her. "I'll be ready."

"Good."

His voice rumbled low, shivering straight through her.

She longed for more, for the feel of his strong arms, for the exciting brush of his mouth to hers.

But heavens, he thought her a loose woman. He was too fine a man, too noble and honorable to want a girl as foolish as she.

His fingers nudged her chin, lifting her face. His eyes looked so sad. His mouth so grim. *He didn't want her.* Her whole heart threatened to crack.

Then he leaned forward, catching her lips with his. He tasted hot, faintly like coffee, the seductive sweep of his mouth coaxing sensations Libby had never felt. Heat pooled in her belly, twisted through her spine. This was like nothing she'd known, not the coolness she'd felt with Arthur. This feeling, this power, could shatter her.

Heavens, she felt hot. Scorching heat rose up in a tide of need. Oh, how she wanted him. As if sensing her thoughts, Jacob enfolded her in his iron-strong arms, pressing her against the expanse of his chest. He felt so good, her bones melted. His kiss intensified, deepened, and she gave herself up to him, helpless.

His kisses grew rough, but good. And so hot she couldn't breathe.

Then, abruptly, he stepped away from her, shadowed, breathing deeply. Libby blinked. She could not think as a coolness slipped between them.

"Jacob?" Panic shivered through her. What had she done? "Y-you think I—I'm...that I always..." she couldn't finish.

She thought of the small roundness of her belly. He must have felt it against him during their embrace. Was he thinking of it, too?

"I'm sorry, Elizabeth. I'm not ready for these feelings."
He stared at his hands. The breeze lifted his hair, mussing
it. "I don't know what I think."

At least he was honest, Libby thought, the hope in her
heart sinking.

She watched Jacob stride away. *Don't be a fool.* When
he felt ready to love again, it wouldn't be to a woman like
her: simple, plain and pregnant.

Chapter Eight

"Good morning, Elizabeth." Jacob stood in the new morning sunshine on the Faded Bloom's porch.

"Jacob." He looked fine in a red flannel shirt and tan trousers. Too fine. Libby's heartbeat doubled, and she lowered her eyes. *Remember last night.* "I see Emma's waiting."

"Miss Hodges! Miss Hodges!" Emma bounced on the wagon seat. "Pa let me ride into town to get you!"

Libby laughed. "You probably woke the entire block, but I'm so glad you came."

"Me, too."

She felt Jacob's gaze on her, heavy and, she feared, condemning. What kind of woman did he think she was? "I brought my sewing box." The wood grip felt familiar, comforting in her hand. "I'm ready to start work."

Jacob tried to smile. "Then we'd best get going. I couldn't leave Emma home alone. I didn't think you'd mind if she joined us."

"You know how I feel about Emma."

He fingered the dark hat he clutched with both hands. "Yes, I know, Elizabeth. Believe me, I know."

As his gaze pinned hers, the weight of last night, of her confession, of her bold behavior kissing him, heated her face.

But Jacob only held out his hand and offered to carry her sewing box. Something that looked like understanding glittered in his eyes, and Libby's anxieties eased. He was such a fine gentleman. Such a gentle man.

When they pulled up to the snug log cabin tucked beneath the deep green boughs, Libby stilled her heart. This was Emma's and Jacob's home, nothing more.

"Here, let me help you."

She glanced up, startled. She hadn't heard him hop down from the halted buckboard, hadn't seen him circle around. Now he stood beside her, holding out his hand, and the knowing weight of his gaze met hers.

Emma grabbed her hand, dragging her to the cabin, chattering all the way. She talked on about her new dress and how glad she was Libby would make it and asked if she'd had breakfast yet. Pa was going to make them all pancakes and eggs.

"Let's go into my room," the girl suggested, marching in the front door and through the cozy main room with its gray stone fireplace and hearth, with the smoothly varnished puncheon floors and the deep honey wood walls.

Libby dutifully followed the child to one of two doors on the far wall. Emma's room was snug and cozy, just large enough for her small bed, neatly made, and a chest along one wall. A doll's cradle fashioned from varnished wood sat on the small trunk holding Emma's rag doll.

"See, she's wearing the red dress you made and the

little apron." The girl carefully retrieved Beth from her cradle.

"She has velvet ribbons tied to the ends of her braids just like you." Libby touched those soft lengths of plaited yarn.

"Pa bought them just for her from Mr. Ellington." Emma gently laid the doll down in the snug cradle, nested with small rectangles of old flannel.

Jacob's boots rang on the wood floor, and Libby looked up. His gaze caught hers through the open doorway. Her heart stopped beating.

"Would you like some breakfast?" he asked.

He warmed her like a fire on a cold day. "Yes, I would."

He tipped off his hat and ambled out of sight. She could hear the bang of a stove's lid and the ring of a skillet. She craved his presence, even if it was wrong wanting someone she couldn't have.

"Pa makes great pancakes," Emma confided, slipping her small hand in Libby's.

She could feel the girl's lonely need for a woman's affection—she could see it in this cozy room, bare without a colorful quilt laid across the bed or without a warm braided rug on the floor.

"Do you want me to start measuring for your dress?"

"Yes!" Excited blue eyes twinkled.

Libby set her sewing box on the blanketed bed. "Then let's get started. I want you to tell me what kind of dresses you like."

Emma launched into a delightful description as Libby pulled out her tape and began measuring.

"Do you like my pa?" she asked abruptly.

Libby nodded. "Sure. I bet he's a good pa to you."

Emma frowned. "Well, so, do you like our cabin?"

"It's snug and safe." Libby marked the inches on a scrap of paper. "I know what you're up to, Emma."

"You do?" Her eyes widened so only honest need shone in them. "I like you very much, Miss Hodges."

Libby's hands faltered and the tape slipped from her fingers. It rolled to the floor, uncurling beneath the small bed.

"Oh, Emma." Libby couldn't stop herself. She reached out and brushed at the soft brown wisps of hair hiding much of the girl's forehead. She let a thin lock curl around her finger. "I'm sorry I came all this way just to get your hopes up. You don't know how I wish I had a daughter just like you."

"Would you want me for a daughter?" Still, that endless-sky hope.

"Oh, yes." Libby's throat hurt, and she pulled her hand away. She knew what the girl wanted. There was nothing she could do to change Jacob's mind. She and Emma had the same dreams, the same needs.

He knocked on the opened door, stirring Libby from her thoughts. "Emma, come set the table."

The little girl scampered off, quick about her tasks, but the sadness clung to the corners of her mouth and shone navy dark in her eyes.

He's angry with me. Jacob would hardly look at her as he filled a platter with pancakes, keeping them warm in the oven, then adding more to the stack. Eggs sizzled with bacon in another skillet.

"I want to help," she said over the clatter of Emma dropping the flatware on the table. "What should I do?"

Jacob lifted the fry pan from the stove. "There's nothing to do. Breakfast is ready."

Then he smiled, and the loneliness lifted from her chest.

"Come sit by me," Emma begged.

She relented.

The sight of gentle-faced Elizabeth in his kitchen tore at his foolish heart. He couldn't get it out of his mind, the feel of her rounding belly pressed against his groin last night, the sight of it beneath her skirts today. And it tore at him.

He knew the kind of woman she was: honest, kind, and hardworking. Despite her innocence and her damn stupidity. What did she expect walking around with her heart so open, her need so clear?

He saw the loneliness in her eyes, how happy she was to sit down at the table next to Emma, how she lapped up affection.

Jacob flipped an egg on Emma's plate and two each on his and Elizabeth's. He stood so close, she only had to breathe to touch him.

He wanted her touch. It was more than sexual—it was deeper than that. He craved *her*. Even now.

Her wheat blond hair was tamed, plaited neatly and pinned around her head. Jacob wondered what it might be like to work his fingers through that thick, silken softness and watch it fall free.

She picked up her fork, and the movement brought his gaze lower, to her lap, seeing the roundness of the small life growing within her. To the reality he could not afford to forget: women died in childbirth.

On the ride back into town, Libby clutched her sewing box in one hand and squinted beneath her sunbonnet's brim into the bright midmorning sun. After eating, she had offered to help with the dishes but Jacob refused, not looking at her. She finished measuring Emma and accepted a ride back into town.

Now Emma chattered merrily at her elbow, between them, talking on about the horses, and it being Sunday and the picnic she and her pa were going on later.

Libby did her best not to care too much. She watched Jacob's gaze slide across her belly several times.

He may understand, but he would not forgive. She sensed it like the scent of autumn leaves on the wind.

Town came into view, a string of three intersecting streets and the buildings huddled along them. Smoke rose from smokestacks in thick gray plumes, filling the town with the cozy scent of wood smoke.

Jacob halted the team at his livery.

"I can walk from here," she said quietly.

"Don't leave," Emma pleaded.

Over her dark head, Jacob's eyes found hers. A similar plea lurked there, between shadows, between what could only be doubt.

"I'd like to stay, Emma, but I have to get started on your dress. Soon, September will be gone and the winter weather will be here. You'll need that warm dress then."

"Aw, pshaw." Emma waved her hand.

"You sound like your grandpa," Jacob commented wryly.

Emma giggled.

Libby longed for such gentle affection, but deliberately turned away and hopped down from the buckboard, spurring Jacob into action.

"I wanted to help you down."

She hated the kindness in his eyes. It only made her want him more. "I don't need help, Jacob. I don't understand why you even want me to sew this dress in the first place."

"Because I don't sew." He shrugged his brawny shoulders. "Because I wanted an excuse to know you better."

"Why? I don't understand." Confusion tore through her. "Emma, hand me down my sewing box."

The girl complied. "You have to come with us."

Libby hated looking into those deep blue eyes and saying the words, but she did it. "No, I'm afraid I can't. I'm sorry, Emma."

Her fingers caught the wood handle and she turned away.

"Emma, stay there." Jacob's command rang in the back yard of the livery. Then came the thud of his boots pounding against the hard-packed earth. "Elizabeth."

She kept walking.

"Elizabeth." He caught up to her. "Why are you walking away? I wanted to ask you to come with us."

"Thank you, Jacob, but I don't need your pity." She walked faster, her entire heart fracturing. *I want your love.*

"My pity? What gave you that idea?"

"Little things. Like that sad little pinched look around your eyes. Like your silence."

"I couldn't talk about this in front of Emma."

"Good. Because I don't want to talk about it at all." She whipped around the corner of the livery, Main Street in plain sight.

Jacob snared her wrist, swinging her around. His im-

prisoning grip felt bruising. "I don't pity you, damn it. I...
You confuse me."

"Well, you confuse me." She wrestled her arm free,
tears stinging behind her eyes.

"Did I hurt you?"

Concern so wide in his eyes. She bowed her chin so she
didn't have to look at it. "Yes. It will probably bruise."

"Oh—" He looked stricken. "I'm sorry."

Nothing mattered, not the bruise, not her silly dreams.
"I appreciate the sewing work, I really do, but don't feed
me out of some misplaced sense of obligation."

"Obligation? Where are you getting these ideas?" he
asked, his dark brows knitting together. "Have I ever said
or done anything to make you think that?"

"You tried to give me money for my passage when we
agreed I would pay my own way." She wouldn't look at
him. *She wouldn't.* Looking at him would break down her
resolve. She wanted him, not to fight with him.

"You agreed to that, I never did. I always intended to
reimburse you, and if you weren't such a stubborn, inde-
pendent woman, then you wouldn't be stuck here without
a way to return home."

"I have no home," she said, too late to grab it back.
She gasped. "I mean, Omaha wasn't a home, as much as
a stopping place."

He said nothing. "I'm sorry, Elizabeth. Hell, I didn't
mean—" He sighed, raking his hand through his hair,
standing it up on end. His hat was missing—he must have
left it in the buckboard.

"I know what you meant." She'd bared her heart to
him, let him know her greatest mistake. And he treated her
so civilly. It enraged her. It shamed her. She spun away

from him. "Just keep your charity to yourself, Jacob Stone. I don't need you. I don't need anything from any man. Not ever again."

She walked fast, trying to keep the tears in, but they burned with rage behind her eyes. Rage at Jacob for being afraid to love again. Rage at herself for needing him more than she'd ever needed anyone.

He hadn't meant to hurt her. She just made him *feel* so much—so hard, so furious. He took Emma on their picnic, stopping by the hotel to pick up a fried chicken meal, and took out the cart he'd made. The mare that had grabbed hold of Elizabeth's ruffle needed a good run.

All week long he avoided her. He needed time to know how to try again to talk to her about what terrified him most.

Once, he was hard at work mucking stalls and he looked up and saw her through the wide doors of the barn. Rain stained the sky gray and stirred the dusty streets to mud. She'd been wearing the same blue calico he'd seen several times and her white apron, carrying a box of groceries from the mercantile. She'd been walking in the direction of Leah's hotel.

Maude Baker from the Faded Bloom stopped by with her stall rent. She insisted Elizabeth didn't need or want his help. Although, when he declined the money, he saw approval in her measuring eyes. No doubt, she wrongly guessed the baby Elizabeth carried was his.

Jacob felt at a loss. He didn't want to go backward to existing without feeling, breathing without living. But he couldn't seem to move forward, either.

Another week rolled by before he figured out what to

do. He would enlist the help of his daughter. Emma, no doubt, would be happy to see Elizabeth again.

"There's a young lady to see you," Maude Baker said as she knocked on the door.

Libby, sitting by the window, looked up. "Come in, Maude. You said a young lady? Who?"

The door popped open to reveal a friendly smile and mysteriously twinkling eyes. "I'm not telling. You'll have to come see for yourself. Oh, and she says to bring your coat and mittens."

"My coat and mittens?" Only a mother would say such a thing...or a child. *Emma.* "Tell her I'll be right down."

"Will do." Maude disappeared down the hall, humming.

Libby grabbed her coat, she had no mittens, and hurried downstairs. Sure enough, a small sprite of a girl waited in the parlor, her blue eyes snapping with excitement.

"Pa says it's gonna be cold," she said, hopping off the overstuffed chair and bounding across the room.

Libby welcomed the innocent hug around her middle. "What's going to be cold?"

"Going on a picnic. It's too darn cold, Pa said, but he agreed to do it anyway."

One look at that grin, and Libby felt trapped. "Where is your pa?"

"Waiting in the cart."

"The cart?"

Emma shrugged. "Yep. Pa got a cart for when the buckboard was too much. He exercises the horses with it. And he takes me on rides in it."

"Does he?" Through the space between the heavy

drapes, she could see a small slice of the street outside. But no Jacob and no cart.

"You have to come. Please? We got extra chicken and everything."

"Say yes." His voice rumbled in from outside.

Libby froze. Jacob. He stood framed in the doorway, the cool gray day at his back, his face shadowed. She remembered how angry she'd been at him. "I should stay home and sew. I have work to do."

"We won't be long."

How his voice touched her, steady like a caress, hot like a kiss. She shivered inside, remembering.

"Yes." The easiest word she'd ever said.

Emma cheered, bouncing up and down, and Jacob held open the door.

Libby brushed past him, resolved not to make more of his invitation than a show of friendship, when she stopped dead still on the porch step. "*That's* your cart?"

Jacob brushed up behind her. "Built it myself."

"Come on. I'm gettin' hungry!" Emma tugged at Libby's hand, and she followed the girl down the steps toward the small horse-drawn buggy at the curb. Her idea of a cart and Jacob's idea of one only proved how different they were, how unsuited.

He helped her onto the padded seat beside Emma, catching her gaze with a smile.

"Why, this is the mare you told me about," she commented as they rolled down the quiet midmorning streets.

"Yes. I need to get her used to driving again. She's not skittish anymore, is she, Emma?"

"No. She's calm as a kitten." Emma leaned back in the seat, grinning wide.

The crisp autumn breeze whispered over them on the ride out of town, toward a low rolling meadow split in half by the river. While it was too cold to play in the water, Emma found plenty of room to run while Jacob carried the basket.

Libby followed, uncertain what to say. She didn't understand why he'd invited her.

"I've been thinking about what you told me, about the baby's father." His voice came gruff, but low.

Libby's step faltered. "I understand how you feel, what kind of woman you think I am."

"You're a damn fine woman, Elizabeth. I know it, and Emma knows it. That isn't what I mean."

"I'm not so fine, Jacob. I'm not like you." She'd been born in a one-room shanty.

"You are fine enough for Emma and me." His gaze held hers.

What was he asking her?

He set the basket in the grass and unfolded the wool blanket that covered it. "I've thought everything over. I can see how a woman as lonely for affection as you were could have been misled."

She blushed. She had been misled. Lied to. She hadn't known what Arthur was doing until he'd done it, laying her over a blanket. She blinked back tears then, so glad it was over. She blinked back tears now. "That doesn't change things between us. You said you don't want more children."

"I don't." His words sounded choked. "I won't be responsible. I just can't be to blame..." *For another woman's death.* He stared hard at the blanket as he laid it over the rock-hard earth. "But I like you, Elizabeth."

"You do?"

"Very much."

Don't read too much into it. Libby wasn't going to be a fool a second time. She knelt to smooth a corner of the blanket. "I plan to have Emma's dress done in two weeks. I'll have all of Mr. Ellington's piece work caught up by then, too."

"Two weeks is fine." Jacob began unpacking the basket. "Emma. The food is ready."

"I'm comin'!" The crisp wind carried her voice across the tall, dry grasses.

Tell him the rest. Libby sat down on the blanket and helped set out the tin plates. "I nearly have enough money saved for the coach ride east."

His head whipped up. "You're leaving?"

"Yes." She tried to sound casual. "At the middle of next month. Two weeks. I won't be around to trouble you any longer than that."

"You're no trouble, Elizabeth." Jacob's gaze held hers, but he said nothing more.

Emma clamored up, breathless and hungry, and he looked away.

"Pa! I saw a deer back there. Think it will eat some of our bread?"

"It's a wild animal, Emma." He spoke gently, but his words sounded tight. "Some things aren't meant to be approached."

"But he's so pretty. Can I take Miss Hodges and show her?" A blue gaze swiveled to hers. "Have you seen deer before? This one has big antlers and everything."

"Go ahead and see," Jacob urged.

Libby stood, trying not to care how he wouldn't look at her. It was truly over between them. She offered Emma her hand.

Chapter Nine

Frost hardened the ground as Libby crunched through the morning-quiet streets. A cold mist fell, chilling her clear through the layers of wool and flannel. She hugged her coat more tightly and kept walking.

She'd given her notice to Leah at the hotel and to Maude at the boardinghouse. There was only one detail left. She'd buy a ticket this morning and be on the stage out of town by this afternoon.

Libby didn't want to go, but Jacob didn't want her to stay. After she told him on their picnic she was leaving, he'd withdrawn from her completely. He'd answered Emma's questions kindly, hitched up the horse, and drove them back into town as soon as they'd finished eating.

But his silence hurt like a blow.

She didn't know what he thought. Was he glad she was leaving town? Was he angry she hadn't accepted the money he felt he owed her?

At a loss, Libby hesitated before the gray barn where the blue sign, Stone's Livery, swung with the brisk wind. One of the large front doors was ajar, indicating he might be in this early.

"Jacob?" She hesitated at the door.

He didn't answer. One horse nickered to her, the small sorrel mare with the single star they'd taken with them on the picnic. Libby crossed through the straw-strewn floor to rub the horse's velvet nose.

A loud hammering, followed by several sharp rings in deliberate rhythm, led Libby around to the back of the livery. She found Jacob in a separate room attached to the stable, bent over his fire. Rolled up shirtsleeves exposed his strong arms. Muscles rippled and bunched as he worked.

He glanced up from the forge. "I'll be done in a minute."

Libby watched as he placed the glowing curve of iron onto the anvil and began a rhythmic pounding. The ringing sound echoed in the small room, hurting her ears.

She didn't want to disappoint or hurt him. Not after how good he'd been to her, paying for her room and board at Maude's. Few men would have been so generous.

Nerves slipped through her, and Libby placed her hand on her growing belly. Jacob dropped the horseshoe into a nearby bucket. Water hissed and steam rose as he walked toward her.

"Good morning, Elizabeth. I didn't know if I'd see you again." He stopped a safe distance before her, his breath a visible white puff in the cold morning air. He rubbed his blackened hands on his thick leather apron.

Libby found her voice. "I couldn't just leave, Jacob. I had to say goodbye. And to give you Emma's dress. I finished it last night."

She unfolded the dress, so he could see it. But Jacob

averted his eyes, studying the nearby horse standing patiently, waiting for new shoes.

"I'm sure Emma will love it. She's with Mrs. Holt these days." He hesitated. "You can find her there if you want to talk to her."

Libby dreaded facing the very proper Mrs. Holt. "I've made you a gift."

"What?" His gaze swung up, revealing the surprise on his face, revealing the bleakness in his eyes. "I don't need a gift, Elizabeth."

"It's in appreciation." Emotion knotted in her throat. "It's not the most expensive or elegant gift, but it's something I made for you."

She held up the blue flannel shirt, extra wide in the shoulders to allow for movement as he worked. "This heavy material is the best Ellington had. It will keep you warm enough so you won't need to wear a coat while you're here in the barn."

He stood framed with the frozen, cold world behind him, a dark figure in black. His face unreadable, his stance stiff and unbending.

"I notice you wear a lot of blue," she said nervously.

"It's a fine shirt."

"I hope you like it. I lined Emma's dress. It will be warmer." Looking away seemed easiest. She folded the shirt along with the dress and wrapped them up in the brown paper.

"Let me pay you." Jacob drew his billfold from his pocket. His fingers, blackened from his work at the forge, eased several bills from the leather fold.

"That's too much," she protested as he shoved a wad of money into her hand.

"It's not enough." His touch blazed through her, and she quieted the fast beat of her heart. "If you weren't leaving, if you had decided to stay—" He paused.

"What are you saying, Jacob?"

"I don't know. I don't want—" He sighed, closing and then opening his dark eyes. "Why the hell are you leaving? Can you answer me that?"

"Because I don't live here, Jacob." Confused, Libby stepped forward, hugging the package to her rounded belly. "I came to visit you, to marry you. Since there's no home for me here, I can't stay. People are starting to think this baby is yours."

She'd felt the whispers at her back. The eager suitors had long since gone. "You don't want me here, Jacob. It ruins your life, and confuses Emma."

"And leaving won't hurt me and my daughter?"

Libby hurt watching him. "Jacob, I thought that was our agreement. If there was no marriage, then I would leave you be. For Emma's sake."

"All I know is when I'm near you, life is easier to live." His voice trembled with sincerity. "I don't want you to go."

"But you said—"

"None of this makes sense to me either, but I know how I feel. Maybe we can keep to our original plans. I'm willing to try again, Elizabeth, if you still want to."

"You'll give me another chance? At what?"

"To find out if we're compatible."

She set the package on top of a straw bale. "Don't we know that already?"

Sadness crept into his eyes.

"I saw what losing my mother did to my father. It destroyed him. He was never the same man again. He never married, he never kept family ties. The last time I saw him, I was four. I can take care of myself, Jacob. I don't want you to worry."

"I know you can take care of yourself, Elizabeth." Jacob's gaze fell to the package. "You've proven that by working hard, without complaint. That isn't the issue."

"No, but the baby is." She laid her hand on the crest of her stomach.

"The baby…" His big hands fisted. He had to try. If she'd had children of her own already born, that would be a different issue. But women died in childbirth. "I can't go through that again."

"I'm not asking you to. Jacob, I don't want this baby to grow up the way I did, out of place, resented."

"I don't resent—"

"You don't accept it, either." Her eyes glistened with understanding.

Why didn't she get angry at him? Why didn't she hate him? Jacob pressed his hand to his forehead. Lord, he couldn't let her go. He'd asked her to stay, yet she still looked set on leaving.

"I'll write you and Emma when I'm settled." She reached up to kiss his cheek.

So much sweetness. He needed her, he needed to absorb her the way a drought-stricken land needs water. How to tell her?

"Goodbye, Jacob. Take care of yourself." She walked away before he could summon up the words to stop her.

His gaze fell to the carefully sewn shirt she'd made him. Tears filled his eyes. He didn't want to care for her, but he couldn't seem to stop the flood of affection in his heart. It hurt to watch her walk away. It hurt damn bad.

The rain had turned to snow. Libby walked carefully down the wet boardwalk and waded through mud as she crossed the street. Her heart felt shattered.

She didn't expect Jacob to stop her from leaving. She didn't expect him to beg her to stay. Life had taught her to be a realist. But saying goodbye…it seemed so *final.*

How long had it been since she had real ties? Her heart ached to spend time with Jacob, to see what could happen between them. But she didn't fool herself. Jacob was not ready to love her. She understood how ties could bind a heart—and shatter it when they ended.

She felt like that. Shattered, grief-stricken at having to leave Jacob. But she could not stay in this town. She would not stand by waiting, hoping he would be able to end his grieving, hoping for marriage.

Her aunt was waiting for her, had said she could come. It would be a difficult situation living with the cold woman, but Libby felt determined to make the best of it.

Gathering every last bit of her courage, Libby knocked on Mrs. Holt's door. Within seconds, the tight-lipped woman appeared, her eyes pinching with recognition.

"What do you want?"

Libby drew her coat tightly over her rounding stomach. "I'd like to see Emma, please. Jacob said it was okay."

"Jacob, is it?" Those judgmental eyes of the very proper Mrs. Holt raked her with condemnation. No doubt she suspected the baby was Jacob's, as many people did. "I'll get the girl, but you'll have to speak with her outside."

Libby nodded, flushing. The falling snow cooled her,

and she let it cling to her shoulders and hair. When she was very small, before Mother became ill, she remembered playing in the winter snows.

"Miss Hodges!" Emma burst through the door breathless without a coat or hat. "Are you done with my dress?"

"Yes, I just left it with your pa. You can try it on tonight."

"That's good. It's supposed to be a winter dress and look, it's snowing really hard."

"Yes. I finished it just in time. And guess what? I have something for you."

"You do?"

She tugged out the carefully wrapped packages, one from each coat pocket. "I made these for a gift."

Emma's small fingers, red from the chilly morning, tore at the brown paper. "Oh, more clothes for Beth."

"I made her a winter dress, too, out of the scraps from your dress. And a good warm winter coat, a hat and gloves. To keep her warm this winter."

Eyes sad, Emma looked up. "You're leaving, aren't you?"

"How did you know?"

"I heard Mrs. Holt talking." The small girl bowed her chin. "I don't want you to go. You were supposed to marry my pa and be my mother."

"I know. It makes me sad, too." *More than sad.*

"But what about your baby?" Emma reached out her hand.

Libby startled at the touch to her rounding stomach, just noticeable behind the wool bulk of her coat.

"Pa said it wasn't our baby." Emma removed her hand.

"No." Libby managed. How was she going to tell this child goodbye?

But she did it anyway, making sure Emma understood. None of this was her fault.

It was Libby's. From the moment in the tailor shop when she'd mistaken a man's interest for love. It was a mistake she would never make again.

As the snow began to accumulate outside and the wind began to howl through the open stable door, Jacob finished his stall work. Sweet straw filled the air, and the horses banged their empty grain buckets against their doors in protest. *More,* they demanded.

The nameless mare with the star on her forehead reached out and nipped at his shirt, catching hold of his sleeve. She wanted attention. He patted her velvet nose before moving on.

Elizabeth wanted to leave.

Standing alone, right there in the middle of his livery, Jacob felt the darkness descend, like a black blanket folding itself around his heart. Memories of Mary, so pregnant she waddled when she walked, she needed help with her shoes and getting out of chairs, these pictures snapped into his mind. He remembered the lifeless Mary, lying so still after such agony. He thought of Elizabeth, just as vulnerable, lifeless in the same way. Jacob saw himself grieving her, as lost as he'd been when Mary died.

He ached to go after Elizabeth, ask her to stay, provide for her, love her. But could he face such loss again? He cared for Elizabeth. He'd kissed her, shared meals with her, hired her to do Emma's sewing. But he wasn't in love with her—yet. He could still let her go and never have to face his fears.

But that was no answer. Jacob grabbed his coat, already thinking ahead. He would find his daughter, he would try to make Elizabeth understand. His hands shook, and he fisted them, wishing he could recapture the blind faith in life he'd once known.

After a morning filled with errands, Libby only had her stage ticket to purchase. She wound up in Leah's kitchen, staring at a plate of roasted chicken. The good food steamed as she stared out the window, watching the driving snow.

"Have some of this warm bread," Leah offered, setting a covered basket and a plate of butter by Libby's elbow.

"You are too good to me," she protested, but judging by the look on her former boss's face, she didn't argue.

"You've been a good employee, Libby. I'm mighty sorry to see you go." Leah tugged out a chair and sat down at the small kitchen table. Now, in the quiet time before the dining room opened, they had a moment to talk. "Are you up to this traveling? I'm worried about you."

"It's just stage travel, until I can catch the train. I'll be fine."

"I worry about you not eating. And getting too cold. Look at this weather. This could turn into a blizzard by the looks of things. Maybe you should stay and catch the stage next week."

"It's time for me to go." She thought of Jacob. "If I don't do it now, I may never do it. I can't stay here."

"Because of him?"

Libby blushed at those wise eyes. "I don't belong here. I never did. I have a future, and I best get started on it."

Leah's gaze slid downward. "Yes, the best kind of future. I wish you luck. And if there is something I can do—"

"I know, I know. I'll ask you first." Smiling, Libby reached to butter a piece of steaming bread.

The wind slammed against the side of the building. She jumped, dropping her knife. The light seemed to eke from the room.

"That wind means business." Leah stood and crossed to the stove. "You have the right idea leavin' this country, but I doubt the stage will be running today."

Libby glanced up. All she could see through the window was blowing snow. "I gave Maude notice."

"You can stay with me, no charge." Leah reached down for the coffee grinder. "You'll be stuck here anyway, if this gets any worse. Won't hardly be able to cross the street. One day last winter I woke up to find my entire hotel buried. Three stories! Think of it. No one came or left from my place that day."

"I guess the reverend and his flock won't be picketing Oleson's next door," Libby joked.

A bang rocketed through the hotel.

"Sounds like the front door," Leah guessed. "I best get this coffee started. People comin' in are bound to be near to freezing."

"I might as well help, since I'm stuck here." Libby stood.

"No, finish your meal. Food is important for a woman in your condition. You eat first, then you help. I'll go—"

"Miz Leah?" The kitchen door swung open. A young

man stood there, snow clinging to his clothes. "I'm look-ing for Miss Hodges. Are you Miss Hodges?"

"Yes." Libby jumped, a bolt of alarm jolted her chest. "What's wrong?" She could see it, smell it.

"Mr. Stone sent me to tell you, he thought you should know. I tried you first over at Miz Baker's place, but she sent me here." The lad tugged off his ice-covered hat. "The little girl could be missin'. Seems she left for home and she didn't make it there."

Emma. Libby wasted no time. She snatched her wool coat and shawl from the small lean-to behind the kitchen.

"Libby, where are you going?" Leah abandoned her coffee making. "This weather isn't safe. You aren't going out in it."

"I have to." Her hands shook, making it hard to button her coat. "If Emma is lost, I have to find her."

"Leave it to the men. They've done this kind of search-ing before. They'll find her."

"Leave it to the men." Libby sighed. "That little girl ran off because of me, because she was upset I was leav-ing. I'm certain of it. And that makes me responsible for finding her."

Leah hesitated, measuring. "I don't agree, but I under-stand. Here, take my shawl and gloves, they are better than yours. They will keep you warmer. And here's my hat."

"Thank you." Libby headed for the door. The last thing she heard was Leah's voice promising to head upstairs and rouse her boarders to help with the search.

Cold ice slapped her face, burning like sharp little nee-dles. Libby tucked the edge of Leah's fine shawl across her nose to protect her face. Only her eyes were exposed to the bitter wind. Bending low, she walked as quickly as the snow-covered boardwalk would allow.

Noises rose on the streets. Through the haze of white, she spotted a knot of men on the street, several on horseback listening to the barked instructions of another man on a big gray. Jacob was not among them.

Her eyes tearing at the cold, she circled around and slipped into the livery. The big stable doors were shut tight against the storm, and several horses were missing. A young boy, bone thin, ambled over to greet her.

"You shouldn't be out in the storm like this, ma'am," he advised.

Libby only looked past him. "Is Mr. Stone here?"

"No. He went off to find his girl."

Of course he would. She looked around. There had to be something she could do to help. But what? She owned no horse to join the search for Emma. She couldn't just stand here.

"You'd better stay inside ma'am and let the men try to find the girl," the boy advised.

The hell she would. She marched toward the door, determined, her chin firm.

Two men stepped in from the storm and he hurried to saddle their horses.

Libby strode around them, ignoring their curious gazes. The driving wind cut straight through her layers of wool. She didn't care about the cold. She cared about nothing but Emma. She watched the men on the street fan out on horseback, the man on the gray still waiting to organize other searchers.

Some were on foot, trudging stoically through the heartless winds.

She could walk, too. She had to. A child could be so easily lost and never found in these conditions. Already the tracks Libby left on the strip of uncovered boardwalk between the livery and the main street hardly showed.

There was no time to waste. She hurried across the street toward the boardinghouse where her bags waited, packed in her old room. She let herself in, stomping the snow from her boots, and tore up the two flights of steps. Once inside her room she layered on every piece of warm clothing she owned. Socks. Two union suits. Two wool petticoats, her oldest flannel dress, her wash-worn sweater, and secured it all with the tight sash of her cloak.

The storm is worsening. Emma doesn't have much time. As Libby barreled out into the street, she worried how well the girl was bundled against this unexpected weather. Jacob drove Emma home beneath a warm blanket every day; she wasn't expected to walk any farther than across the street to the livery.

Libby walked north toward the steep slope of the hillside, leaving the town behind. She could hardly see through the heavy snowfall. Men on horseback marched past, not noticing her, others on foot overtook her. Wind drove ice straight through the thick wool of the shawl and froze the shawl to her face.

Hurting from the cold, Libby kept walking. Even when she couldn't feel her toes. Even when her lungs burned sharp and raw from the wind and she couldn't draw in enough air. She wouldn't stop, squinting against the driving snow, watching for any sign that might lead her to Emma.

Men crossed off on the road all around her, shouting to be heard above the roar of the wind. They marched off into the dense undergrowth, looking for the child. As the wind rose, blocking them from her view, Libby feared she would lose sight of the road and become lost.

What had happened to Emma? Had she become confused in the snow and wandered off the road? Had a wild animal found her? A little girl with only a wool coat for warmth wouldn't last long in this cold.

Emma couldn't be dead. The thought made Libby stumble. The driving snow blinded her, burning numbing cold straight into her bones. She refused to think she'd never see Emma again.

All around her, the storm thundered into a blizzard. Libby couldn't see anything, hear anything, saw only colored blurs of men's coats. Some were heading home.

She didn't give up, but kept walking. The road split through the steep evergreens, offering some shield from the wind, but it wasn't enough. Libby crept from one cedar to the next. Her teeth chattered violently, ricocheting through her jaw.

Her body screamed at her to stop. She shook from the inside out, so cold she couldn't feel herself breathe. She had to go on. Libby refused to stop and took one more determined step, then another.

She would find Emma. She would not leave the child to freeze.

Chapter Ten

Jacob wheeled his mount around in the whirling chaos of snow and ice. He'd ridden the trail twice now, and still he found no sign of his daughter. She wasn't in town; she wasn't at home. He feared the worst. That Emma had wandered off the trail and froze to death.

A suffocating sorrow gripped his lungs. He couldn't think it. He couldn't let it be true. He couldn't bear to lose his precious daughter, the last piece of his heart.

As he started his bay on a third dangerous trip up the trail, he spotted a flash of muted red in the solid wall of white—the flannel coat of one of the merchants who'd helped organize the search. Jacob rode up next to him.

Still, he had to shout to be heard over the roaring wind. "I want to spread out into the forest. She might have taken shelter there."

"I'm telling the men to go home." Gatz shouted too. "The temperature is dropping and the wind is rising. This will be a full-blown blizzard before long. We can't risk more lives."

Jacob knew that. He understood it. But as he waved the man on, anger grew with each step of his tired horse.

The search had lasted several hours. No one harbored hope of finding Emma now. She wasn't dressed for this weather. Had she run off, hurting because of him, because he hadn't asked Elizabeth to stay, and headed off on her own? Fear gripped him. He couldn't lose his Emma. She was out here somewhere. He had to find her. He couldn't give up hope. It was all he had.

Jacob turned his horse toward home. He'd planned to stop Elizabeth from leaving, but he'd waited. He should have made her understand how he felt when he had her alone in his livery. He should have made her stay. Now, he'd failed Emma. She hadn't come to him with her grief but had run off on her own. It was his own damn fault.

The wind howled with the same desolate determination in his heart. Chunks of ice beat at his face and chest, driving through the layers of wool clothing. Both hands numb, he switched reins, nesting his right hand in his coat pocket.

He could not give up, yet common sense told him he would freeze before long. But how could he stop searching for his Emma, for the tiny drop of sunshine in his lonely life? Feeling lost, he turned the horse toward town for another search down the trail.

His heart broke as he saw other men heading toward town, heading home, moving like defeated shadows in the whirling, beating gray-whiteness. They were giving up. To them, Emma was as good as dead.

But not to him. Jacob's eyelids bled from the driving ice, yet he rode on, searching, hoping, refusing to give in to defeat. As he rode, he saw fewer and fewer men until there was only one smudge of tan against the unrelenting, driving snow. The figure struggled slow and steady, heading away from town unlike the other men, stopping to search beneath one tree's heavy boughs, then the next.

The tan wool twisted around in the wind, and Jacob stopped his weary horse. No, that was a woman's cloak. That was the hem of a woman's dress.

Elizabeth.

Jacob nudged his horse closer. The worsening storm drove him from the animal's back, hurling him to the ground. He landed on his booted feet and lifted a hand to protect his aching eyes from the scouring bits of ice.

His heart broke at the sight of Elizabeth stooped, searching beneath the tree's bottommost boughs. She turned, startled by his presence.

"Jacob!" She yanked down the ice-stiff shawl from her face, but the angry wind snatched her words.

How long had she been out in this cold? he wondered. Alarm speared through him. Her face looked beaten, red from the cold, her nose frosted with her own breath.

She lumbered closer. "Have they found Emma?"

He shook his head. *God, how it hurt.* "The search has been called off."

"What? That's impossible. If no one's found her, we can't—"

"The search is over." *At least for Elizabeth.* He caught her by the arm. "Come with me. We have to find shelter or we'll freeze to death."

"No." She stomped her feet, her gaze hot enough to melt the driving wall of ice beating between them. "I'm not going anywhere until I find her."

Grief, fear, frustration battered him like the wind. "This is no place for a pregnant woman, Elizabeth. You have to stop and let me search—"

"I can't." Her teeth chattered. She covered her face, tucking a shawl snugly between the folds of her worn cloak. To his horror, she strode away, disappearing in the wall of white-grayness.

Elizabeth! She was a fragile, pregnant woman. This cold killed men like him. He had to stop her. He couldn't lose Elizabeth, not even for Emma's sake.

Jacob pulled the horse after him, searching for Elizabeth's tan cloak in the blinding storm. The wind pounded, howling like a lost soul between the stand of trees. Finally, he saw the smudge of wool against the driving ice where she knelt and gazed beneath another tree's low boughs.

Jacob's heart broke. This strong, loyal woman would freeze to death searching for his daughter rather than save herself. Only a mother would risk her life for a child.

He grabbed her arm and spun her around, forcing her to look at him. "Be sensible. I can't have you hurt. You have to stop."

Elizabeth planted her feet solidly in the knee-high snowdrift. "Not until I've found her."

"Think of your baby." He shook her. "You could lose your baby."

"I can't lose Emma." She jerked free from his grasp and marched straight into the wall of driving snow.

Jacob could feel his whole world crumbling about him. Ice froze in her hair and her eyebrows, caked her clothes and froze her cloak stiff. She had to be as cold as he was. The danger terrified him.

"I don't need your help. I'll give you my horse and you can ride back to town."

"No."

Elizabeth's stubborn denial shook through him, knocking loose the hard quaking deep inside. "Don't make me take time away from searching for Emma to keep you safe."

"She could be sheltered in these trees, don't you see?" Even inches away from his face, the howling, greedy wind snatched her words and broke them apart. "I will not give up on her. Will you?"

"No."

She stopped, searched his face with her fiercely determined gaze. "Then we'll search together. It's my decision, Jacob."

"Hell—" He couldn't allow Elizabeth to risk her health, her life, yet he needed help.

He watched the wind increase in velocity, driving all of the world from his sight. A search now was as impossible as seeing anything through this unrelenting beat of ice upon ice, but he could not stop. He would not stop until he'd found his daughter.

The worsening storm could not tear apart his determination. He kept walking, kept searching despite the cold driving its way so deep inside him that even his guts felt numb. Jacob couldn't stop the deep, violent quaking, a warning he could not survive this cold much longer.

Elizabeth was just as cold. Troubled, he followed her through the blinding storm.

Emma wouldn't have wandered off the trail and into the dark shadows of the forest, Libby was sure of it. If she were a little girl afraid of the storm, she would have found shelter beneath the trees.

Determined, she kept looking. She had no other choice. How could she give up on Emma?

The driving, cruel wind snatched her skirts, winding them about her knees as if to stop her from searching. Libby couldn't stop. Ice beat at her like nails driven from the sky. Wind hurled the bitter cold straight through her, but she wouldn't quit, she wouldn't allow a howling wind to stop her. Emma could be hiding beneath the next tree, frightened and cold.

She kept to her methodical search of each cedar along the edges of the road. The earth was frozen but dry, and the thick needles shielded the ground from the snow like a roof. It would be a cozy and safe shelter.

Libby rubbed her hands until she could feel the pain in them. She stomped her feet until her toes burned and prickled. She kept going. When Emma wasn't under one tree, she looked beneath the next.

As she knelt, her numb feet lost traction in the ice. She caught herself before she landed on her stomach, hitting her hand on a sharp bough. Blood warmed her mitten and oozed into the wool, darkening it.

She felt solid hands grab her arm, then help her up. Jacob. She recognized his dark coat, but that was all she could see of him, just a smudge of navy in the white whirl that cocooned her.

She heard one word. "Home."

"No." How could she tell him why she couldn't give up? She couldn't stop, she couldn't abandon Emma.

Wind roared, ice crackled. She lost sight of him in the wall of white that had become the world. Had he left her? Truly alone and losing her sense of direction, Libby felt her determination begin to wither.

Hopeless, she knelt down, her knees bending clumsily,

searching beneath the tree's boughs. A smudge of red caught her eye.

"Jacob!" Libby screamed with the forceful strength of her entire being. "Jacob!" She snatched up the knit cap and fell back to her knees. Without daring to hope she eased up the bough and looked beneath it.

There was only bare ground and a thatch of old pine needles.

He grabbed her from behind, helping her up. Her heart beating as fast as the wind, she shoved the cap at him. Libby couldn't see his face through the thick veil of white-gray ice.

"Emma!" Jacob's scream was torn into bits by the howling wind. He stood up and away, disappearing in the dizzying, unrelenting snow.

"Emma!" She screamed with all her might. "Emma!"

The driving ice scoured like sand, but she didn't care. She wouldn't stop now. Jacob disappeared, a hint of a shadow, his shouts already beaten into silence by the horrible wind.

Libby kept screaming for the girl, not daring to move until Jacob returned and they could search together. A slight smudge of gray burst out of the blinding ice, and she reached for it already crying, feeling the tears freeze to her eyelashes.

"Emma!" Libby wrapped her arms around the shivering, miserable form huddled in Jacob's arms. She leaned her face to nudge the girl's and touched her dear chin just to make sure she was real.

"Have to get her in," Jacob shouted.

Libby grabbed his coat sleeve and was surprised when he stopped, searching for his horse. The animal was tied to a bough, and she grabbed the reins. The bay stumbled, straining to breathe in the smothering storm.

She followed Jacob, trusting him to bring them safely home through the battering ice and wind. It blocked their sight of the sky, of the great forest of trees and the road at her feet. Jacob would see them to safety. She trusted him to.

The cold beat at her in steady waves. She fought against it, straining with every step. Libby forced her legs to work. She had to keep going. They had to get Emma to shelter. Without warning, she slammed into the side of a building. Jacob's stable.

Thank God.

Safe in Jacob's house, Libby knelt in the pool of lantern light, struggling with her frozen wraps. Her numb fingers fumbled with stiff buttons. Her coat crackled, driven full of snow.

"I—I'm so c-cold," Emma sobbed, slumped on the floor.

"I know." Libby knelt close. She felt the frozen stiffness of Emma's dark hair. "Your pa is lighting the fire. You're going to be warm soon."

"Let me take her." Jacob, still cloaked in his icy wraps, knelt down to cocoon Emma in a thick wool blanket. The little girl cuddled up to his chest, sobs catching in her throat.

Father and daughter. Libby's heart tightened. They sat together before the glow of the building fire. Cuddled in his strong arms, Emma's tears quieted.

Libby tugged off her shoes and walked on painful feet

toward the dark kitchen. She filled a kettle with water and set it on the hearth to heat.

"Are you feeling warmer?" Libby asked.

Emma's teeth chattered in response.

"Let me get these frozen shoes off your feet." The simple act of taking the child's small foot in her hand fired up Libby's affections. Affections she vowed to keep quiet. She bent to her work.

"Thank you, Elizabeth."

His rumbling voice, warm and inviting, beckoned her gaze. She remembered how he'd held her in the storm, how he cared for her, wanted to protect her from danger. Desire for him fired in her blood, warming her straight through.

He didn't invite you here, remember that. Libby busily chipped at the ice frozen into the leather tongue of Emma's right shoe. But she felt Jacob's gaze like a bold touch to her face. They were stuck in this cabin together. Did he regret it? Did she?

Her half-frozen fingers fumbled, but she managed to get Emma's feet bare.

"How do they look?" Concern vibrated in Jacob's words.

Don't look up. Looking at him would only make her want.

"I see bright pink toes." She kept her eyes down, rubbing Emma's small feet, grateful for the healthy skin. A child could lose toes, even an entire foot to such cold.

"We are lucky."

So very lucky. Tucking away her heart, she stood, turning from his presence. Emma was alive and safe. Libby vowed to focus on that and not the handsome father seated before the fire.

In Emma's cool bedroom, she gathered up warm wool underthings and a pink flannel nightgown. Libby dreaded going back into the main room where the fire licked warmth into the cabin and Jacob waited for her. But Emma needed warm clothes.

The brisk flames crackled, radiating delicious heat as Libby approached the hearth. She set the clean clothes on the nearby chair, avoiding Jacob. Looking at him would make her wish—so she left for the dark kitchen. Without much trouble, she found a match and lit the glass lamp, adjusting the wick.

"Let me help you," He strode into the room.

"*No*—I mean, I can do it. You need to stay with Emma." She stiffened. "I don't mind preparing her bath."

He studied her. She didn't know if he meant to lecture her, if he regretted her presence here. Then his eyes warmed.

"My hands hurt, Pa," Emma whined, alone before the fire.

"Take care of your daughter," Libby instructed softly. "She needs you. I don't."

He clenched his jaw, stiffening as if she'd slapped him. "Fine." He turned and limped away.

He wanted to reach out to her, Libby felt it. He'd been terrified today, afraid of losing the child he loved. He wanted comfort, reassurance, a warm woman. All men were the same. She didn't blame him, but she wouldn't be foolish a second time.

Soon the tea was ready and she joined Emma and Jacob in the front room. The cups in her hand teetered just a bit as she walked, but she didn't spill as she knelt before the snapping fire. "Emma, this will warm you right up."

"B-b-but I—I'm s-s-shak-king," she sobbed, hiccuping miserably. "I c-can't d-drink."

"I know. I'll hold the cup for you. Then it won't spill." Gentleness gripped her heart as she leaned closer, so close to Emma, to Jacob. She felt raw with the need to love them.

If only they would let her.

"I brought the second cup for you, Jacob." She wouldn't look at him as she held Emma's cup, tipping it slowly forward for her to sip from.

"I don't want it," Jacob said, his heart set.

"You're still in your frozen clothes," Elizabeth answered in her gentle way. "You should drink it. It will keep you from getting sick."

His chest pinched. She'd been out in that storm, damn it. "No, you should drink it,"

"Well, I'm not still wearing my half-frozen clothes." She looked worn and battered. The driving ice had scraped the skin on her eyelids. Exhaustion clung in purple shadows beneath her eyes.

He hated arguing. "I may be cold, but I'm not pregnant."

Her face paled. She turned away. "I'm not important. Emma comes first."

She didn't understand he only meant— This woman would have frozen to death searching for Emma. Her heart was big enough to love a child not her own.

His Emma. She shivered in his arms, her bird-small bones knocking against him. Naked, wrapped in the scratchy blanket, this tiny daughter of his was all scrawny arms and legs, all bony elbows and knees. There was hardly anything to her.

She was so delicate, so easily lost. His heart cracked at the realization. *He could lose this child, too.*

He wanted to run, to close himself off from the fear of living. *It's time to stop hiding.*

Jacob lifted the cup from Elizabeth's chapped hands. "You sit with her. I hear the water boiling on the stove."

"The bath water." Elizabeth's gaze lifted. "I'll be right back."

"No, let me—"

She'd already gone. Damn stubborn woman.

"P-Pa?"

"Hmm." Jacob could just reach the cup's handle on the hearth.

"I—I d-don't w-want M-miss Hodges t-to l-leave." Emma's teeth chattered.

"I know." He felt inadequate beneath her innocence-filled gaze. And so blessed, too. "You need to drink this all up. Miss Hodges made it just for you."

The shivering little girl obediently sipped the hot, soothing tea. A warmth ebbed into Jacob's heart. He couldn't stop the rush of love for his daughter, couldn't hold back the tides of his heart.

"M-miss Hodges m-makes g-good tea," Emma said, draining the last of her cup.

"We can ask her to make more."

Before he could stop her, Emma twisted and wrapped her arms tight around his neck. Jacob buried his face in her wet hair and held back burning tears.

Chapter Eleven

Even in flannel she was beautiful.

Elizabeth sat across from him, the oak table between them. Frozen and wet clean through, she'd bathed in the kitchen, after Emma. The entire time he'd put Emma to bed and read aloud from *Moby Dick*, waiting for her to fall asleep, he could hear the quiet splashes of the water as Elizabeth washed herself—naked in his kitchen—hell, the image taunted him for long hours, even now at the supper table.

"These beans are good," she said, her hair wet and loose, framing her face. "You're a mighty fine cook, Jacob."

"I'm fair to middling. When I first moved out here, I had to learn. I couldn't let Emma starve."

She smiled. He could see how she'd been preyed upon by a wolf of a man.

He could forgive her anything.

"Why did you choose Montana Territory?" She sliced into the fried salt pork.

Too personal. Jacob wanted to bolt up from the table

and get as far away from her as possible. But he stayed; faced it. "Because it wasn't Kentucky."

"Kentucky. It sounds like a beautiful place."

"Yes." Kentucky was home. Sweet bluegrass and the scent of horses, his mother's apple pie baking in the kitchen. "After the war, I couldn't settle down. I needed a change."

"You served?" She set down her fork. "You never told me."

"I don't talk about it. Ever."

"I see."

So gentle. She didn't demand more than he could give. "I didn't mean to sound gruff."

"You didn't." She set aside her napkin. "You cooked. Let me do the dishes."

"You need your rest." He laid his hand over her wrist to stop her—a mistake. He felt the heat of her soft skin beneath his. "You're exhausted. I can see it. Tomorrow you can make it up to me."

"Make it up to you?" Confusion clouded her eyes. She thought...she feared— Jacob blushed. "I meant, you can wash the dishes all you want tomorrow when you're rested."

"Oh." The wariness slipped away, replaced with a shy smile. "I didn't think you meant—"

"I know. After all, we are stuck here together until the blizzard blows itself out." He withdrew his hand.

Elizabeth slipped hers beneath the table, as if she'd felt the heat, too.

"I can be a gentleman, if I have to be."

A genuine smile twinkled in her eyes. "You are always a gentleman, Jacob. I admire you for it."

His gaze roamed to her mouth. A tugging need urged him to lean closer, to taste her lips. Too fast. Much too fast. He looked down. "Trust me, there's little to admire about me."

Trust. It shone in her deep soft eyes, steady like the North Star, unfailing.

"I think I hear Emma," he lied. He needed room to think, to breathe. He wasn't ready for this.

"Really, I—"

The fire snapped, spewing out a chunk of burning ember onto the wood floor, rescuing him. Jacob jumped up, his body relaxing as the distance between them grew. He'd reacted to Elizabeth like a bear scenting a female and it shamed him, scared him. He knelt before the smoldering ember and flicked it back into the hearth.

She walked past him. "Let me take a plate into Emma if she's awake. She should be hungry by now."

Jacob's conscience winced. He bowed his head. He'd lied to the woman. What was next? What would he do to avoid the one person he feared most?

Elizabeth.

She pushed the door open. A small lantern sat safely in the corner, far from the bed, the wick turned low. A faint glow caressed Emma, who immediately sat up in bed.

"So you are awake." Libby smiled.

A tentative nod. "I tried to sleep, but I just can't. It's too early."

"I know, but we can't have you sick." Libby bent to turn the wick. Stronger light filled the room, illuminating Emma's fluffy cloud of hair, dry after her hot bath. "I brought your dinner."

"I like Pa's baked beans. Jane had to teach him how to make 'em. He couldn't cook, you know."

"He told me." Libby sat down at the foot of the bed. "Can you eat this without spilling?"

Another nod. "I'm glad you're here, you know."

"I'm glad, too. That storm sounds terrible. I couldn't make it back to town." Outside the sturdy logs, thick and strong, howled a demon of a storm. The ice scoured the walls above the power of the wind.

Emma balanced the plate on her knees. Libby reached a hand to steady it.

"Do you think Pa is mad at me?" she asked with a rushed whisper.

"He's much too scared to be really angry." Libby took the napkin and caught a drop of baked bean that landed on the wool blanket. "You scared all of us near to death. Most of the town was out looking for you."

"Oh." Emma stopped chewing.

She looked small and afraid. Libby brushed a hand along Emma's chin. "I think your pa will forgive you."

She sighed. "I sure hope so. I don't want Pa to send me back to Granny and leave again. Do you think he'll send me away now?"

"No, I don't." Libby knew what it was like to be afraid. "I think your pa loves you very much."

"I'm sorry." Great tears brimmed her eyes, and her lower lip trembled.

"I know."

"I was just so mad. I wanted you to stay." Fat tears rolled down her cheeks. "I didn't know about the storm."

"Neither did I. I couldn't take the stage today because of the blizzard." Libby's heart tightened. She saw herself, a little girl in a strange family, unsure if her aunt would keep her. She understood Emma's fears.

"Really? I was afraid you would be mad at me, too."

"I could never be angry with you." Libby grabbed the plate when it tipped again. "Now eat up. You look a little feverish."

"I'm fine, now that you're here."

Libby's entire heart filled. She felt fine, too.

Jacob stood and padded on stockinged feet to the fire. He saw her womanly things drying there, and he reached for a split log to toss onto the flames.

"Sweet dreams." Elizabeth's words rang solid, like a promise to be kept. When she closed Emma's door behind her, he looked away.

"She's promised to sleep now. She kept yawning, so I think she will." Elizabeth, clutching the plate in both hands, crossed the room.

He watched her go, looking so different without her calico dress. While her clothes dried, she wore his blue flannel shirt, hanging clear to her knees, over his long johns. She looked beautiful even in gray wool.

He listened to her in the kitchen as she rinsed the plate, dried it, stacked it. Then to the soft pad of her bare feet as she walked back to him.

"It's getting late."

Her voice rippled up his spine. He couldn't look away from her slender ankles, nicely shaped thighs, or the cling of fabric across her unbound breasts all perfectly hugged by clinging blue flannel. He could see the nub of her nipples nudging the soft flannel, and he felt a hardening, a thickening in his groin.

Jacob turned to drop another log on the fire, ashamed of his thoughts. "There's a room upstairs behind the chimney where you can stay, if you'd like."

"Yes. It sounds perfect." Elizabeth stared down at her red, rough hands. A nasty gash on her left palm had scabbed, and now she studied it. "I don't want to be a bother. I know you aren't comfortable with me staying here."

"I'm not—"

She interrupted. "You can't stop avoiding me, Jacob. I understand. You didn't invite me here."

"That doesn't mean—" He *did* want her here. Frustrated, he walked away, disappearing into the kitchen and returning with a stack of clean sheets. "I haven't thanked you."

"Thanked me? For what?" Her eyebrows rose.

His heart beat so rapidly, he was barely able to look at her. "If it hadn't been for you, Emma would have died today."

She shrugged one thin shoulder. "I didn't do all that much."

"You did everything." He ached to brush her face, to feel the heat of her satin skin against his hand, but he held back. "You saved Emma's life."

"I didn't do anything more than anyone else would do, than you did."

Couldn't she see what she did to him? She thawed his heart like sun after a winter's frost. "You wouldn't give up when the other searchers did."

"What can I say? I'm stubborn. It's my worst trait."

"Your best."

"Oh, Jacob." Libby swallowed, unable to find words.

"I did what I had to do—the same thing you did. I couldn't leave a little girl to freeze alone in the cold."

"You couldn't let *Emma* freeze," he corrected her gently.

Feelings she was too afraid to acknowledge ached in her throat. *Remember what you are to him,* she reminded herself. No matter how much it hurt. "You said there's a room upstairs—and a bed."

"Yes." He looked as uncertain as she felt. "If you don't want to climb the ladder, I can give you my room."

"Oh, no." She couldn't sleep in his bed. "I don't mind a ladder."

"It's just as well. The upstairs is warmer. I'll show you."

She had noticed the narrow ladder tucked between the back kitchen wall and the cookstove. Now, Jacob climbed that ladder, pulled open the half door on hinges and disappeared inside.

Libby saw a glow of light and she carefully climbed after him. He'd lit a small lamp and now it tossed a warm puddle across the smooth varnished boards. She eased to her feet. "This attic is so snug and warm."

"The chimney heats it. It's the warmest place in the house besides the kitchen."

At the sight of the small unmade bed tucked beneath the peak of the roof, Libby lowered her gaze. She thought of Jacob and that bed. Her entire body flushed.

He spread out one muslin sheet on the straw tick. "Jane often stayed here when I worked late. I'm afraid it hasn't been cleaned since she left."

"What's a little dust?" Libby looked anywhere but at

Jacob—at the fitted rafters, the solid logs, the stone chimney walling one end of the room.

"Some women would complain about a little dust. They seem to think it's an evil needing obliteration."

He caught her gaze. His grin stopped her heart. She smiled. "I'm not one of those women."

"I remember you spoke of it in your letters." Jacob's face softened, warmed with the memory. "You thought baking cookies with a little girl much more important."

"Yes." It hurt to remember now.

She looked up and caught him studying her body. His flannel shirt she wore showed the sway of her full breasts and the soft rise of her abdomen.

Libby bent to smooth the sheet.

"I've got a few extra blankets," he said quietly, proceeding stiffly across the room toward the ladder.

He was here, yet felt so distant. She felt so distant. As soon as Jacob disappeared from sight, she slipped to the straw tick, so tired she could hardly sit up.

She was here, trapped in this house with him. What did he think? Was he remembering her stupid, embarrassing story? Did he think her easy? Her heart broke.

No, Jacob would never think that about any woman. He was honorable. He was different from other men.

His steps on the ladder announced his approach, and Libby rose to take the thick wool blankets from his arms.

"I meant to make the bed for you," he protested.

"Let me, Jacob. You haven't rested tonight, either. I'll be fine without your help."

"I see." His eyes saddened. "Then it's good night."

"Yes." She ached to pull him back, but he climbed down the ladder, wordlessly, favoring one leg. Libby had no doubt what she was looking at: the most gentle man she'd ever had the privilege to meet.

Jacob checked on Emma when he heard her cough. The small child huddled beneath her thick pile of blankets, still asleep, curled on her side facing away from him.

Concerned, he stepped into the room and swept his hand over Emma's small forehead. Too warm. *It was nothing serious, right?* She'd been caught in a storm without a winter coat or dress—nothing more, he hoped. It wasn't surprising she might catch cold.

"My throat hurts," she whispered, sounding so small in the darkness.

Jacob sat on her bed and tucked her head beneath his chin. She felt so fragile. "I'll make you some tea and honey. That will cure what ails you."

"I'd like that."

He left her door ajar so the heat from the fire would warm her room. Emma was so young, and he was fortunate she'd been spared today. Fortunate he hadn't been alone in his search, and that Elizabeth had found Emma's cap. Together they'd shared the same determination to find a lost little girl in the snow.

Jacob opened the back door to the lean-to. Furious, bitter cold wind snatched the breath from his lungs as he filled his bucket with fresh snow. He'd been outside less than a minute, but the wind had sucked the warmth right out of him.

He bumped one shoulder against the ladder and thought of Elizabeth sleeping upstairs. His entire body heated at the image of her wheat blond hair fanning the snowy white pillowcase.

The kettle whistled, interrupting his thoughts, and he brewed tea, then mixed it with milk and honey as Elizabeth had done. Out of love.

Emma's cough echoed through the cabin. Grabbing the cup, Jacob skirted the corner and pushed into her room. She sat up in bed, snug in her pink flowered nightgown, her hand to her mouth.

"Pa? I hate coughin'."

"I know." He sat down beside her, awkward, not knowing what to do with his own daughter. He handed her the cup. "This tea is pretty hot. Do you want to drink it out by the fire?"

She nodded against his chest.

"Then let's get you roasting warm."

"I'm not a steak, Pa."

He laughed as she cuddled against him. He closed his eyes, breathing in the soap smell of her. His little girl. He felt struck by the power of simply holding her.

"Where's Miss Hodges?"

Balancing both the cup and the girl, he rose slowly, careful of his wounded leg. "She's upstairs sleeping."

"In Jane's old room?"

"Yes." He halted before the old rocking chair and set her down, light as a bird.

"She needs extra sleep because of the baby that's growing in her stomach, right?" Emma asked, gazing up at him knowledgeably.

"That's right." He didn't want to think of the baby. Or Elizabeth's fragility. But knowing she slept upstairs, in his house, satisfied him deeply. "Here, drink your tea."

"I'm very sorry I walked home in the snow," she said

now, clinging to his shirt, the fabric fisted in both little hands.

"You scared the life right out of me. I thought I'd never see you again. Don't you know how important you are to me? Emma, you are all I have in this world, and I love you more than anything."

"I love you, too, Pa," she whispered, her eyes full of tears. When she wrapped her arms around his neck, he'd never felt anything sweeter.

Through the web of sleep, Libby heard the stove lid rattle. She sat up, orienting herself in the pitch-black room. She could hear the faint snap of the hungry fire in the hearth down below.

Why was Jacob up? It had to be past midnight. The storm still howled outside, scouring the house. She heard a faint cough and flew out of bed. Emma.

The kitchen was dark. A clock bonged the time, declaring it three in the morning. The front room felt warm; a fire blazed in the hearth. Emma's door stood open, and Libby hesitated in the threshold.

Jacob sat on Emma's bed, and a low lamp cast a sepia glow to the small room. His face shadowed, his head bowed, he held a cup to his daughter's lips.

Emma whimpered, and his low voice soothed her. He took the cup away, set it on the floor and wrung out a washcloth in a pan of water.

Libby watched as Jacob bathed the girl's face, and her breathing slowed.

"She's asleep," he whispered when he stood.

Libby backed out into the main room where the fire threw dancing light and shadow. "She's got a fever?"

"Yes." Jacob's mouth closed tightly, compressing his lips. "I've been up with her all night."

She touched his arm. "This is more than just a cold and a simple fever. Could it be the croup?"

"I don't know." He stepped away from her touch. "Go back to bed, Elizabeth. You need your sleep."

"I'm pregnant, not sick, Jacob." Libby looked down at her bare hands. "I feel rested. But you—you've been up all day and most of the night. Why don't you catch some sleep while I tend her?"

"No. I won't leave Emma."

"It would be foolish for you to wear yourself out when I'm here to help."

"But you need your sleep and I don't want any argument." Without explanation, he turned his back to her, heading for the kitchen.

"Jacob, I'm not a child and I don't want to be treated like one." She marched after him. "I care about Emma, too."

"I know." Yet his jaw looked as tight set as his mind. He lifted the stove lid and lit a match. "Emma is *my* daughter."

"I know she isn't mine." Her heart broke a little. "But I can care about her, can't I?"

He bowed his chin. "That isn't what I meant. I want you to take care of yourself. You can't become ill the way Emma has."

"I won't get sick." She laid her hand on his arm. His sleeve, rolled to his elbow, revealed a stretch of muscled forearm dusted with dark hair. He felt wonderful beneath her palm.

Fire crackled to life inside the belly of the stove. Jacob's face changed in the shadowed room, relenting a little.

"I think Emma's very ill," he whispered. The silence between them was broken by a little girl's hacking cough. "I lost her mother and I can't lose Emma, too. I can't go through that again."

"I know. I couldn't bear it, either."

Jacob's throat worked, as if he couldn't find the right words. His fingers reached out to wind around hers. He held on to her, needing her touch.

"I don't know what to do," he whispered, ashamed of his own inadequacies. "With this storm, I can't risk heading to town. And even if I made it, there's no guarantee I can talk a doctor into coming back through that blizzard with me."

"It's foolish to leave, Jacob."

"I know." Elizabeth's eyes warmed, and he wanted to feel her heat, feel whole again. "I feel helpless. Maybe a doctor—"

"I know what to do. I helped my aunt take care of all her children, remember?"

He hadn't needed anyone in so long, it clawed at him now. Needing came with a price to his heart. How could he tell her? How could he thank her?

"I guess this means you aren't sending me to bed like a six-year-old." A smile played along her soft mouth.

He pulled her against him, finding her lips and kissing her hard, binding her to him. Trying to drive out the darkness inside.

Chapter Twelve

As the storm raged outside, Jacob watched Emma's condition worsen. The fever weakened her as cough after cough raged through her lungs. He and Elizabeth took turns bathing her brow with cold water. Emma clutched her rag doll in one arm and slept fitfully.

He hauled wood from the lean-to to the hearth and filled the grate with dry split logs. The fire roared, keeping the cabin toasty warm. Elizabeth suggested bringing Emma's bed out into the main room, closer to the fire.

He felt so helpless as he watched the girl's fever progress, it felt good to do something with his hands. He carefully laid Emma on a blanket while Libby tended her, then he dismantled the wood-frame bed.

While he worked, he worried. He tried not to think of what could happen. It wasn't easy. He listened to Elizabeth's gentle humming—it gave him hope. She knew what to do with a very sick child. He had to trust, he had to believe in her.

Jacob did what he could. He set the bed up in the middle of the front room, safely from the fire but close enough to benefit from the constant, blazing heat. As he smoothed out the sheet, he watched Elizabeth. She sat on the floor, her legs drawn neatly beneath her wool skirt. Her light hair plaited into one thick braid, hung down her back to brush the floor.

She looked so delicate from behind. He could see the bumps of her spine and the vulnerable thinness of the back of her neck. He wanted to touch her there.

His heart kicked. He ought to be worrying over Emma, but he couldn't forget the way Elizabeth felt tucked against his body, firm and supple, yet so soft. She tasted like heaven, like desire, like something he could never deserve again. His body hardened just thinking of her, and he looked away in shame.

"Is the bed ready?"

"Yes."

"Good. I've got Emma asleep again. You can move her."

He looked directly into Elizabeth's soft eyes, they were almost a pale lilac. Such a gentleness lived in her. He could see it in the careful way she tended Emma, in the undemanding way she treated him.

His senses burned as he knelt beside her.

"Her fever is still rising." Elizabeth brushed a hand across Emma's small forehead.

"Do you know how to bring it down?"

"I can try."

Elizabeth twisted to look up at him. His hands shook as he gathered Emma in his arms. Sniffling, the child clung to him, and he concentrated on that.

"It's all right, little one." He brushed her forehead with

his cheek. Her fine, wispy hair clung to his unshaven whiskers.

"My throat hurts real bad," Emma complained in the smallest voice.

"Would you like some more tea?" He gently balanced her against his chest.

Emma nodded.

She was so precious. He couldn't bear to see her ill. As he slipped her between the clean sheets, his whole heart began to rend.

"I'll make you something for your throat, precious," he said with a solemn promise.

Emma's deep blue eyes, Mary's eyes, smiled up at him.

Jacob's throat tightened. Life was so uncertain. He brushed his big hand over her small, hot forehead.

"You shouldn't be lifting like that."

His voice startled her. She straightened from the stove. "It's just a few pieces of wood, Jacob."

"Wood is heavy." He strode into the small kitchen, all powerful man, unyielding muscle and will. He'd changed into an emerald green shirt that darkened his eyes.

"I'm not going to break," she chided.

His face tightened. "You need to take better care of yourself. You've been working who knows how many hours a day in that hotel's kitchen, on your feet. It's demanding work, Elizabeth, it can't be good for you."

"Being unemployed would be worse." He didn't want to talk about her pregnancy. *Fine.* She checked on the fire, then closed the lid, turning her back to him.

"I would have helped you."

"You wanted to give me money, not help." Her spine

stiffened. She didn't want to fight, especially when she saw the purple circles beneath his eyes. "You've been up last night and most of today with Emma. Let me take care of her while you rest for a while."

"No, *you* need to nap." He looked down at his empty hands. "You've been cooking and preparing and carrying water, now what are you up to? It's too much, Elizabeth."

"I thought I would wash Emma's sheets." She rested her hand on her stomach, small as a gravy bowl, but life thrived there. A life he didn't want to acknowledge.

"I planned on stopping you from taking the stage," he said now, hardly audible above the snapping fire and the scouring wind. "I didn't know how to tell you when we spoke in the livery. Deep down, I'm afraid. Do you want a man like me?"

"What?" Not want him? She adored Jacob. "Why do you think I was leaving?"

"Because of me. Because you think I can't accept..." His gaze slid to her belly. "Because it's taken me so long to let myself tell you how I feel."

Libby reached for an empty kettle, but his hand was there first. He towered behind her so close she only had to breathe and her back would touch his chest. "Jacob, I can get it. Emma needs you." *I need you.*

"She's sleeping for now. The bean soup you made was delicious. She liked it. I'm grateful to you—she managed to get some down."

"It's just bean soup."

"It's more than that. It's you." His hand cupped her jaw.

Shivers of need rippled through her. "Emma's sick. I've

done nothing amazing, Jacob. Just cooking and keeping her warm and fed and dry.''

''It's everything.'' He pulled her hard against the solid wall of his chest.

She shrugged. ''I figured, since I was snowed in here, I might as well be useful.''

''You are no trouble, believe me.''

She wanted to. Closing her eyes made her want to believe. He smelled so good. She breathed in the scent of him, of wood smoke and tea. His strong arms engulfed her and she felt so small against him, so helpless against his goodness, his strength.

She didn't know how to help him, to reassure him, to be someone he could lean on. She only knew she wanted to try.

''I need you,'' he said, his voice rough. ''I'm so glad you're here.''

She knew how overwhelmed he felt, how afraid. Emma was so sick.

When his mouth found hers, Libby felt a kick of fear bolt through her. Not fear at his touch, but fear of what his touch meant. Need drove his kiss in a slow, sensual caress of his mouth to hers. Libby felt her heart pulse and heat curl through her stomach.

She dared to lay her hand along the rough texture of his jaw. A day and night's growth of whiskers tickled her palm, and Jacob moaned at her touch, deepening the kiss, pulling her hard against his body.

How could he find her attractive at all? She was carrying another man's child. When her rounded belly pressed against his solid abdomen, Jacob didn't pull away; he drew her arms up around his neck, holding her closer. Her fingers played with his collar length hair.

She wanted him. It wasn't right, yet she couldn't stop it. Loving him felt so *right*.

The hard length of his arousal nudged against her abdomen, and a heady excitement kicked through her. *Don't stop*. Emotions unknotted in her heart, emotions long unused. As if he knew, Jacob softened his mouth against hers, tracing her bottom lip with his velvet-moist tongue.

"Oh, Elizabeth," he said as he drew his lips from hers and hugged her to him hard, pressing them together, man against woman. Libby had never felt so safe or more alive.

"I need you," Jacob whispered in her ear. "Please, just hold me."

No one had ever wanted her like this. Libby held on to him with all her might.

Emma slept fitfully. While Jacob tended her, Libby found onions down in the cellar and began the smelly task of slicing them up. Night deepened as she worked at making a batch of thick paste. She lit a lamp as the brew simmered over the stove.

"What stinks?" he asked, stepping into the kitchen.

"This should knock the congestion from her lungs." Libby lifted the pan from the stove. "I'll let it cool for a few minutes. Then I'll rub this on her chest."

"I'm glad you're here. I wouldn't want to touch that stuff. It smells rancid."

"It smells bad enough to clear up her lungs," she corrected. "Here, carry this pan for me. I'll get some clean towels."

"I'd rather get the towels." Jacob winked.

His teasing made her smile, although there was so little to smile about with Emma's fever worsening. Libby didn't want to think what would happen if her aunt's concoction didn't work. The storm still raged with no sign of stopping. When it did, it could be too late for a doctor's help.

She returned to the kitchen, laden with fresh towels. Jacob stood by the table, the teasing glint in his eyes faded.

He held the pan. ''I'll carry this in to Emma.''

''Fine.'' She hugged the soft towels. He looked—he *felt*—so distant. ''Are you angry with me?''

''With you?'' He whirled around. ''No. I'm not angry, Elizabeth.''

''Scared?''

''I'm damn scared.'' His gaze fell to the bed where Emma slept fitfully, breathing hard, coughing painfully in her sleep. The hacking sound filled the cabin, hollow and desolate.

''She can't get worse,'' he said, determination in his voice. As if he could will it, and Emma could be well soon. He knelt beside the bed.

''We're doing all we can. We're keeping her warm. We're fighting the fever and the congestion.'' Libby knelt, too, setting down the towels to unbutton the front of Emma's pink flannel nightgown.

''She's so very ill. So very small. But she's strong.''

''Strong like her pa.'' Libby covered his big hand with her smaller one. ''Don't torture yourself with those fears, Jacob. She could become worse, but she also could recover. Don't borrow trouble.''

He closed his eyes. She could see the hope in him. She could see the darkness. Like the storm howling outside, he struggled.

"She'll be fine, Jacob. Because she has you." Libby dipped her fingers into the pungent paste. "Hold her nightgown open so I can apply this to her chest. I made a very strong batch. This ought to clear her lungs."

"Or suffocate us," he said wryly.

They worked side by side for hours, as they had done all day. Libby at the stove, brewing soothing honeyed tea for Emma's throat when she woke, boiling coffee for the two of them to sip while they worried, heating water and warming a quick meal, then making another poultice for Emma's chest.

Exhaustion weighed Libby down like an anvil, but she pushed herself hard, unable to stop the creeping worry. Emma wasn't getting better.

The howling storm still battered the cabin, cutting them off from town and the doctor. Jacob brought in great piles of snow-covered wood to burn. It was a struggle to keep the main room warm enough for the sick little girl.

When she wasn't in the kitchen, Libby sat beside Jacob at Emma's bedside, watching the fear settle deeper into his face. She didn't know how to comfort him. She doubted she held that much power over his heart.

Jacob looked up at the whisper of Elizabeth's stockinged step. She balanced two coffee cups, steam rising from both.

She'd left her hair down and it curled down her back, shimmering like fine silk. Her pretty blue dress was wrinkled from drying near the hearth overnight, but the rumpled fabric could never detract from her gentle beauty. A beauty that radiated from the inside.

"This is the last of the pot. I can brew more." She handed him one of the coffee cups.

The welcome heat burned his hand. At least he could still feel. "No, don't go to the bother. I won't want more."

She settled down awkwardly beside him. The floor was hard. She looked uncomfortable, but there was no complaint. He watched as she checked Emma's forehead, listening to her breathing.

"It sounds better," she announced.

"Perhaps."

Silence.

"I'm glad you're here, that you were forced to stay." His gaze caught hers. "If the storm hadn't done it, I would have. A stage ride isn't what you need in your condition."

"You keep worrying over my health, Jacob, and there's no need." She kept her voice even, but she twisted away from him to look at Emma.

"Why not? You've hardly eaten. You've been without sleep. I feel damn guilty."

"Guilty?" She shook her head, scattering soft wheat blond curls that shimmered in the firelight. "I don't understand. Emma is sick. She needs me. Where else would I be?"

Emma was very sick. Despair swam in his heart, but he had to fight it, to refuse to give in to the fear. He could feel the darkness descending, but then Elizabeth smiled. Saving him.

"Jacob, look." She moved gracefully, reaching across him. "Emma's fever is broken."

The words were magic; from her lips they were a miracle. He laid his hand on Emma's forehead. No fever.

None at all. His daughter slept peacefully, except for the rattle of congestion.

Tears spilled into his eyes, hot like hope, clear like dreams. "You did this."

Elizabeth looked up, her eyes wide and bright. She didn't know how she saved Emma, saved him. How she made life easier to live.

Unable to find words, he reached out, tracing her jaw, holding her face in his hand from the hollow of her ear to the curve of her chin.

"I owe you everything," he rasped.

Emotion trembled in her eyes. "Don't be silly. I'm not a doctor to be paid. Emma is well. Let me get the clean sheets I washed this morning. They ought to be dry by now. Oh, and another nightgown."

She scrambled to her feet before he could stop her. Jacob stood, catching her by the shoulder. "Let me do those things for my daughter. It's time I took care of her myself. I haven't been a good enough father."

"Jacob, you are wonderful to Emma." The lamplight glowed against the soft contours of her face and the deep luminous shine in his eyes. "You are always too hard on yourself."

His throat closed. He would be nothing without Emma. Without Elizabeth. He realized it now, at the sight of beauty in her eyes. "I almost lost you, too."

Something precious burned in her gentle blue eyes. He leaned forward, catching her mouth with his.

The storm broke somewhere near dawn. With Emma safely sleeping, Jacob climbed up the ladder into Elizabeth's attic room, warring with himself.

He needed her. His mind kept telling him to stay in his own bed. His feelings told him to keep climbing.

Lamplight from the kitchen below tossed enough of a glow into the snug room for him to see her by. She slept on her side, breathing regularly and softly, her light hair fanning the pillow in a curly cloud.

"Elizabeth."

She stirred, shook her head, then bolted upright. "Jacob. How's Emma?"

"I made her some oatmeal and now she's sleeping soundly." He took one step toward the bed, and another. "Nothing is wrong."

"Good." She threw back the blankets and climbed to her feet. In the faint shadowed light he could see the shape of his too large wool union suit stretching over every curve of her body.

Need kicked through him.

He knew he should turn away and head down the ladder. He knew he should do anything but stay in this room with her, seeing her sleep-soft and her hair tousled by the night. Long wisps had escaped the single braid and softened her oval face with gossamer curls.

"I can't tell you how happy I am," Elizabeth breathed, then slipped into his arms.

Heavenly sweetness pumped through his veins—an intoxicating combination of need and loneliness and affection. Her arms tightened around his back, and he enfolded her gently against his chest, this woman who loved his daughter as fiercely as he ever could. She felt so light in his arms, small despite her strength.

"That's something else we have in common," he whispered into the soft curls of her hair. "Remember the letters we wrote? We discovered we had more and more in common with each letter?''

"I remember.''

"Our mothers had the same pattern of dishes.'' He started.

"We both broke our right leg when we were young.'' Laughter softened her mouth. "I was six. You were...ten.''

"Yes.'' His heart squeezed. He could no longer hide from life, yet he'd been afraid to live. Well, not anymore. "Come sit with me.''

"Downstairs?''

"No. Here.'' He held out his hand.

His gentle hands.

Libby trembled as she lifted her palm. His fingers caught hers, easing her toward him. Heavens, she couldn't breathe. He sat down on the bed, pulling her down beside him so close her thigh brushed his.

Libby had never known such powerful feelings. She'd been terrified of the storm, terrified of losing Emma. Now in the webby light from the kitchen below, she could see the same realization in Jacob's eyes. He was scared, too.

"I swore I'd never be like this again with a woman,'' he whispered, "if you will have me.''

Her throat closed. She wanted him, even though she knew better than to want him.

"You aren't saying anything. I guess I—'' Jacob bowed his chin. "Forgive me, I'm exhausted, I'm shaking with emotion. I—''

"I don't want to mistake human need for love.'' She'd been lonely, needy, so hungry for affection, she'd been blind once before. But not this time.

"There is no mistake," he said.

His gaze caught hers, and Libby saw the weight of his need, the size of his heart. Lying with Jacob could never be a mistake. To feel his strong yet gentle hands on her body, to know the weight of him inside her. That would be heaven.

Jacob's eyes darkened. He reached out and unbuttoned her long johns with stiff, quick movements.

He needed her. And she needed him.

She stood when the shirt fell open and she slipped the garment over her shoulders, down over her full breasts and her thickening waist. By the time the fabric puddled at her ankles, Libby's heart beat too fast to speak.

She stood before him naked in the faint light. She hoped he couldn't see her tears. They blurred her vision and she felt helpless to stop them. She waited while he removed his shirt and stepped out of his trousers. He stood naked before her, unashamed of his body and its proud, full shaft.

She warmed shamefully. *How she wanted him.*

Jacob took her hand, laying her gently on the bed. A softness burned in his eyes, an affection she couldn't believe in. He eased beside her.

"Can I take down your hair?" His whispered words sounded rough and strained. Full of need.

"Yes."

His hot, hard body pressed against hers while he ran his fingers through the braids, loosening the long silken length of her hair. He felt so good, so gentle. Libby pressed her face into his shoulder, holding back her heart.

Chapter Thirteen

She wanted him. She didn't deserve him, couldn't have him. And if nothing else, if he hated her afterward, then at least she had this: tender love with a real, gentle man.

"You don't know how I've been wanting you," he whispered once her hair spilled free down her back.

Libby could feel the hard pulse of his shaft against her pelvis, mysterious and throbbing with his life. "Ever since you kissed me that first time," she answered.

"Yes." His hand skidded down her throat and he gazed at her bare breasts. "I saw you with Emma and I thought what a good mother you would be."

Libby pressed a bold kiss to the hollow of his throat where his heart beat hard and quick and steady. What might have happened between them if she were coming to him untouched? What if he had planted the life that now grew within her?

"But I could never do that to you, get you with child," he whispered, his throat strangled. "I can't get you pregnant now."

"No," she agreed as his warm hand closed over her left breast, so full and aching.

Sensation bolted through her, twisted tightly around the life inside her. She put her hand there, but the baby was safe. It was just pleasure. Tender, loving pleasure.

Then Jacob caught her nipple with his mouth. He suckled, deepening the strange twist inside her. She caught a groan of pleasure in her throat and held it there, afraid to let him know.

"Relax, Elizabeth. It's all right."

He nibbled along her jawbone. His hot breath fanned her cheek, tickled in her ear. All resistance fled. She whimpered, relaxing into his arms as he brushed her mouth with his.

Aching kisses teased at her own needs, physical and emotional. Open kisses explored her mouth, leaving her breathless. Libby mated her tongue with his, gasping as he pressed her back onto the bed, nudging her legs apart with his knee.

She opened for him, feeling the hard length and breadth of his body move over her, and then his erection as it nudged against that part of her. She stiffened, but he kept kissing her, hot, wet.

Libby closed her eyes, knowing what would happen next. The pleasure, hot and loose in her core, faded into something cold. Jacob touched her face.

"Open your eyes," he said tenderly. "It's just me. Jacob."

"Jacob." She looked into his dear face, so familiar now, and precious. "I'm afraid."

"I know." Sadness crept into his gray eyes. "But it will be different with me. I promise."

A man of honor. Her throat tightened, and she pressed her face into his chest to hide her tears. She wrapped her arms around his strong back, holding him tight. Only he could ease all the pain of her heart.

Jacob cradled her in his strong arms and positioned her on the bed so that they lay on their sides, facing one another. Libby held on, afraid to let go.

"Let me show you," he said, kissing one tear from her cheek. "Will you trust me?"

His gaze held hers, and she could see such affection, such tender caring. No one had ever looked at her that way. Libby reached up to catch his mouth with hers, kissing him as deeply as he kissed her.

Love. She could feel it in his touch. His hand cupped her breast, squeezing, kneading deliciously. That warm tightness coiled itself back around her stomach, twisting wondrously taut as his hands burned sensation across her bare skin. Her breasts. Her stomach. Her inner thighs. The soft damp entrance to her body.

"I need you," he whispered, rising back over her when she feared he might move away and stop. Libby gazed up into his face as he pressed her thighs apart. Then he smiled, lighting up his eyes.

"Oh, Jacob." How could she tell him all he meant to her? She could find no words, only feelings. Powerful, frightening emotions wavering in her heart.

She wanted him. All of him. No matter how afraid she was, how unpleasant she knew this intimacy could be. But when he whispered into her hair and she felt the hard thickness of his engorged shaft pressing against her, she wasn't afraid.

It didn't hurt, yet. Libby gasped, unprepared for the stretching full sensation of him filling her. She moaned as he trailed tender kisses along her forehead. She felt so small beneath him, but her body felt so incredibly full.

Libby held him to her as he moved, pulling delicious sensation through her with each withdrawal, pushing frighteningly intense pleasure with every satisfying thrust. A thrilling tightness twisted through her, able to snap her in two. At Jacob's gently murmured urgings, she relaxed, moved up to meet him, accepted him so deeply she lost her breath. Explosive light burst in her spine, shattering her entire body, breaking every piece of her heart.

Breathless, Libby clung to Jacob as his body tightened, and he plunged faster, deeper. The groan started low in his throat and she held him tightly, unable to let go, feeling the hot pulse of wetness spilling deep inside.

So this is what love feels like. Tears burned in her eyes.

He rained kisses across her face. She felt too full to speak. When a drop of wetness dotted her forehead, Libby knew Jacob was crying too.

After he loved her a second time, he slipped from the bed, granting her one needy, lingering kiss before pulling on his trousers.

Libby sat up, tired but sated. Her body thrummed with his touch, her heart felt full with his loving. He stood beside her bed, dressing. She did not want him to leave her, even to go downstairs. Sitting up, she reached for her clothes.

"Would you like some coffee?" Jacob took her by the hand.

She wanted more than coffee. "Yes." It was a start.

He led her across the room and down the ladder in silence. Even in the kitchen, as he set the coffeepot to boil on the stove, he didn't speak.

The sweetness between them was enough.

Light washed over him, limning him like moonlight in the windowless room. He worked without looking at her, kneeling to throw more small shreds of wood into the black stove.

Libby stood staring. She could still remember the feel of his body filling hers and the tender, tear-stained kisses along her brow.

Jacob closed the stove's little door and faced her. The silence between them was broken only by the sounds of the fire. They were alone with what they'd done. Alone to face separate futures.

As if he were aware of this, too, Jacob crossed to the table and set two tin cups on its polished surface. He said nothing, busily putting out the sugar bowl and two spoons.

He kept his back to her while he worked. She felt so close to him; still, a part of him felt so distant.

"The coffee's nearly done." His low voice hummed with a small tenderness.

Somehow that loving touch in his voice hurt more. "Thank you." Woodenly she sat in the chair he offered her like a polite southern gentleman.

"I suppose we need to talk about this." The other chair scraped as he pulled it out. "About how I compromised you."

"You didn't—" *He thinks you lie with any man you get close to,* she chided herself. Libby stared at the cup he placed before her, wet on the outside from a washing, brimming with steaming black coffee.

"I did. I wanted you, and you were there." His hand covered hers with a firm certainty.

Did he blame her? No, the honesty in his eyes said differently. "I hope you don't think that I..." She couldn't finish.

"No."

Tears burned behind her eyes. "You needed me." He would never know the depth of her affection for him, changed now after the love they'd made.

His hand over hers didn't pull away. Libby stared down at the contact of their fingers as if it held personal significance.

"Jacob." Tears glimmered in her eyes. "You must think..."

She bowed her chin.

"I know the kind of woman you are, Elizabeth." His gaze latched onto hers. "Loving. Decent. Honorable."

Elizabeth was alone in the world, full of need, quietly aching to love someone. The thought of her lying with another man enraged him; he wanted to unleash all his anger at that bastard who used her loneliness to his gain. *Hell, he was no better.*

"The storm has stopped." She fingered the steaming hot cup, testing the temperature. "It's morning, and I need to figure out what's happening with the stage."

"You still plan on leaving?"

She snapped her gaze up to his. "Yes. I have to think of my future. There's no one I can rely on. I need to work all day, and I can't take care of a baby at the same time. I need help."

"You don't have to go."

"I do. I care for you, Jacob." She tucked her bottom

lip between her teeth. "That makes it more difficult. Can't you see?"

He did. But he didn't want her to leave. His heart felt raw. "Maybe I could help you."

"Jacob, thank you, but no." Pride shimmered in her eyes.

How many women would have manipulated to stay with him, to marry him? But not Elizabeth. And he wanted so much more from her than he knew how to ask.

"Elizabeth, you don't need to be alone to fend for yourself."

He covered his face with his hands. Why was it so hard to say what burned in his heart? It felt so risky to be that vulnerable. He didn't know how to begin to tell her.

"You didn't leave me alone." Her soft voice soothed like morning light. "You paid for my room and board even when I didn't want you to."

Jacob ached. "It was the right thing to do. Your condition surprised me. I needed time to think, to make sense of my fear."

She lifted her chin. He saw confused pain in her eyes, and it matched what tore at his heart. He wanted her—but what about that baby?

He loved babies and he hated himself for his feelings—the child Elizabeth carried was an innocent life, not to blame for its existence just as it would not be to blame for what could happen at its birth. Emma was not responsible for Mary's death—he was.

Lantern light glowed across Elizabeth's face. She was a beautiful woman with a big heart and large eyes the color of a morning sky. He remembered the untutored way she had lain beneath him on the bed. He remembered her strangled, surprised gasp of pleasure.

She'd given him her innocence, even if she hadn't been able to give him her virginity. Jacob had seen enough in this world to know the difference between taking and giving.

"Stay here with me. With Emma." The words—risky and vulnerable—caught in his throat. He wanted to ask for more, but this was enough to risk. For now. "We need you here with us."

Her face crumpled. "Jacob, I just can't stay." Heat crept up her face.

Lord, she thought he just wanted sex. Anger ripped through him. He pushed back the chair, wood grating upon wood. "That isn't what I meant." He didn't know how to speak from his heart.

"I don't expect you to marry me, Jacob." Her voice quivered.

He paced away to the main room and tossed more wood on the dying fire. Even now his body thrummed with the heat of their passion. He ached for more. How he ached for more. But at what cost to Elizabeth?

He marched back into the kitchen. She was standing before the pantry, pulling out the makings for breakfast.

"I just can't walk off without speaking to her." Elizabeth didn't turn around.

The lamplight shone on her unbound hair, floating freely down her back, curling at her knees. Her dress shivered around her slender form as she carried his biggest bowl to the table.

"I didn't mean I wanted—" Hell, he didn't know how to say it. Sex wasn't something a gentleman discussed with a lady. Neither was his heart. "I don't want you to leave. If you think I only want to use you, if that's the reason you're determined to leave, then I'll make you a promise. I won't touch you again, if that's what you want."

"Oh, Jacob." Her mouth trembled. "I can't stay. You can't give me what I came here for."

"I want to try." He meant it with his entire soul.

"Trying isn't what I need." She gestured to her abdomen helplessly, to the baby within.

He took her hands in his. Her palms felt cold and clammy, betraying her feelings. How did he say it? How did he reach past the fear and the words he couldn't find to let her know he needed more than sex, more than just her presence in his life. "I have to know. Do you need me? Am I enough to keep you here?"

"Yes." Tears sparkled in her eyes. "You are more than enough for me, Jacob Stone. I've never met any man as good and as gentle as you."

Grateful tears spilled silently down her soft cheeks.

She was so wrong. He felt as if he were standing on a cliff's edge, the earth crumbling beneath his feet. He'd been falling with nothing to hold on to for so long. Now he had Elizabeth.

"Do you want sausage and bacon, or just bacon?" she asked, her chin set, pride steeling her spine.

"Emma likes both."

He pulled her into his arms right where she belonged, tucked beneath his chin, close to his heart.

Libby stood over the hot stove, frying sausage and bacon, listening to Jacob coaxing Emma from bed. With the storm gone, the silence felt loud and the smallest noise traveled through the snug cabin, even Jacob's low voice.

Emma answered. She sounded cranky, but strong.

This is what she'd traveled so far to find: the cozy sounds of home, the snug feeling of belonging. It seemed so little now compared with what she might have with Jacob, if he wasn't so scarred inside.

No, meeting him, seeing what might have been was not the worst thing that could have happened. She could have fallen in love with him. No man had treated her with such respect, such amazing gentleness. The strength of him, all steel-muscles, power and tender heart. The combination intrigued her, just as it had in his letters.

He was no longer fantasy, no longer a flesh-and-blood stranger, but a man filled with pain. She felt it in the tender way he'd loved her. She knew only lies before Jacob; now she knew how love felt. What she didn't know, that was a risky thing. Would he ever heal his broken heart? Would he love her?

More importantly, would he come to love her baby? Babies were vulnerable. They required love and care. Things Jacob did not feel he could give his own daughter—why else would he advertise for a wife he never meant to love?

"You're still here!" Emma padded into the kitchen, her dark hair disheveled, her face drawn. Pleasure sparkled in her eyes.

"I am." Libby turned from the pantry. "I guess the stage can't leave with all the snow outside."

"It's deep! I wish you could take me out to play."

"I doubt you'll be going out to play anytime soon,

missy.'' Libby couldn't hide her smile. ''Not with that cough.''

''I just had to ask, you know.''

''I know.'' Her heart felt light as air. ''Sit up to the table. I'll have pancakes for us soon.''

''Do you know how to make 'em in shapes?''

''Yes, I know how to make shapes. How does a cat sound?''

''Good. But do you know how to make a horse?''

''Hmm. I bet I can figure it out.'' Libby turned to lift the last of the bacon from the sizzling pan. She felt so happy.

Playing house did not make this her home. She needed to remember that. This happiness was temporary; it wasn't hers for a lifetime.

''Can I watch?'' Emma had already hopped off her chair and stood ready.

''If you're very careful of the stove,'' Libby consented. She could never say no to Emma, just as she could never say it to Jacob.

Did that mean she would stay? What would she sacrifice for another man's needs? What would she sacrifice for her own?

''Goody,'' Emma cheered, dragging the chair across the floor with an ear-breaking racket.

Libby helped her climb up near the stove. At Emma's trusting touch, her heart filled. A daughter of her own. Would she be so lucky?

''Pa likes horses,'' Emma said, mischief dancing in her eyes.

Libby wasn't fooled. Emma wanted her to stay. Jacob wanted her to stay. Her heart twisted, felt torn. She could only guess at the depth of Jacob's grief, only imagine if he might one day overcome his past.

As Emma leaned closer, Libby cradled the pitcher filled with batter, cold against her hands. What if she stayed, only to find the wounds in his heart too deep to return her love? Libby was strong; she could live without love. It wouldn't kill her. But she would not risk her heart again. She'd made a mistake with Arthur by wanting him desperately to be what she needed. And he was not. If she stayed, would she make the same mistake with Jacob?

The tight knot in Jacob's chest softened a bit at the sight of his daughter standing on a chair beside Elizabeth, helping make the morning meal. The rich scent of coffee and bacon filled the air, making his mouth water, awakening more than just his hunger.

"We've made a surprise for you, Jacob." Elizabeth turned, her face flushed from the heat.

A hard hammering pounded behind his heart. He wanted to touch her, lay his hand against the sweet curve of her face. "A surprise, for me?"

"It was my idea, Pa." Emma covered her mouth with her hand, coughed, then jumped down from the chair.

Elizabeth's hand reached out, settling on Emma's back, to keep her from falling accidentally against the stove.

"Your idea, huh?" he acknowledged. "I can't imagine what you've come up with this time."

"Look at the pancakes!"

Horses. He met Elizabeth's gaze over the plate. But he was thinking of the spinning excitement he'd felt in her arms.

"Emma tells me you have real maple syrup." She

brushed past him, her gaze falling, suddenly shy. "I've never had it before."

"It was my mother's favorite—she always had maple syrup. It just came into Ellington's. I had to special order." The memory came rushing back. Elizabeth made him remember times he'd come to Montana to forget. Connections to family, to home. "You'll like it."

She granted him a small smile. "Everyone sit down. I'll get the eggs from the oven. Emma, you forgot to get the napkins."

"Sorry." The girl sauntered to the pantry, making noise as she went.

Jacob grabbed the coffeepot and began to pour two cups full, keeping his back to Elizabeth. He could smell her, a soft rose water scent that warmed his blood, hear her as she deftly carried the plates of food to the table.

"Jacob." Her sweet voice rippled across his back like a touch. "Let me do that. It's the least I can do."

"The least?" He should be figuring out what to do for her, how to make her stay, how to make this strumming need for her end.

He'd promised not to touch her if she stayed. It was for the best. He had to keep his heart protected. Losing Mary—the memories choked him even now. What if he lost Elizabeth, too? His gaze slipped to her belly.

Emma dashed back, and the two of them began talking. So warm, filling the snug cabin with a life he'd been missing for years.

Numb, Jacob sat down at the table. "Thank you for the horses."

"It took some practice. Emma said the first ones I made looked like dogs."

Then her smile shone bright enough to break his heart. "I've decided to stay. For a while."

Chapter Fourteen

For a while, Libby reminded herself, that's all. It wasn't a hard decision. Not when she thought about it. Not when she wanted to take care of him.

"Let me do the dishes, Elizabeth." He covered her hand with his. "You worked side by side with me when Emma was sick. You've done so much already."

"I haven't done nearly enough." She felt it in her heart. She owed Jacob so much. Knowing him was a privilege. And loving him…she owed him for wanting her, despite her baby and his own wounded heart.

"That's not true." His hand brushed her face.

Fire rippled across her skin. "We can work together. We do that well."

"Yes. We do." A smile warmed his eyes; a genuine smile that made her grin.

"I'll get the water heating." She turned.

His hand snared her wrist. "No, I'll do it. I don't want you doing any heavy work."

"There's no need to treat me like glass."

"There's every reason in the world." His gaze slipped to her waist.

Libby placed her hand there. "Emma needs me. I have her bath to draw and her bed to change."

It was the least he could do for this woman who worked hard fixing for Emma, tending her, washing sheets, grinding onions no matter her own exhaustion, no matter her own condition. She'd been such a help to him, and he didn't know how to tell her. "I'll get the bed moved back into her room for you."

"That would be wonderful." Despite the exhaustion ringing in her eyes, Elizabeth's smile shone bright. "Now that the blizzard has passed, the cabin feels so snug. Emma's room will be more than warm enough for her."

"I'll get started then," he said, instead of saying what burned in his heart.

"Jacob?" Elizabeth caught his hand. Affection snapped in her honest eyes.

She's staying. For a while, she'd said. He still felt rocked by the news. Joy stirred in his heart, lightening him. This was an opportunity to see what might come of their relationship. He felt drawn to Elizabeth like no woman he'd known—even Mary.

That shamed him, and saved him. The responsibility of caring for another settled on his shoulders, gave him purpose.

"Are you going to work today?"

"I—" He hesitated. "Yes." It would give him time to think. To make things straight in his own mind. "I've got a lot of men to thank for helping with the search. They don't know Emma's been found."

"Of course." The soft morning light touched her face like he wanted to: gently, intimately.

He stepped away. "I'll get to the bed right away. And

the wood. I want to carry in enough to see you through the day. How much wash water do you need?''

''Jacob, you don't need to do so much for me.''

Affection. Admiration. He didn't know what it was twisting in his heart, but if felt like more. ''I want to.''

Then she smiled, and it was enough to light the world. ''My bags are waiting at the Faded Bloom.''

''I'll grab them for you and bring them home tonight, if that's not too late.''

''No.''

He turned before the way her mouth moved when she spoke, the way her body moved when she walked, made him reach out and pull her hard against him.

She padded off to the kitchen, and he yanked the sheets off Emma's little bed.

''Pa?'' Emma strolled to his side. ''Aren't you glad she's stayin'? I sure am.''

He looked down at the rag doll clutched in her small hands, and his entire chest deflated. Glad? He was glad, all right. Hell, he was terrified, too.

Libby watched a sparrow dive for the bread crumbs scattered in the peaceful blanket of snow, then squinted through the fog from Emma's breath.

''Now I can't see,'' the girl complained.

''Then don't huff and puff so close to the glass,'' Libby teased.

A grin widened Emma's face. ''I wish I could go outside and play.''

''I think you were outside enough the other day.'' Libby rubbed the glass with her sleeve. ''In fact, the entire town was.''

"I know." Emma sighed. "I don't like storms."

"I used to be scared of them when I was little, too." Scared in her aunt's home. It hurt to remember.

"I'm not little, not anymore."

"Sorry." Libby laughed. "Look, there's your pa. I'd best get his coffee boiling. He looks cold."

"He's got a different horse!" Emma clung to the window. "Please, oh please, can I go out and see it?"

"Not today." Libby stood. "Maybe tomorrow, if you're well enough."

Her heart made a funny skip when she saw Jacob tucked beneath blankets in a small sleigh.

"It's the horse with the star on her face!" Emma cried, nearly toppling off the chair.

Libby caught her by the elbow, steadying her, then leaned close for a better look. She squinted against the sheen of bright sunshine reflecting off the shrinking snow and saw Jacob, solid and dark, untying a horse from the back of his sled.

"Pa, is that pretty horse ours?" Emma asked the instant Jacob stepped into the lean-to.

He only grinned at her as he tugged off his boots. "I'm not telling."

"Pa!" Emma hid a cough in her hand. "Is she ours?"

"No. I brought the horse for Elizabeth." Jacob smiled, and when he caught Libby's gaze her heart kicked again.

"For me?"

"Yes." He bent down to tend to his boots. "I'll have the team with me at the livery. You need to drive Emma back and forth from town every day."

"I have to go to Mrs. Holt's to *school*," Emma sighed.

"It's a good thing I'm too sick to go for weeks and weeks, right Pa?"

"I don't think you're that sick." Jacob winked.

"Oh, Pa." Emma sighed, clearly tortured by the thought of school.

"I won't need a horse, Jacob," Libby said. "Emma can go to town with you in the mornings."

"But she's done with Mrs. Holt by two. Would you pick her up for me? I guess we haven't discussed what you'll do here." He looked down at his hands, confusion twisting his face.

"No, I guess we haven't." Nerves fluttered in her chest. What did Jacob expect? What did he need from her?

"She's supposed to take care of me, Pa," Emma interjected, then coughed. "That's why we wrote her that letter in the first place."

"I guess that says it all." Jacob straightened, then shrugged out of his coat. "Elizabeth, you will take care of us, won't you?"

"Oh, yes." It hurt inside where she'd been lonely for so long.

"Then the horse is yours." The sheer size of him shrunk the small lean-to.

"To use," she clarified.

"No. I'm giving her to you."

"But I can't..." She froze.

Jacob walked past her as if the gift of a fine horse were nothing. It was too much, more than she would ever deserve. She stayed because she could not leave him, not because she needed a gift.

But he'd already dismissed it, walking through the kitchen with Emma at his side.

He poured himself a steaming cup of coffee from the pot on the stove. "Emma, go find the book in my room. I'll read to you until dinner."

"Yes, Pa." She scampered off, short sharp coughs punctuating her trip across the cabin.

Tell him now. Her knees shook as she stepped forward. "I can't accept the horse."

"A woman needs a horse. It's a long walk to town, Elizabeth." Jacob poured her a cup, too.

"But she's valuable." She fisted her slender hands. "I'm not in the habit of taking gifts from men. I know I've been too innocent, too easy to fool in the past, but..."

"Do you think I brought you this mare because of what we did upstairs?"

She blushed. "No, it's just..." Her blue eyes darkened like the sky before a thunderstorm. "I didn't stay here to get something for myself."

"Then why are you here?"

Her face fell. "Because I have to know if we can make this work. Why did you ask me to stay?"

"Because I can't let you go." If his heart gripped, he refused to feel it. "Don't read too much into this. The mare has been abused and needs someone gentle. You need a horse to get you to town and back. It's that simple."

He needed someone as gentle as her. Jacob grabbed the sugar bowl. "Besides, I wanted to give you this mare for the same reason you gave Emma her doll."

Tears, clear like diamonds, rose in her eyes, and her clenched jaw trembled. "No one's ever given me anything like that before," she managed to say.

Jacob's throat tightened. He reached out his hand and cupped her dear face in his palm. "I've been saving the mare for you, Elizabeth. It was hard to find the right time to give her to you.''

She leaned her cheek against his hand. ''I owe you so much, Jacob. For the horse. For allowing me to stay here with you and Emma. I won't make you sorry.''

''I know.'' And he did. ''I want to make this work, for Emma's sake.''

She stepped away, and the smile in her eyes dimmed. Jacob didn't know why. He wished he could have told her the truth. He wanted her to stay for him, too.

While she checked the soup simmering on the stove, Libby listened to his low voice above the crackling of the fire. There were a hundred different chores she needed to do, but she couldn't seem to budge herself from the kitchen.

Jacob's low voice spoke of a faraway ocean, an ocean she knew nothing about. She closed her eyes, enchanted by his words. His voice rumbled low and affectionate, caught up in the joy of the story. Libby couldn't help herself. She peered around the corner just to watch him.

He bowed slightly over his open book, tucked in the chair before the hearth. His red flannel shirt matched the happiness in his voice, deepening his gray eyes and ebony hair. Her gaze traveled lower, remembering the feel of him. Comfortable cotton encased his powerful thighs, and his stockinged feet were crossed at the ankles.

She wanted this man like nothing else—to love him. The emotion burned in her heart. Making love to him had changed her. She could see how love—how romance—was possible between a man and a woman. It wasn't based only on need.

Emma sat enchanted on the floor at his feet, gazing up at her father with rapt eyes. *Jacob enraptured her, too.* It was all Libby could do to keep from snatching up the dress she was sewing and join them. It would feel so right to sit in the other chair at the other side of the small fireplace and work on a few buttonholes while Jacob read, Emma at their feet. It would feel like a family at home for the evening.

But they weren't a family. It pinched Libby's heart to remember that. But maybe, in time, she could make it so.

Whether she was foolish or not, she didn't care. Libby stepped into the lean-to and began organizing the shelves of food, listening to the warm tone of his voice.

"Your soup was delicious." Jacob ambled up to the worktable where Elizabeth was sudsing dishes. "I've been eating my own cooking for so long, I forgot what real food tastes like."

"You're exaggerating. I've eaten your meals before." Elizabeth plunged her bare hands into the dish tub, her sleeves rolled up to her elbows. "You are a fine cook— for a man."

He chuckled. "Hey, I'm best with horses, but I learned a thing or two watching my mother and sisters in the kitchen."

"You watched your mother and sisters in the kitchen?" She lifted a skeptical brow.

"Okay, I was usually eating whatever it was they made, but I saw things."

"Sure. That's why Emma told me the only thing you could make was pancakes." Elizabeth shook her head at him.

"But I'm a damn fine cook now." He grabbed a dish towel and began drying. "I never thought to ask if you liked books. We never discussed it in our letters."

"No. What was the story you were reading to Emma?" She sounded wistful.

"*Moby Dick.* Mother always teased me how I lived for books." Between horses and reading, his only other love had been Mary.

"I've never read a novel," Elizabeth said quietly. She reached for the soup bowls with soapy hands. "I never had much of a chance to go to school."

"You write a fine letter."

She shrugged. "I worked at it, mostly at home. I always hoped I could be a schoolteacher one day."

Her lost dream saddened him, a dream he could not give her now. "I'm going to see if Emma's ready for an early bed."

She only nodded, scrubbing hard at each bowl. Doing the same thorough job she seemed to do with everything. What other dreams had she lost? he wondered.

He listened to Emma's chatter as he tucked her into bed. Her cough was still thick and raw, but she was recovering. That was all that mattered. He'd sent for the doctor from town—only to learn Emma would be fine.

His worries eased, he fetched the book from the front room and read to her in the lamplight until her eyelids grew heavy.

Such a vulnerable child. He'd almost lost her, and it tore at him with a fury, with a knowledge.

"I love you, Pa," Emma said when he leaned to kiss her forehead.

Jacob's throat swelled as he cupped her little chin in his big hand. "I love you too, precious."

He would not be afraid to love.

Elizabeth sat in her chair before the fire, her head bent over her work. She held a dress in her hands, patiently pressing a needle through the soft fabric. She glanced up from her sewing, twisting around to see him.

"Emma's a lot better today," she said casually, facing her work. "I told her she couldn't go outside until her cough was gone."

She belonged here. He knew it in his heart.

"Would you like to go meet your new horse?"

She looked up, her needle poised in midair. "You mean, now?"

It was dark and cold out. Maybe it wasn't best for her health. He wasn't sure. "I wanted to check on her. She doesn't take well to change. Besides, I just realized I forgot to bring your bags in from town."

She set down her needle. Smiled. "I don't want to bother you. My uncle always had this idea about the stable."

"What kind of idea?"

"It's a man's domain."

Her heart lifted when he laughed. "I guess I can say a woman's domain is the kitchen, but I'm there as often as my stomach gets empty. Will you come?"

Yes. "I still don't feel right about the gift of the mare."

"Then just don't think about it." His smile could knock her clear to the stars.

Libby carefully set down her mending. She stood, washed in the firelight. He stepped forward and took her hand. Nothing in her life had ever felt so right.

"I shouldn't leave Emma," she said.

"She's sleeping. She'll be fine." Jacob's hand stayed, warming her skin. "Come with me."

The sensation of being beside him, of being touched by him pounded a vivid memory into her brain. Of Jacob standing naked before her, the thickness of his erection mesmerizing her. Of his touch to her breast and the amazing fullness she felt as he joined them together.

The man was like whiskey, intoxicating her, muddling her mind. She couldn't think straight as he led her into the kitchen, then into the lean-to. He lit a lantern, and the dancing light tossed eerie shadows around the small room.

"Tell me more about the mare," she urged, just to hear his voice.

"She's a little mustang. I'm guessing about four or five years old, too damn young to have been treated the way she was. It's taken most of the year to teach her to trust me."

He held out a heavy wool coat, large enough to be his own. "Here. Wear this. It will keep you warm."

So caring. "Thank you." No one had ever treated her like this. "How did you teach her to trust you?"

"Patience. It was something I learned from my father."

"No. It was your hands." She caught his fingers, studying them in the wobbling light. "You have the most gentle hands. Just your touch feels like comfort."

She said the wrong thing. Jacob's eyes darkened and he stepped closer. Without one word, he helped her into her wraps, then knelt to button her boots.

"I can do it." She bent to do the task.

"I want to." Jacob's gaze stopped her. Tenderness burned, taking her breath away.

He was a man she could depend on. She'd never had that, never trusted anyone so deeply.

"Will you be warm enough?" He caught her hand with his.

She could only nod.

He led her out into the night. Snow crunched beneath her shoes. Frigid air burned her face. The night felt so dark despite Jacob's lantern licking a pool of light across the frozen vastness of the yard. Tall black trees, solemn in the dark, stood silent sentries indiscernible with the night.

"It's so breathtaking." Libby tipped her head back to study the black canopy overhead. The sky was as dark as sleep and scattered with thousands of white stars.

"Yes. When it's warmer, I can stay out here for hours."

"It's a little cold tonight," she agreed.

"The stable will be warm."

With Jacob's firm grip on her, she didn't slip on the ice. But she'd never leaned on anyone before. Once inside the small stable, she was glad when he released her arm.

"This door is strong enough to withstand a bear attack," Jacob said as he barricaded the door behind them.

"Have you had any trouble with bears?" She thought of Emma alone in the house.

"Not tonight," he said, then smiled. "I'm teasing. We only had one last year, and when he figured out he couldn't get into my stable, he gave up and hasn't been back."

"Good." Libby sagged against the wood wall, then jumped.

A cow immediately poked her head out of a stall and curled out her long pink tongue.

"Oh, you nearly scared the life right out of me." Libby

laughed as the cow deftly caught the edge of her coat sleeve between her teeth.

"That's Jane," Jacob explained, "named in honor of our last housekeeper."

Libby made herself smile, but her heart tightened a little. Did he consider her simply their current housekeeper?

"I brought her with me from Kentucky." Jacob rubbed the cow's neck. "Since I was bringing Emma, I figured a little girl needed milk to drink."

Libby nodded. He had brought stock all the way from Kentucky. A fine cow and the most beautiful horses she'd ever seen.

"Look, she's watching you." Jacob gestured.

The sorrel mare peeked down at Libby with her fudge brown eyes. She was a pretty animal with a velvet nose and intelligent, pricked ears and a thick red mane. Now that she knew the animal was hers, Libby realized how big the horse was, how powerful.

"She hasn't quite trusted me to get up on her back yet, but she will drive just fine. If this snow holds, she'll let you pull a sleigh to town and back."

"She seems gentle." Libby worried about driving all the way to town.

"As a kitten." Jacob turned to grab his coat from the mare's mouth. "It's a good thing. Some animals never overcome bad handling."

"The past is a powerful influence." Her heart twisted. *For all of them.*

The mare reached out, begging for a treat. Libby had nothing. Other than hay, she didn't even know what a horse ate.

"Here, she loves this." Jacob handed Libby a short

length of carrot. "Hold it flat on your palm so she doesn't accidentally bite your fingers."

"Like this?" Nervous, she held open her palm for Jacob to see, but the mare was quicker. That velvet soft muzzle nibbled her hand, tickling her, and Libby felt completely enchanted as the mare seized the chunk of carrot.

"She seems to like you." His gaze caressed her with the same tangible weight as if he'd brushed her face with his tender hands. Something began to expand just beneath her heart, and she tried to stop it.

"D-do you really think I could drive her?"

"Yes. You are gentle, Elizabeth, and that's all she requires." Jacob's gaze never relented, kept brushing her like a touch. "Do you know how to handle a horse?"

"No. I've never been around one."

"That's hard for me to imagine. I've been riding since I was two."

"Since you were two?" Libby tried to picture the strongly built, very masculine man before her as a little boy on a pony. She couldn't.

"My father bred and sold horses," Jacob explained, his voice warm, his eyes lighting. "I grew up knowing nothing but horses. They used to be my whole life."

She knew so little about Jacob, what life had been like for him growing up, what his parents were like, what were his dreams. She felt closer to him, knowing even this small piece of his heart. "I don't know how to care for her."

"I'll teach you." Jacob focused on her face, his gaze narrowing on her lips.

Libby's mouth tingled.

"Of course there's a lot of pitchforking involved, but I won't make you clean stalls."

"You're such a gentleman."

"Yes."

His lips caught hers, gentle at first as if he wanted to kiss away past hurts, old wounds. Libby needed his kiss, his comfort, and she opened up to him. Her heart exploded as his kiss deepened, grew wilder. Heaven help her, but she felt an answering twist of need deep inside her.

Yes. Libby tipped her mouth up, needing more. Jacob folded his strong arms around her, backed her against the solid stable wall and pinned her there. His tongue laved her bottom lip, then pressed inside her mouth.

Need speared through her. He felt solid, comforting, exciting. His powerful hands could hurt her, but instead they reached up to cup her face, never asking more from her just as he'd promised.

Libby didn't believe in happily-ever-afters, but when she tipped her head back and saw the gleam in his eyes, she began to believe.

Chapter Fifteen

He'd asked her to stay for Emma's sake, Libby thought as she washed the breakfast dishes. She didn't fool herself, yet she knew he cared for her, too. She clung to that thought, knowing it had to be enough. She'd traveled all this way to meet and marry a man she hardly knew—back in her lonely rented room in Omaha, a friendly relationship with a kind, intelligent man seemed like heaven.

It ought to be good enough now.

"Look, my new dress is perfect," Emma chimed, pounding into the kitchen with bare feet.

Libby turned from the basin. "It looks beautiful on you."

Emma grinned. "You sewed it up really good. I wanted curtains for my room, but Jane said she was too old to sew a lot. Her fingers hurt all the time."

"Let me guess, you want me to make you some curtains for your room." Libby wrung out the rag and bent to wipe the table.

"Yes."

"We'll see."

Since Emma was not well enough to go out in the cold to school, she spent the morning at home, wandering around bored. So Libby put her to work helping sort the wash. By then, Emma was ready for a nap and Libby changed the other beds alone, blushing when she stripped her straw tick and remembered Jacob's lovemaking.

She had supper ready minutes after Jacob came home, tugging off his boots in the lean-to. He told Emma of the melting snow, of the latest antics of the horses in his stable, of the funny news from town.

Libby kept her heart still as she drained the water from the potatoes. Steam rose in her face. Jacob said hello to her and thanked her for cooking. All she could remember was his heated, tender touch. Did he remember, too?

She watched him sit down to the table and listened to Emma's questions about his day and it filled the silence between them.

Libby set the potatoes on the table and caught Jacob studying her. She would give every penny she'd earned over the last few months to know what he was thinking.

Libby held tightly to Emma's mittened hand as they crossed the icy street from Ellington's store.

"What do you suppose your pa will say when he sees all the material you wanted?" Libby asked.

Emma shrugged beneath her tightly bundled layers. "He won't mind. He says it's a womanly thing to want lace and ruffles."

"So, what did you cost me?" Jacob leaned against the stable door, framed by solid wood. The tiniest snowflakes fell like sugar between them.

His dark hair looked rumpled from his work, and the

blue flannel shirt she made him hugged his wide shoulders. It was his smile that made her stop in her tracks.

She loved him. It hit her like a brick.

Yet the earth didn't move, the sky didn't open, the world remained exactly the same.

"Your daughter cost you a bundle." She hefted up the thick package for him to see. "You should have come with us, because I have a hard time saying no to her."

Emma grinned. "That's why I like her, Pa. She's so easy."

Jacob tipped back his head and laughed.

Libby blushed. The child had no notion of what she said. "I'm a pushover for sweet blue eyes," she muttered instead. "Jacob, it's not that funny."

He winked at her. Humor warmed his voice. "Let me guess. We're getting curtains."

"In every room of the house."

Jacob lifted the bulky package from her arms. His gaze snared hers. "I guess I can resign myself to a few curtains."

Affection filled her. Did he want her the same way she wanted him?

"Pa! I'm starving. Are you gonna take us to the diner?"

Libby leaned against the corner post separating the stall from the wide aisle. Jacob felt so distant, yet he stood so near.

"How about it, Elizabeth?"

He wanted her with him. She could see that in his eyes. "I'd love to."

His smile stretched across his mouth, and she wanted to touch him there, to kiss him again. Need for him simmered in her heart.

"Pa, you got a new horse!" Emma announced with heart-deep excitement.

Jacob knelt down to talk about the new boarder, and Libby glanced out on the street. Another stage would leave tomorrow at noon. She wouldn't be on it. When she asked at the counter, she'd been told the route would be closed in a month due to the harsh winter snows.

She had a month. It wasn't enough time to decide the rest of her future.

"You look tired, Elizabeth." He touched her arm. "Are you feeling all right?"

"I'm just hungry."

Her hand felt right tucked in his own. When he looked up and saw hope in her beautiful eyes, he felt almost whole again.

The cabin eased into sight as the horses climbed the slope, pulling the sled along the snow-crusted ground. His day had been long, but lunch with Elizabeth and Emma had brightened it.

He'd been lonely for so long. But not now.

He reined in the horses in front of the stable, surprised when two bundled figures crunched through the snow.

"Pa!" Emma launched herself at him.

He caught her, laughing. "You're covered from head to toe. What did you do, bury yourself in the snow?"

"Miss Hodges said I was well enough to go out to play. We've been having snowball fights."

"It looks like you've been losing." Jacob's gaze landed on Elizabeth.

Slim, shy, she offered him a smile. Her face, pinkened

by the cold, looked pretty. More than pretty. He ached to take her into his arms and keep her warm.

"Pa, can you take us for a sleigh ride? Please?" Emma tugged at his hand. "I promise my cough won't get worse."

"Emma, you've been outside a long time." Elizabeth tucked her gloved hands into her coat pockets. "You must be half-frozen by now."

"Pa?"

His throat constricted. He could see how they would make a family: Elizabeth caring for Emma, Emma between them like a bright shining star. This is what he wanted, a loving home for Emma. This was why he'd taken that terrible risk and placed the advertisement last winter. Jacob's heart filled with hope.

"I could take Elizabeth's mare for a run. She's been in that stall for a few days," he said at last.

"Can we, Pa?" Emma clapped her gloved hands. "It would be so fun."

How could he say no? "I have to unhitch the team first and tend them."

"I can help!" Emma volunteered.

He nodded. Elizabeth stepped closer to lay her hand on Emma's shoulder. So protective. So loving. He could barely manage to utter an agreement.

"The fire is getting low," she said quietly as tiny bits of snow filled the air between them. "I'd best head inside and stoke it up, so it's warm enough to thaw out a certain little girl when she's frozen solid."

Humor sparkled in her sky blue eyes, and it meant the world to Jacob. Few women could be so gentle, so loving to his little girl.

"I can carry in the wood for you," he offered.

"There's plenty in the house." Pleasure lit her eyes. She was glad he asked.

There was supper to check on—the beef vegetable soup was simmering on the stove, and the fire needed wood. She swept the hearth and stopped by the brown-wrapped bundle on the table. A warm feeling slipped through her chest when she fingered the yellow flannel Emma had chosen for another dress, then the flowery muslin folded beneath. How would Jacob react when he saw the tiny pink roses with green stems on white frilly curtains at his window?

She felt a tiny flutter, and she placed her hand over the spot on her abdomen. Would he feel any different about this baby when it was born?

A delighted shriek filled the air and Libby hurried to the window. She gazed out at the winter landscape as Jacob led the sorrel mare by her reins. Emma sat on the horse's back, laughing wholeheartedly. Jacob broke into a jog, and the mare trotted after him.

Emma spotted her through the window and waved wildly. There was no mistaking that signal. Libby waved back and hurried to the lean-to where she tugged on her wraps.

"Pa is gonna hitch up the sleigh and teach you to drive!" Emma announced the instant Libby closed the door behind her.

"It's true." Jacob halted the mare only steps away.

"I've never driven before. Is it hard?"

"Not at all." Jacob reached into his pocket and withdrew a carrot. "Here, feed your mare. You need to let her know how much you like her."

"Like her? Why, I love her." She could feel Jacob's gaze on her face as gentle as the snowflakes brushing her skin. Emotion wedged in her throat. The mare nickered in recognition, and Libby dared to reach for her velvet warm nose.

"What are you gonna name her?" Emma asked.

"I get to name her?" Libby looked up.

Right into Jacob's eyes. "Yes. She was meant for you all along. I always figured you would decide what to call her."

Libby's throat felt so tight, she couldn't breathe. Her heartbeat thudded dully in her ears. He wanted her. She read it in his stormy eyes. He'd wanted her from the very first.

"I—I have no idea what to name her," she finally replied.

"I'd name her Star," Emma decided with infinite wisdom.

"Star, it is." She felt so happy.

Jacob's hand covered hers. "I'll show you how to hitch her up."

Libby wrapped her fingers through his.

At the stable, Jacob hauled out the leather harness and let Star sniff it before he laid it across her back. He talked about buckles and Libby tried to pay attention. His thick, nimble fingers worked over numerous straps and then stopped to reassure the mare with gentle pats.

"Can we go fast?" Emma asked.

"We'll see." Jacob promised.

Libby's heart skipped when he smiled, a slow sweet curve of his lips, and helped her onto the sleigh's low board seat. Excitement thrummed through her. She'd never felt so happy or her heart so full.

Jacob squeezed next to her, his strong shoulder tight against hers. She tried to fight the tingling thrill of awareness possessing her. It was hard. Every touch, every glance reminded her of loving him, of how she wanted him to love her.

"Now, watch what I do," he said, leaning close.

Watch? Heavens, she couldn't even think.

Snow floated down in small airless flakes, filling the air with their gentle whiteness. He moved the reins just enough, and the mare tugged the sleigh forward. Soon they were whizzing along the road to town, gliding like air over the ice-slick snow.

"It feels like flying," Libby cried out, filled with delight. The tall lengths of the evergreens whipped by with dizzying speed. Cold air rushed against her face. Emma laughed, and Jacob smiled.

"Here, you try it." He leaned closer and gently placed the reins in Libby's hands.

"Oh!" Her fingers closed around the leather reins, and instantly the thrilling feel of Star's mouth vibrated against her fingers. She wasn't just holding leather reins, she was feeling the mare.

"That's right. You have a gentle touch." Jacob's voice rumbled in her ear.

His hand covered hers, and she felt his scorching touch through the yarn of her gloves. At Jacob's urging she tightened the reins just a bit, and Star changed smoothly from a trot to a canter.

Wind drove the snow into her eyelashes, and Libby blinked against them. Jacob's large hands fell away from hers, and she urged Star faster all on her own. They flew toward the cabin, and Libby slowed the mare into a trot to turn her around, then raced her down the long road lined with noble cedars.

Emma's laughter doubled. Even Libby found herself smiling. She felt the thrill and the strength of her mare through the reins, the power and the grace. Pride swept through her. This was her mare, Jacob's gift to her.

All her worries melted like snow to the sun as the world whizzed by in a blur of white and brown and deep green. They flew over the frozen ground earthbound, but for the first time in her life, Libby felt free.

She leaned into the wind, her eyes tearing from the cold, and let herself join in Jacob's and Emma's joyful laughter.

When it was too cold for both the sweating horse and Emma, whose cough did worsen despite her promise, Libby left Jacob to tend the horse while she hurried Emma inside the cabin.

The soup simmered on the stove, ready to eat, scenting the kitchen.

"Grandpa used to take me for sleigh rides when I was little," Emma said as she sat down on the nearest chair.

Libby knelt down before her and tugged off those small winter shoes. "When you were little, huh?"

"Yep. He would put bells on a real sleigh and they would sing the whole time."

Libby tucked the shoes neatly near the stove to dry. "So, you lived with both of your grandparents back in Kentucky?"

Emma brushed away the melting chunks of snow that

had driven past her muffler and coat. They hit the floor in a sloppy mess. "I had my own pony, too."

"It sounds like you had a nice life with your grandparents."

Emma nodded. "But I wanted to be with my pa."

"Of course." Libby tried to smile at the girl and failed. Jacob had kept so much to himself, even now, when they were forging a friendship. How much would he ever trust her?

Forcing lightness into her voice, Libby unwound Emma's muffler. "You're not kidding when you say you know how to ride."

"Nope." Emma's nose ran from the cold and she sniffed.

Libby pulled a handkerchief from her skirt pocket and handed it to the girl. Emma was a lucky child, kept safe and loved and protected by people who could afford such things as a child's pony. Why was she here in the middle of this rugged territory? Why had Jacob left Kentucky?

She stood. "Come to the kitchen with me. The milk is warm by now."

Emma took her hand. "Miss Hodges?"

"Yes?"

"Pa calls you Elizabeth. Can I?"

Libby stopped and stared down into those honest eyes packed full of need.

"You can call me Libby," she said through a tight throat. It was the best she could do for Emma.

All through supper, he watched her. Gray eyes, unreadable as a storm, followed her every movement. Even when he answered Emma, he didn't look at the girl. He paid attention, he just didn't move his gaze.

He complimented her cooking. He told her what a good job she'd done on her first attempt at driving the mare. She told him she'd never driven in a real sleigh before. He said he'd made it himself; it was too much hassle to get one shipped out from back east.

The evening felt perfect. He dried the dishes by her side as she washed them. He carried the conversation, telling her how Maude Baker dropped by to check on her horse, and asked after Libby. How Mr. Ellington wanted to know if she still wanted to sew for him, if she intended to stay in town.

Yes, Libby said, thinking the extra money would come in handy. She had the baby to think about and baby clothes to start making, although she didn't say that aloud to Jacob, afraid of what he would say.

Emma couldn't wait until the dishes were done. Libby put coffee on to boil while the little girl dragged her pa across the shining puncheon floors to the rocking chair before the fireplace. Emma had the book out and ready.

While Jacob read aloud of an adventure Libby had never heard before, she gathered her mending. Finally, when she could delay it no more, she carried Emma's dresses and her sewing box to the empty chair before the fire and settled into it.

Jacob didn't look up, so she began mending. Listening to his low voice rumble in the lamplight, feeling the coziness in the room, she felt sad and happy at the same time. Why? This was what she'd traveled here to find, wasn't it?

Yet she couldn't stop the nagging doubt in her heart.

Jacob made no promises, they had no agreement between them. It was best not to hope too much. So, Libby concentrated instead on mending the hem of Emma's red dress.

Once, she looked up, and Jacob smiled at her. And the world, if only momentarily, felt just right.

The next evening, when she climbed the ladder to her room, Libby found a crisp twenty dollar bill on the small bureau. Her hands shook. He'd paid her, as if she were a housekeeper.

Shame swept over her like a cold wind.

After checking on the fire and on Emma, snug and asleep in her bed, Libby pulled on her wraps, lit a lantern and headed out into the cold night.

She found Jacob in the stable, brushing down one of his bays. Star turned at the sound of her footsteps, nickering softly. Without a carrot, she had only an affectionate pat to offer the horse, but Star seemed satisfied.

Jacob looked down at her over the mare's withers. "Did you put Emma down for the night?"

"Yes. She was exhausted." Libby didn't know what to do with her hands. She touched Star's warm side and felt the strong power there.

"You seem happy with the horse," he said quietly, and she looked up.

"Happy?" The single word caught in her throat. "Oh, Jacob, nobody has ever given me something like this. She's magnificent."

"Yes." Something gleamed in his eyes. "I'm glad you like her. Not everyone cares about horses the way I do."

Libby thought about the man who had beaten Star and said nothing. "You paid me, didn't you?"

"Yes. Wasn't it enough?" He didn't turn around. So friendly, so polite, so damn respectful of her feelings.

"It's more than enough." She'd never before made that kind of money in a week. "It isn't necessary to pay me at all."

"Of course it is. This is only a trial period. We both know that." He stopped brushing. "I like having you here. Maybe we have a chance."

"At what? A business relationship?" She thought of the money in her room, in the same room where he'd lain beside her, made love with her, taught her to ache and want like nothing she'd ever known.

"No, damn it." His face tightened. "I don't want to take advantage of you. I've already done so. I care about you. You're a good woman. I just can't *use* you."

The struggle showed in his eyes. "I'm trying hard to make this work, for Emma's sake."

"That's the only reason?" She couldn't believe it. She thought of his touch, of his emotional needs she'd felt when their bodies joined.

He lifted the brush, returned to his work. "It's the only reason that matters."

Twenty dollars. She was nothing but a housekeeper to him. She didn't want to believe it; she refused to believe it. Sadness rang in his voice—and she realized what was wrong, what was missing between them.

Love. Jacob Stone didn't believe he could ever love again. That's why he went to the trouble of finding a mother for Emma, someone who could love her in case he failed, but someone who wouldn't love him.

Tears filled her eyes. "I won't accept your money. You can't pay me for the privilege of knowing you."

"I made a promise, and I meant it. I won't touch you." He turned around, his face set, his mouth grim. Pain lined his face. "I know I made a mistake, and I won't use you again."

"I don't understand. You haven't used me, Jacob." Libby looked down at her hands, reddened from work, chapped from the cold. "But I do know why having me in your home is so painful. You're a widower. You've suffered a heartbreaking loss."

His throat worked, though he remained silent.

"It just takes time. Not to forget, but to learn to live again. It can happen, Jacob."

"No." He turned his back to her and started brushing, the rhythm filling the silent barn. Not even the animals moved. "I meant what I said when we first met face-to-face. I don't want romance. Love doesn't survive in this cold world."

"That's not it. That's not it at all. You are using excuses, Jacob. You just want a convenient woman, someone to cook and clean for you, to care for your daughter, someone without any emotional needs to fill." Anger fired through her. So fast, so swift. She spun around, wanting to do something with her hands. Anything with her hands. Like break something.

"You're wrong, Elizabeth. I don't mean to be so unfeeling." Sorrow stood in his eyes, silent like deep water. "I've been lonely for so long. I need a friend. I need you."

He could twist her inside out so quickly. Libby felt the molten anger just slide away. Friends. It was so little; it was so much.

Chapter Sixteen

Jacob sat by the fire late, reading his book by lamplight. He had long ago accepted he couldn't read *Moby Dick* without Emma, who seemed thoroughly enchanted with the laborious novel, so he was reading Dickens. Maybe, when they had waded through Melville, Emma might enjoy the *Pickwick Papers*.

Night claimed the corners of the main room, and Jacob held the novel flat so it would catch the steady glow of the lamplight. Upstairs he heard a loose board squeak where Elizabeth was probably standing, working hard as usual, and he felt his conscience bite.

Everywhere he looked, he saw her touch. Her frilly curtains with starched ruffles edged in lace graced every window in the cabin, including his bedroom. A pile of material lay in a heap by the other rocking chair. According to Emma, she was helping Elizabeth make a braided rug.

Now, Jacob could hear her footsteps light on the ceiling above. He had listened to her boil water and didn't need to ask what she was doing up there.

She had scrubbed the place from corner to corner so

when he came home today, the cabin shone. Exhaustion rimmed her eyes and pinched around her mouth, but she smiled, pleased with her work.

Guilt hammered through him, and he set down his book. She was working too hard. Didn't she know a woman in her condition needed to be careful?

Jacob wandered into the kitchen. Should he go to her and tell her to stop working? He wasn't sure what to say. He didn't want to talk about the baby because it reminded him of everything standing between them—his own fears, his own responsibility for Mary's death.

He made a pot of coffee before working up the courage to climb the attic ladder. As he ascended out of the lamplight toward the dark ceiling, he climbed into the warm pool of light in Elizabeth's room, light gleaming off the polished floorboards and into his eyes.

He looked up and froze at the naked image of Elizabeth reclining in the washtub. Her honeyed hair spilled over the drab silver side of the tub, pooling on the floor like luxurious blond silk. She sat in profile so Jacob could see the intelligent plane of her forehead, the slight tilt of her nose, the rounded firmness of her jaw and full curve of her bare breasts.

Move, damn it. But his body refused to obey him. Too stunned to move, he could only watch the lamplight glow like honey on her smooth skin. He couldn't tear his gaze from the dark disks of her nipples peaking her full, firm breasts.

She hadn't seen him yet. If he just slipped silently back down the ladder, she would never know he'd been peeping at her like...like...he couldn't think what. Desire slammed through him like a freight train, delivering memories he could never forget. She'd been so...*everything* lying beneath him. Exciting. Loving. Thrilling. She had genuinely wanted him.

Ashamed as he felt over touching her in such an intimate way, Jacob had loved being bound to her, loved the glorious texture of her skin, the taste of her breasts, the feel of her body accommodating when he entered her.

She still hadn't noticed him. Jacob glanced down at the ladder, placed his foot on the nearest rung and almost moved...Elizabeth stared at him with surprise rounding her mouth.

"Jacob!" Water splashed everywhere like little prisms of light. She covered her beautiful breasts with her arms, shock lighting her eyes.

He fumbled for an explanation and felt his foot slip on the ladder rung. He fell, tumbling down several rungs, knocking his bad leg painfully in the knee, jarring his old injury. Pain shot through him like a lance.

"Jacob!"

He heard her cry out in alarm as he caught a rung with his good leg. Then he heard splashes and the patter of wet bare feet on the floorboards above. Lord, she was naked. He kept his eyes low and, by using the strength in his arms, edged his way down to the kitchen floor.

"Jacob! Thank God. You didn't fall all the way."

He heard her voice from above. Elizabeth was already kneeling at the head of the ladder, he guessed, without her clothes. Lord, she had to be naked—she hadn't the time to dress. How could he look up and see—? A man could take only so much temptation. He couldn't survive seeing her naked again.

"Are you hurt?" she persisted, her concern genuine.

He would not look up. No matter how beautiful she looked. Just the thought of the water blushing across her bare silken skin heated him to the deepest core.

"I'm fine," he managed to reply. "Just a foolish man."

Foolish? It didn't begin to describe the fire burning in his blood. He turned his back to the ladder, fighting the temptation to look up. He took a step, intending to grab the coffeepot, but his bad leg buckled, refusing to hold his weight.

Caught by surprise, Jacob fell against the stove. Pain shot to his brain, and already he'd pulled his hand away. Biting back a cry, Jacob didn't dare move to find cold water for fear his leg would fail him again.

"Oh, Jacob," Elizabeth's voice soothed as she hurried down the ladder. He listened to the soft thuds of her bare feet on the wooden rungs.

His breath wedged sideways in his chest. Lord, she was coming to him naked.

"It's nothing," he said quickly, but not fast enough to stop her.

She reached with bare arms, colored a soft peach in the lamplight. And he kept his gaze low so he only saw her bare fingers catch his wrist and hold his burned hand up to the light. He felt the swish of fabric against his arm— *thank God.* She'd tugged on a chemise.

He winced at his own foolishness. Of course she wouldn't come down naked. He snatched a sideways glance to verify it. His eyes widened. His breath caught sideways in his lungs.

She might as well be naked. Elizabeth wore only a thin shiver of fabric that hugged her unbound breasts and clung to her skin. He could see the round disks of her nipples, her full breasts and every curve of her body.

Jacob concentrated hard on the ugly burn on the palm of his hand.

"It's already blistering and look, you've lost some skin." Elizabeth gazed up into his face, her morning-sky eyes wide with sympathy. "It must really hurt. Can you make it to the table?"

Make it to the table? Hell, he wanted to run all the way to Texas just so he wouldn't have to look her in the eye. He forced himself to nod.

"Good. Here, lean on me. You must have hurt your leg."

His leg? Right now it wasn't his hand or his leg that gave him the greatest discomfort. And if she moved closer, she was bound to discover it, too.

But she took firm hold of his arm and said nothing more. Grateful, Jacob tested his bad leg. Pain shivered through the bone, but he managed to hobble the length of the kitchen and, with Elizabeth's help, ease down into the closest chair.

"I'll be right back," she said. "I'll get dressed and then I'll tend that hand for you."

He nodded. Heavens, she could tempt a saint, smelling of rose-scented soap and with that chemise clinging to her wet skin, although she didn't realize it. She turned away, offering him an inspiring view as she climbed up the ladder. Jacob closed his eyes, breathing deeply, calling himself all sorts of names.

Elizabeth returned wearing a hastily put on dress that had been hardly buttoned in the back. She set the lantern on the table and a bucket of snow on the floor. Jacob watched her wrap some of the snow in a towel.

"Hold this to your hand," she said quietly. "This will take some of the heat out of that burn."

No wonder Emma loved her so. Jacob swallowed. "Thank you."

All business, Elizabeth said nothing as she slipped away into the darker part of the kitchen. He heard her working at the stove, heard a rattle of the pan and the sound of her bare feet padding into the lean-to.

The pain in his hand was enough to jam those naked images of her right out of his head—temporarily. As she worked, the only sound between them was the tick of the clock and the snap of the fires. Was she furious with him?

"I thought you were washing the floors," he said, knowing it was a lame excuse. "That's the truth."

She said nothing as she stood with her back to him at the stove.

"I'm sorry." The words sounded so powerless compared to the way he'd invaded her privacy. "I'd wanted to ask you down for coffee."

"I see." She set a cup of coffee on the table for him.

"I wasn't peeping at you." Jacob looked up at her, and with the fall of her long hair like a silken curl against her soft face, desire kicked through his loins. "I mean, I was watching you, but I didn't mean to. I thought—"

"You thought I was washing the floor?"

"Yes." He'd never felt so stupid.

"Well, that does explain it. I didn't think you would spy on me." She turned to walk away, leaving him to watch the straight line of her slender back.

Jacob closed his eyes. Life was a lot simpler before she rode into town. But this was better.

Elizabeth returned. She knelt down at his feet, keeping her eyes low. He watched the luxurious fall of her hair and how it shimmered in the lamplight. Her soft touch tugged the towel away from his hand, and she bowed her chin to study his injury.

"This is a bad burn." She piled more snow on his palm and rewrapped the towel.

"Yes, I can feel it."

Elizabeth smiled, an amused grin curving her lips. "You should have seen the look on your face when you fell down the ladder. Oh, Jacob, you looked so surprised." Then she started to giggle.

It wasn't funny. But then, he could see her side, see how the joke was on him. He started to laugh, and that only made Elizabeth giggle harder. She laid a hand to her belly as it shook with each breath.

"Oh, you nearly fell all the way to the floor," she gasped. "You thought I was naked, didn't you? That's why you wouldn't look up at me when I came to check on you."

"Yes," he managed. His stomach muscles ached, but he couldn't stop laughing. "I'm so sorry, Elizabeth. I had no idea. I expected to see you on your hands and knees with a scrub brush."

"What a shock I must have given you." She laughed even harder, leaning over, both arms wrapped about her thickening middle.

A shock? The laughter died in his throat. The sight of her naked in the tub, the wash of light on her skin, the shimmering beauty of her hair, the tantalizing curve of her full breasts filled his head.

Looking up into his eyes, Elizabeth stopped laughing, too.

"You're a beautiful woman," he said quietly, emotion so thick in his throat he could hear it tremble in his voice.

"Oh, Jacob." Her voice melted, warm with wonder. Her morning-sky eyes sparkled in the lamplight, those tears winking like diamonds. "No one has ever said such a thing to me."

"I can't believe it." His gaze slid to her midsection.

The wonder in her eyes faded. "Believe it. Not every man is good."

"No, I guess not." Jacob started when her warm hand brushed his chin, rough from a day's growth. Guilt stabbed through his heart. He wasn't a good man, he didn't deserve the affection soft in her eyes. "Don't look at me like that. I'm not—"

"Oh yes, you are," she interrupted. "You are the gentlest man I've ever met. You rescued Star. Emma adores you. I can see how much you love her. Not every father would stay and care for a child."

Shame struck him like a blow to his head. Jacob bent over, unable to look her in the eye. He couldn't tell her the truth. He couldn't watch the respect he didn't deserve fade from her eyes.

Instead, he stared hard at the bucket of melting snow. "I climbed the ladder tonight because I wanted to talk with you."

"Well, we've got the coffee." Elizabeth carried hers from the stove. "We've got the time. I can sit down and we can talk."

Talk? After what he'd done tonight, he wanted to sink into a hole in the ground. But he faced her. "I think you work too hard."

"You've told me that before." She studied her steaming cup of coffee. "Besides, I don't mind hard work. It's good for the soul."

But not good for you. Jacob bit back his worries. "I appreciate what you've done—it isn't that. The cabin looks wonderful. Emma is pleased to death with those frilly curtains you made."

A smile tugged at Elizabeth's gentle mouth. "So you don't like the rosebuds and lace?"

"Well, not in my bedroom. But Emma's happy, and that's what matters."

"Yes, it is." She met his gaze, but sadness filled her eyes.

He looked away. "Are we agreed, then?"

"About what?"

Women, they were so stubborn. "About you not working hard. I know you haven't touched the money I've been leaving for you. It's still in a stack on the bureau."

Her spine stiffened. "I consider myself to be working for room and board."

"You're worth more than that to us, Elizabeth." Jacob stared down at his wrapped hand. Pain throbbed there, and something deeper in his heart. "You don't need to try so hard."

"But I don't want you to regret letting me stay. I couldn't bear that." She met his eyes with all of her honesty shining in them.

"Regret having you here? Impossible." Jacob's chest ached. "Will you slow down a little, for me?"

She nodded, her long, unbound hair shimmering, burnished by the light.

He felt his throat tighten. Despite the singe of pain throbbing like fire through his hand, Jacob still couldn't forget the sight of her in the tub touched by the lamp's mesmerizing glow or the feel of her beneath him so wonderfully new, moving in an age-old rhythm of love. How he wanted her.

Jacob jumped up; he had to get away. Hauling the wet towel with him, he crossed the room and kept walking. The frantic beat of his heart pounded in his chest. He stopped by the fire and watched it burn. Hell, he felt the same, hot and hungry.

He dropped another log into the grate, watching the flames snap greedily around the split wood.

He needed her so badly he shook. How sweet it had been seeing her in her bath. How beautiful. It was low and coarse of him to think of sex, of making love to such a noble woman. Yet it was all he could think of.

Friendship? Hell, he wanted more than that. He wanted the woman, and the friend.

He padded into the cool darkness of his bedroom. The white curtains at the small window simply glowed with the reflected light from the fire. Ruffles and lace in a rough wilderness. She'd changed his life with so little.

He grabbed up the package with his good hand and walked on his sore leg back to the table. Elizabeth lifted her chin, meeting his gaze.

"How's the pain in your hand?" she asked.

"Fine." He thunked the paper-wrapped bundle on the table. "Do you want more coffee?"

Her grip tightened on the nearly empty tin cup. "Jacob, you don't need to wait on me."

"Why not?" He grabbed the pot and returned to fill both their cups. "You do so much for Emma and me."

"And it's been such a hardship." She smiled.

"We've tried to make it tough for you."

She cared for them because she wanted to. What reason could be greater? It filled her heart.

A lopsided grin tugged at his mouth. "I wanted to do something for you." He nodded toward the package. "Go ahead. Open it."

She didn't move at first. The tremble began low in her stomach. "You didn't need to do anything for me, Jacob."

"Don't I?" His dark gaze held hers.

"You seem mad at me." Her feelings pinched at the possibility.

"No. Just grateful you are here. You've done so much for us. For Emma." Shadows edged his face where the lamp failed to throw light.

For Emma. It was the child who brought them together and it was her need keeping them together now. And as much as she adored Emma, Libby wanted Jacob to want *her*—even just a little.

"I don't do so much, Jacob. Emma goes to town to Mrs. Holt's school for most of the day. I hitch up the little sleigh and bring her back home in the afternoons."

Jacob sighed and reached down into the bucket for more snow. He piled it on his burn, and she held her hands in her lap to keep from helping him. He didn't look as if he wanted her near him.

He'd seen her naked upstairs. Was he remembering making love to her? Was he angered by how easy it had been to get her into bed? The memory still shamed her, and saved her, too. Love still beat for him in her heart.

"Aren't you going to open it?"

His gray eyes pinched, and she had to look away. "You've already given me the mare."

"Somebody has to be good to you."

Her fingers felt stiff and wooden as she tugged off the white string and began unfolding the paper. The lamplight revealed fine, soft blue wool the color of fading cornflowers, and Libby's hands froze. "There's more than enough for a dress. Oh, and ribbons and braid for trim. I can't accept this."

"But you have to." He reached forward with this left hand and covered hers. "You deserve something new for yourself after all the new things you've made for me and Emma."

"It's too much."

"It's not enough." When the lamplight caught his eyes she saw the truth in them. "I want you to have a new dress. Nobody deserves to have as little as you do."

But she had so much.

"Besides, not every man in Cedar Rock has white lace curtains hanging in his bedroom."

"Emma insisted." Libby shrugged. "I should have asked you, but it's impossible to say no. At least, the curtains seemed like such a joy to her."

"I love them." The emotion in Jacob's eyes deepened, capturing her whole heart. "This cabin has been empty for so long. It feels like a home now."

She shrugged. "Curtains are simple to make. And the braided rugs take no time at all."

"It feels like a home because you are here." He ached

to draw her in his arms and feel the heat of her body. He wanted her comfort, he wanted her warmth, he wanted that soothing compassion in her eyes to nudge away the cold hard fear in his heart, to make him live again. She had that power. And it terrified him.

"I've got a salve cooling in the lean-to. Let me rub that over your burn and wrap it for the night." She moved away into the shadows of the kitchen.

He listened to the efficient, light pad of her bare feet as she returned with an oily paste in the smallest fry pan. She knelt before him, the lamplight kissing the soft honey satin of her hair, and he ached to do the same.

How he ached for it.

"This should stop the pain so you can sleep the night." She sat down and laid his injured hand on her skirted knee.

He could feel the solid heat of her through the layers of cotton. Her fingers gently soothed cool salve across his heated burn. It hurt, but he hardly noticed, too mesmerized by the gentle love lighting her face. A love for him.

He needed it like spring needed sunshine. Leaning a few inches closer, they were face-to-face. Elizabeth looked up, and he covered her mouth with his.

Sweet heat filtered through him as she parted her lips, accepting the sweep of his tongue. She tasted of rich coffee, and he kissed her harder, deeper, needing her comfort—no, it was more than comfort. It was naked need, raw affection and it burned inside him with shameful brightness.

He reached out for her, and she fell against him, her hands sliding around his neck, catching his hair. He felt the little tugs of her fingers, and his heart gripped.

Loving hurt so much.

Chapter Seventeen

Libby set aside the quilt block when the front door banged open. Emma, her button face chapped by the cold, burst into the room, covered with snow.

Laughing, Libby carefully hid her work from sight and rose to help with her icy boots.

"Pa let me go to town with him on the bays," Emma nearly shouted with her glee. "I got to ride Repeat. All by myself and everything!"

"I see." Tugging the red knit cap from Emma's head, Libby shook the snow from it. Bits sprinkled and melted on the floor.

"It's been ever so long since I got to ride," Emma sighed.

"Go warm yourself by the fire. Did your pa get the windowpanes?"

"Yep." She skipped across the room.

Holding back her smile, Libby hung up the little coat on a wall peg and fetched the broom from the lean-to. She swept out the water and slush from the snow on Emma's coat.

"Pa bought us a surprise, too." Emma pounced the minute Libby stepped back into the cabin. Her bright blue eyes shone with the secret.

"A surprise? That sounds mysterious. Do you know what it is?"

"I have my suspicions," Emma admitted.

Libby laughed, snatched up her sewing and hid it in her basket. "Maybe you'd better come help me set the table. I have a surprise for both you and your pa."

"Cinnamon rolls!" Emma hopped up and down. "I can smell them."

"You're right." Libby tugged one of Emma's stiff brown braids. "Let's eat first and then you can help us switch the rooms."

It had been Jacob's idea, since he had so easily fallen down the ladder. Libby could not argue. As the babe inside grew, her own balance became awkward and she feared falling from the narrow rungs.

Jacob insisted, before an accident could happen, she and Emma would switch rooms. And because Emma wanted a pretty room and a place to hang her curtains, he had promised to install a window in the end wall of the small attic.

She heard Jacob stomp into the lean-to as she handed down the soup bowls for Emma. He was quiet at dinner while Emma chattered on about town and the cinnamon rolls and the surprise her pa had bought for them, a new book to be read after supper before the bright fire.

It was a fun day of rearranging the rooms. Jacob moved items upstairs and down. Emma delighted in deciding where to lay her very own braided rug and in hanging her ruffled curtains at the new window and choosing the prettiest blanket to cover her bed.

Then they tromped back downstairs to make up Libby's room in Emma's old space. There were the dresses to hang, the small bureau drawers to rearrange. Then her mother's quilt to lay on the bed.

With a sigh, Emma traced the colorful blue-and-pink rings against the quilted white background. Her eyes shone with admiration, and it was all Libby could do to keep her secret.

Before supper, Jacob pulled Emma aside and gave her the surprise. Libby watched from the corner as Emma squinted at the parchment envelope.

"It's from Granny," he explained quietly.

Libby saw the lines pull into his face and the shadows darken his eyes, and she felt her own heart squeeze.

"I'll be in my room," she said quietly.

He didn't stop her.

Libby sat down on her bed, the room warmed by the wall of stones that backed the fireplace. Outside her window the day's light drained from the horizon, and snow turned blue-gray as it fell from a twilight sky.

She could hear Jacob's low voice as he helped Emma read her letter. Libby tried to close off her ears, but she couldn't help hearing the loving words from a home so far away. It must hurt for him to remember Kentucky.

Jacob often kept his distance from her, always with a polite regard, with silence. He never talked about his life or his past. They had pleasant meals, cozy evenings, busy mornings getting everyone out the door.

Was it enough? She'd never been so happy. And yet, as she sat on her bed, her heart ached with loneliness.

The baby moved, and she placed her hands over her bulky belly. The life inside demanded more of her attention, and she could no longer pretend differently. This baby would be born, no matter if Jacob was ready. Would she have to leave?

Maybe. Nothing had changed in his heart. Was his grief so deep? Sometimes she saw it lurking in his eyes, the need to protect himself, the fear of relying too heavily on another human being.

Would he love her enough to overcome such fears, to put aside his past? As if that somehow lessened the love she felt for him, Libby hid her face in her hands. But she would not cry.

By the end of the week, the house was bursting with secrets. Joy filled the air like the smells of Elizabeth's delicious baking. While Jacob read, long after Emma had gone to bed, Elizabeth stayed with him, frantically finishing a small quilt for his daughter's bed.

Emma was wound as tight as a pocket watch. She skipped through the house instead of walked. She looked near to bursting with their special secret gifts for Elizabeth. She sat still only after supper when they settled down together at the table to work on her reading.

The excitement brought back memories, and he couldn't stay long in the house. He worked extra hours at the livery, smithing when necessary, helping the hired boy clean the stalls, working with his own horses.

When Jacob came home, all he saw was Elizabeth. In her soft wool dresses, she filled the small cabin with the feel of home. She often hummed while she worked, had taught Emma any number of songs, and together they baked in the kitchen. Gingerbread scented the air and little decorated cookie men cluttered the table so they had to eat supper as a picnic on the floor.

At night, when he read aloud *Jane Eyre*, the book he had special ordered for Emma half a year ago, Elizabeth sat in the other chair working at her sewing, and her presence was a gentle reminder he couldn't escape.

He thought of her throughout the day. Dreamed of her at night. Hungered for her touch. It was all he could do to concentrate on his own reading.

"I'm going to bed now," she said quietly, startling him from his daze.

He blinked and saw the yellow-orange lick of the flames in the hearth, saw the swish of her blue skirt as she left him with his silence.

Should he call her back? But he said nothing as her bedroom door closed. He shut his eyes, imagining Elizabeth's graceful movements as she lit a lamp, sat down at the bureau and brushed her knee-length hair until it crackled.

Her bedroom door was only five paces away. It took everything he had to remain seated, his hands clenched and his jaw tight. He no longer wanted Elizabeth to stay for Emma.

He wanted her for himself.

Libby awoke to the pound of Emma's bare feet on the ceiling above. Christmas morning. She tossed back the covers and climbed out of bed. A quick peek out the window showed a blanket of snow over the forest, making the morning as solemn as peace.

Emma banged on Libby's door. "Santa came! Santa

came!'' Not waiting for an answer, she banged on Jacob's door.

Laughing, Libby wrapped her old housecoat around her—it didn't cover her rounded middle—and stepped out into the main room.

Emma hopped with uncontrollable joy, her long brown-black tresses dancing as she did.

"Look!" She pointed to the stuffed stocking at the cold hearth and the large wrapped packages beneath. ''This one has your name, Libby.''

"My name?" She laid a hand to her throat. A present for her? She'd never expected—

Then Emma grinned. ''There's lots of presents with your name. Come see.''

Jacob's door opened, and Libby, too stunned to react, allowed Emma to pull her through the room. She looked over her shoulder, and their gazes met.

He stood in the open doorway, his ebony hair sleep-tousled and dark stubble hugging his jaw. He wore wrinkled trousers, hastily tugged on, and a flannel undershirt, the gray fabric clearly delineating his very masculine chest. Libby's breath lodged somewhere in her throat.

"Come on!" Emma tugged her over to the hearth.

Packages wrapped in plain brown paper were heaped over the cold stone. When she'd retired late last night, there hadn't been as many gifts. She glanced up at Jacob, who only smiled.

"Merry Christmas." His gaze held hers.

"Merry Christmas." The words felt like honey in her throat.

"Pa! Hurry! Let's open the presents now." Emma bounded across the floor.

Now? She'd love nothing more. "Perhaps I should get dressed first."

Jacob's gaze dropped to her stomach, and her heart sank. Libby tried to tug the housecoat more completely over her stomach, only making her pregnancy more evident.

"You look fine," he said quietly.

"*Pa.*" Emma sounded ready to explode.

"All right. We'll open our gifts now, right after I get the fire started." Jacob's smile lit his whole face. "I guess breakfast can wait. We probably won't starve to death while we open a few gifts."

"Oh, Pa."

Libby glanced around the small, cool room. Thin morning light spilled through the windows, despite the falling snow. *Christmas.* The word had never meant so much.

Jacob took her hand and escorted her to the rocking chair, and she felt like a princess. She smiled up at him, and there were no shadows in his eyes when he smiled back. While Emma danced around impatiently, Jacob sorted out the presents. A pile grew at her feet, another at the foot of his empty chair, and a much larger third stack of gifts waited for Emma on the braided rug.

Soon the fire snapped merry warmth into the room, and Jacob handed her the first gift. A soft thick package that felt like fabric beneath her fingers.

"This is all from Emma and me," he said quietly. "You open yours first."

"Hurry, Libby," Emma cheered.

Her throat knotted. A real present given from the heart. She carefully unwrapped it so as not to tear the paper, to make it last as long as possible.

Inside was a variety of soft flannel.

"So you can make clothes for your baby," Emma explained solemnly. "I got to pick them out."

"I see that." Libby fingered the bright yellow and red and greens, many dotted with flowers. "This will make beautiful baby clothes." As long as the baby wasn't a boy.

Emma rewarded Libby with her hugest smile. "There's more." She pointed to the stack of packages on the floor.

"These can't all be for me."

"They are." As if more excited by those gifts than her own, Emma clapped cheerfully. "Shouldn't she open all of them, Pa?"

Jacob's gray eyes shone like a winter sun through clouds. "Yes. Open all of them."

Anyone could see the gifts were bundles of fabric. And so much of it. Soft white cloth for diapers, flannel for gowns, muslin for sheets, yarn for knitting little socks and hats. Finally Libby opened the largest bundle of all, a length of delicate pink calico with small white flowers.

"So you have another dress that fits," Emma explained with grave eyes. "You've got a fat tummy."

"I guess I do." Libby smiled through the horrible pain of happiness. "I don't know how to thank you."

She'd put off buying fabric for baby clothes. Her savings weren't so large and she didn't dare risk taking anything out of the funds reserved for her passage to her aunt's house in Chicago. And she wasn't making wages now. Libby refused to touch Jacob's money, although he faithfully placed a twenty-dollar bill on her bureau every Friday. The stack was huge and still untouched.

But this fabric, these gifts, she could accept.

"Open your gift from me, Pa!" Emma squealed. "I picked it out myself."

"Oh you did?" Jacob grinned down at his sprite of a daughter. Libby's heart warmed at the careful way he unwrapped the girl's gift.

"Elizabeth helped you with this," he said quietly, studying the blue wool shirt.

"We made it together. Look in the pocket." Emma hopped forward to eagerly pull out the pipe and the sack of tobacco. "You broke your other one last summer."

His throat worked, but he didn't speak.

"Don't you like it?" Emma sounded crestfallen.

"Yes, precious. I love the shirt. I've never had a nicer one."

"But do you like the pipe, too?" She wasn't going to be easily convinced.

"Yes. I can't believe what a good memory you have." He reached out and hugged his daughter tightly against him.

"Now you go open your gifts." His voice sounded gruff, as if tears knotted his throat.

"I have so many!" Clearly delighted, Emma picked through her packages, laying them all out in a row on the floor, trying to decide which to open first. "I'll go from small to big," she announced.

"Leave the smallest package." Jacob caught Libby's gaze. A secret twinkled there. "It's your best present and you should save it for last."

"My best present?" Emma thought about that, enchanted. She reached for the next smallest gift. A collection of brightly colored ribbons for her hair. Emma squealed happily, thanking Libby with great enthusiasm.

Libby felt her whole heart slide open as she watched Emma discover Christmas candy and several shiny new pennies stuffed in her stocking, a slate to learn to write on, a colorful book of Mother Goose stories and a small felt cowboy hat with silver trim. Gifts Jacob had bought for his daughter.

"That one is from me," Libby said, almost afraid, as Emma turned to the largest gift of all.

Hope burned in those eyes. "It's too big to be a dress," she guessed.

"You'll have to open it and see." Libby leaned forward, watching the little girl's face.

Emma tore away the wrapping paper and squealed at the bright colors of the yellow-and-blue quilt. "It's just like yours! Except it's yellow! My very favorite color!"

Emma ran into her arms, and Libby hugged the girl hard, this daughter of her heart, and she could not keep back the small brush of a kiss along the crown of that soft brown hair.

"I love you, Libby."

Her throat squeezed, but she managed the words. "I love you too, Emma."

She caught Jacob's gaze on her, and she didn't need to wonder if he would approve. The shine in his eyes told her everything.

"You have one more gift," he told his daughter gently.

"You said the best gift." Emma stepped out of Libby's arms.

"That's what I said." He knew what Emma really wanted couldn't be wrapped in paper.

The little girl bounced over to tear the wrapping off the smallest gift. She stared at the hand-carved figure of a horse, her eyebrows pinching together.

"Thank you, Pa," she said, trying hard to hide her disappointment.

"No, the wooden horse isn't your gift. It's supposed to tell you what Santa Claus brought for you and left in the stable."

"A pony?" Emma's eyes filled with happy tears. "Did Santa bring me a pony?"

"No." Jacob stood. "Santa brought you a real horse."

"A horse!" The child stood staring at him, the surprise vivid in her eyes.

Jacob held out his hand. "Come with me and let's go take a look at your Christmas horse."

Emma's small hand felt so binding in his. He could feel how much she needed him, how lonely she had been, how much love filled her small child's heart.

The three of them tromped out into the morning with their coats pulled hastily over their nightclothes. Emma hopped the entire way to the stable, her excitement as tangible as the bits of falling snow.

The small black mare he'd traded for early this winter stood in the end stall. She was a sturdy mustang, gentle and even-tempered. Now she gazed at Emma with curious and welcoming eyes, as if she could sense the well of love deep in the girl's heart.

"Here's a piece of carrot," Jacob said, slipping a chunk into Emma's hand.

She let go of Elizabeth and walked slowly up to the horse.

Other animals nickered and begged for a treat, but Emma walked right past them to the little mustang in the corner. She held out her hand quietly, offering the bit of carrot.

The mare daintily accepted the offering and welcomed those small, eager fingers along the soft velvet of her nose.

"She's beautiful," Emma breathed. "I'm going to name her Holly."

Jacob closed his eyes, the pain so great it could cripple him. Holly was his mother's name. The granny Emma loved so much.

Jacob had fought hard to ward off the memories. Images of Mother decorating the house for Christmas, the hot eggnog treats she mixed with rum or whiskey to warm the end of a cold day, the good china, a ham roasting in the oven, a tree to trim and decorate.

Jacob opened his eyes to the gray stone wall of his fireplace. Flames crackled greedily, generating enough heat to melt him where he sat.

Emma sat on the beautiful blue-and-white braided rug Elizabeth had made, changing her doll's clothes. She wore her new dress in the sunshine, yellow flannel with red and blue daisies. Her new cowboy hat crowned her head and two new ribbons tied her braids, one bright red satin bow and one bright blue one.

"Will you read from my new book now?" Emma asked him.

He smiled down at those bright eyes darkened with purple smudges. They had spent the afternoon riding horses, he and his daughter. The new mare had proven to be a good mount for her. Now, with supper behind them, Jacob could see the tiredness in Emma's face.

"If you get ready for bed, I'll read you to sleep," he said quietly.

"I guess. Let me change Beth into her new nightgown,

too.'' Emma readied her doll with great care. More clothes had been part of Elizabeth's Christmas gift to her. She ran through the cabin and climbed up into her attic room to find the new nightgown.

Jacob set aside his book. ''She's so wound up I may be a long time reading her to sleep.''

''She's had an exciting Christmas. That little mare you brought means everything to her.'' Elizabeth set down her knitting. ''You're a good father, Jacob.''

He looked at his hands. She didn't know the truth. ''Don't worry about turning down the lamps. I'll tend to them when I come down.''

She nodded, her eyes puzzled, hurt. He ambled away, the hard wall he'd put around his heart ready to crumble. The loneliness of years and the power of the day had teased alive his feelings, brought to light his fears.

Loving came with such risk. There was so much to lose. But as he felt Elizabeth's gaze on his back, gentle as a loving touch, he felt torn. Need coursed through him, swift like a river and just as hard to control.

Libby could hear the low rumble of his rich voice through the ceiling above as he read Emma to sleep. The cabin shone with her careful cleaning, the fire snapped happily in the hearth.

She listened to Jacob's footsteps cross overhead, then descend down the ladder. She lifted her knitting up to the light to count her stitches.

''Emma was so worn-out,'' Jacob said as he strode into the room. ''She was too tired to fall asleep.''

The sadness in his voice pierced her. Libby knew, when he sounded like that, he would keep his distance. After today, she didn't want a polite exchange. She didn't want to see him hurting without knowing how to help him.

"I suppose I'd better get to bed." She set down her knitting.

"Please. Don't go." His quiet voice rumbled low beneath the sounds of the fire snapping and the tick of the clock.

His voice held her. She saw the need like a painful shadow dark in his gray eyes.

"I could make coffee," she offered, unsure what he wanted. Unsure how to give it to him.

"I don't want coffee." He settled into his rocking chair. "My mother used to make Christmas into magic. Songs and scented candles and days spent making candies and cakes. The whole house smelled like joy."

Libby tried to imagine it. "You must have a very loving mother. You must be missing her today."

"Yes." His answer was immediate and his eyes troubled. "She wrote me. She's been writing me faithfully since I moved out here. I don't answer her letters."

She studied the tense line of his jaw, the tight press of his lips, the firm white-knuckled fists of his big hands.

"Do you want to talk?" she asked quietly.

"No, I don't. I don't want to feel. I don't want to remember." He stared hard at his empty hands. "But I can't stop."

Libby saw his sorrow and something that gripped him so tightly. "Perhaps you could have Emma write. She's been wanting to learn to write letters."

Jacob shook his head, moving toward her, his heart shining full in his eyes. "See how you do that? Everything is so much easier with you here."

She didn't do so much. She made curtains, cooked meals, scrubbed floors. "This has been a painful day for you."

"Yes." Firelight threw orange-and-black shadows across his face. "This is my first real Christmas since Mary died."

"How you must have loved her." Libby saw Jacob's face fall, felt his heart crumble.

"I loved her very much." Tears rimmed his eyes and he cleared his throat, but couldn't push them away. "I'm so tired of being alone."

"You're not alone, Jacob." It seemed so obvious to her. "You have Emma, who is enough to light up an entire life."

"Yes." He unfisted one hand and laid his warm, broad palm along her jawbone, cupping her face. "I have you."

Libby held her breath. She knew what he wanted, could see what he needed. She loved him. And she could see how he cared for her in his heart. He cared for *her*.

Jacob stood. Libby stood. He cradled her face in his hands, his fingers at the back of her collar. In one small movement his mouth found hers, kissing her with a hungry gentleness that tugged at her every aching need.

His arms folded her against his chest. His tongue caressed her lips, then dipped past to explore deeper. She curled her hands in his shirt and held on. Desire for him rolled through her, leaving her unsteady, unable to think. She could only feel. She wanted him. All of him. As much as he would give her.

Her breath caught as he began working the buttons at the nape of her neck. Each tug of his fingers worked a button free. Her collar fell loose, the fabric of her bodice relaxed, the girth of her waistband slipped. Pure, honest desire shivered through her. He slipped the dress from her shoulders.

Libby heard his sharp intake of air at the sight of her in her chemise, her breasts against the white muslin, her belly firmly shaping the cloth. Jacob breathed out that air in a hiss of desire, and his eyes shone as he slipped one thin strap of her chemise down her shoulder, exposing the top of her breast. The hot, firm tip of his finger brushed down the other strap, and the chemise caught and held on the tips of her full breasts.

He shook with need, with the effort of holding himself back. He knew what he wanted. Elizabeth. He wanted all of her, but he made himself go slow, wanted to make it last. He reached with one finger and freed the fabric, exposing her ample breasts.

The glow of the firelight brushed her sweet skin into an alluring peach, and he bent down to cover the pebbled tips of her beautiful breasts with his mouth. Need kicked through him. He suckled lightly at first, tasting her, teasing her with his tongue. With a surprised moan of pleasure, Elizabeth wrapped both arms around his neck, holding him to her breast and rained kisses along the top of his forehead.

With his hands, he freed the fabric around her stomach, and the dress and chemise whispered to the floor. He squeezed his eyes shut at the sight of that belly, full and ripe, nurturing a life so fragile inside.

"I'm sorry I'm so...so fat," Elizabeth whispered quietly, taking one step back.

"No." Jacob grabbed her arm, unwilling to let her slip

away. "I think you're beautiful. And brave." She had no idea of what birthing that life may require.

He knew. And it killed him. Fear for her battered him like a blizzard. Suddenly he didn't have enough time with her, and he couldn't waste another moment being afraid.

He kissed her with the whole of his being. Tasting the lingering coffee on her tongue, exploring the hot velvet moistness of her mouth. Jacob hugged her to him, delighted in the feel of her breasts against his chest and the solid strength in her arms as she wrapped them around his neck.

Elizabeth kissed him back, ardently pressing her body against his, twining her fingers through his hair. He moaned first at the tug her fingers made along his scalp, then again when her tongue dared to meet his, first tracing the shape of his lips, then slipping shyly into his mouth.

Control snapped. He couldn't raise his lips from hers, couldn't lift his hand from her breast. He backed her to the open door of his dark room. He didn't bother to light a lamp as he pulled back the rough wool blanket and sat her on the edge of his bed.

Slow down. He had to force himself to breathe, to step away from her. He ought to ask if she was certain about loving him, but she grabbed hold of his shirt with both hands and tugged him by the collar to kneel between her knees, mating her mouth with his.

Desire coiled in his groin and he rubbed his hands along the smooth line of her parted thighs. Her skin was so soft, so private there even through the soft muslin of her drawers. He found the string along the span of her rounded waist and untied the bow.

She released her fistfuls of his shirt and began unbuttoning him. Her hands fluttered over his chest, traced the line of his wide shoulders, tickled down the flat of his abdomen.

He felt solid. Libby slipped her hands across his bare chest to feel the pelt of dark curling hair, covering his male nipples. She traced one with the tip of her finger and felt him shiver. He shivered again when she traced down his solid abdomen to the first button of his trousers.

Once she had him naked, Libby leaned back in the bed, slipping off her drawers, glad for the dark room that cloaked her awkward pregnancy from his sight. But not from his touch. His hand settled on her belly.

Her breath caught in her throat, worry punched at her mind. But when Jacob stretched out beside her, whispering sweetly, she melted. She gave him all her trust.

His mouth caught hers, and she wasn't prepared for the tenderness of his kiss. He moved over her, touching her with gentleness as if she were more precious than blown glass. When his erection nudged her, pushing into that welcoming place in her body, Libby wrapped her arms around his back and held him with all the strength in her heart.

Chapter Eighteen

Morning dawned cold enough to freeze her breath to the blankets. Libby huddled beneath the covers, awakening to the realization she was not only in Jacob's bed, but stark naked besides.

Jacob rolled onto his side and stared at her.

"Good morning." She couldn't hide her smile. No matter how cold the room, in her heart she felt warm and toasty.

"Morning," he said quietly.

Libby's happiness faded a notch. She put aside the images of last night, of how gently excited he'd been in her arms, how considerate he'd been making love to her. Dawn nudged at the darkness in the room. "It's late. We slept in."

"Yes, I'd better get a fire started. It's damn cold this morning." Jacob hopped out of bed, his own nakedness causing him to shiver in the frigid air. "Stay beneath the covers until the cabin warms. I'll bring your clothes."

"Jacob—" She wanted to argue, but his gaze met hers. He wanted to take care of her. The luxury of it kept her silent. She smiled, but he didn't return it.

He tugged on long johns, thick socks, a shirt, his trousers and returned with the same clothes she'd shed before the fire last night. Libby blushed in memory as he laid her garments on the bed, but his gaze didn't catch hers.

She shivered until she was warm again. The snapping crackle of a fire popped in the hearth, and she waited until the muffled sound of the outside door closing echoed through the house before she tossed off the blankets, braced herself against the icy air, and pulled on her clothes, her teeth chattering.

The fire burning robustly in the hearth gave very little heat. But it didn't matter. Her heart felt warm.

Humming, she glanced out the front window and saw clear, crisp skies. A brand-new day.

"Libby?" Emma's voice called from upstairs.

She hurried to the kitchen. "Stay in bed until the cabin is warmer."

"But Pa was supposed to get me so I could feed Holly."

Libby heard the disappointment in the girl's voice. "I guess he decided it was too cold this morning. I bet he'll ask you to help him tomorrow."

"Oh rats."

Libby smiled as she hurried with her morning work. She ground coffee, sliced salt pork, mixed pancake batter.

Jacob clamored into the lean-to just as a wall of wind slammed into the cabin. "It's freezing out there. The milk froze solid in the pail."

"I'll thaw it over the stove." Libby reached out.

His gaze met hers over the tin bucket. "What do you think of our Montana winters?"

"They could be warmer." The icy bucket burned cold

straight through to her bones. She set it on the floor by the stove and warmed her hands.

Jacob laughed, but not deep and rich like he always did. "I hope it warms up enough for us to go outside."

"Yes, 'cuz I want to ride Holly." Emma's head poked out from the attic door. "Can we go to town, Pa?"

Jacob shivered out of his heavy coat. "We'll see what the temperature does."

Emma sighed, deeply disappointed. "I hate waiting."

"Here, this will warm you." Libby handed him a cup of steaming coffee.

Jacob's hand touched hers. Sparks of sensation sizzled up her arm. "How are you feeling this morning?"

Happy. Did he feel the same? She read the worry in his eyes. "Fine."

He nodded. "I thought I'd do some reading aloud after the morning work is done, since it will be too cold on the horses to head for town just yet."

"Yippee!" Emma disappeared from the attic door. Her feet pounded against the floorboards above.

Jacob smiled. A real smile. One that brightened his eyes and changed his entire face. "You look beautiful this morning," he said, then he kissed her long and hard.

All day long he thought of her. Shoeing horses, cleaning stalls, buying oats at the feed store. The hired boy had taken good care of the animals over the holiday and so there was only the most basic chores to keep him busy. He had plenty of time to think.

Snow blew in with the wind, and by noon Jacob found his hands empty. Images of last night battered him. He remembered the feel of her, the taste of her, the amazing rush of emotion. He couldn't stop wanting her. All of her.

Jacob knew he didn't just have sex with her, he'd made love to her. Love. There was no mistaking it. His heart began cracking like ice on a frozen lake. Emotion lived there. Sorrow and hope. Grief and joy.

Elizabeth had done this, taking his hand and helping him to love again. She had broken wide his heart with her gentle loving, with her tender acceptance, with the press of soft lips against his throat.

Friendship? Companionship? Is that what he wanted from her? Hell, he was only fooling himself. Elizabeth lit his life like the sun, warmed his heart and his bed. She was the reason he hurried home at night. Even if it was just to see the smile in her eyes.

He shut the barn doors against the frigid wind and wandered to the back. His tools lay in an organized disarray on the table, pieces of lumber stacked neatly by the outside wall.

He sorted through the wood, made plans, picked up his smallest hammer. There could be friendship between him and Elizabeth. And, maybe, there could be something more.

"Pa!"

The instant he opened the lean-to door, Emma jumped off the chair and ran straight for him, rattling all the lamps in the room.

"Hi, precious." His voice rumbled low, sounded alive. *He was home.* Happiness spilled through her. "We have a surprise for you."

"Don't breathe too deep or you might guess it, Pa." Emma warned.

"I can't smell a thing. Honest." But when his gray eyes met hers, they sparkled with humor. It was hard to miss the scent of fried chicken.

Libby closed the reader and stood. "Let me get the table set and we'll eat."

"Hmm. It smells good," Jacob teased.

"Pa, don't breathe or you'll guess!" Emma pleaded.

His laughing gaze met Libby's across the room and her heart beat wildly.

He needed her. She could read it in his face, see it reflected in his eyes. No one had ever made her feel complete, whole the way Jacob could. She'd never needed anyone so much.

Libby trembled with the knowledge. For even Jacob could leave her and she would be alone again.

Night had long since crept in to darken the small cabin. He should be in bed holding Elizabeth while she slept, sated from their lovemaking, so beautiful in sleep.

Tonight, she'd known what he wanted. Offered herself to him with a small smile that twinkled in her eyes. Her hand had been so warm in his, so pliable, so accepting as he led her into his bedroom. He laid her down and undressed her slowly in the dark, fearing what she thought of his base, physical needs.

But Elizabeth had welcomed him with a loving warmth he didn't deserve, pleasured him with an innocent attempt that doubled his guilt, accepted him into her body with one quiet whisper. "Please."

She'd given him her heart, and he took it. Wanted to

take it. Wanted to give his to her. Now, what did he have to protect him? Jacob stared into the dying fire. Too much pulled at him. Emma's needs. Elizabeth's love. His mother's letter. Mary's memories.

He buried his face in his hands. For so long, he'd lived each day like the next, bleak and unfeeling and as cold as a winter's snow. But now she was here.

"Jacob?" Elizabeth stood framed in his bedroom doorway, her nightgown glowing eerily in the dark corner of the cabin. "Jacob, are you all right?"

The concern in her voice came gently, as open and as caring as her heart. He'd long since forgiven her for loving another man—she loved easily, cared so much. Loving easily was the same reason she saved him, guided him with her loving acceptance. And now he could no longer deny his feelings or how she warmed his soul. Fully. Completely.

His heart cracked open, melting more each time.

She knelt on the floor before him. The low red-orange glow of the dying embers licked dark shadows over her, glinting like molten gold in her hair. She lifted a tender hand and gently wiped one tear from his cheek.

"It's a lot easier to be alone than to love someone else. People disappoint you. You can disappoint them." He didn't move from her touch. "People die."

Her eyes watered and he saw the hurt there.

"People also live to be old, gray and very wrinkled." Her warm hand slid down his throat and rested on the crest of his shoulder. "The question is, will you love me when I'm so old I don't have any teeth?"

Pain so pure it broke shuddered through him. Jacob took her hand in his. "As long as you can love me."

He stood, taking her in his arms. Cold stiffened the air in the cabin, but Elizabeth felt warm in his arms. His mouth covered hers as solid as a promise made.

"What I have, I want to give to you," he said quietly. "My heart. My soul. My life. It's all yours."

Jacob's touch was like fire even in the cold room, and Libby gave herself up to the spellbinding heat. Like flame, his kisses claimed her, leaving hot tingling trails where his lips nibbled along her skin. His touch consumed every part of her, igniting the desire in her belly coiling tighter and tighter.

Oh, Jacob. She marveled at the sensations swirling and twisting deep inside. As his kisses nibbled at her throat, lined her jaw, circled her mouth, she leaned back in the pillows pulling Jacob with her. As his lips brushed hers, she reached out to seal the kiss.

Both of his hands framed her face, holding her tenderly. His tongue traced the curve of her lip, laved the sensitive inside of her mouth, tickled her tongue. Every part of her ached for his touch. She felt restless, then lost when he touched her. He bunched up her nightgown and the burning, tantalizing brush of his hands kneading her breasts stunned her with intimacy. Then, the exquisite pleasure built, amazed her, threatened to break her into pieces.

She squeezed her eyes against the burn of the tears, against the too-much feeling in her heart. Love sizzled there like water on a hot fry pan. Emotions licked through her, tentative at first and then burning bright. He had to love her. And it felt too much to endure, too much to accept, yet Libby couldn't help reaching for more. *So much more.*

Jacob's mouth slipped from hers, nibbling down her throat to her breast. Laving, suckling, nibbling. She closed her eyes, feeling the deep vulnerability of trust grip her heart. She trusted him not to hurt her. She trusted him to love her in this new, gentle-exciting way that rushed through her blood like fire.

Libby didn't know where this would lead, what love would be like, how long it would last. She only knew she could never deny what Jacob wanted from her. He loved her; she could feel it in the way he clung to her, in the desperate yet gentle way he spanned his big hands over the girth of her waist.

He rained kisses along the curve of her stomach, and Libby couldn't swallow the tears. They wet her face as his lips dampened her skin. Jacob's breath fanned across her belly, hot and fast.

His fingers slipped through the tight curls at the juncture of her thighs. White-hot sensation buzzed through her, tingling in the very tips of her fingers. She felt near to exploding, certain she would fracture at the thrilling mix of pleasure and sweet pain.

Jacob's hand explored her, finding a hot, delicious spot that spiked bolts of unbearable pleasure through her. Libby couldn't hold back the pleasure, couldn't hold back her heart. Tears squeezed from her eyes as he drew her up to him. He kissed her so thoroughly, so tenderly she could only cling to him.

No one, nothing, had ever mattered to her this much.

Jacob rubbed one tear from her cheek. He knew. As if he could heal all her scars and every old wound, he brushed back the hair from her face.

"Oh, Jacob." She loved to say his name. Loved the way it felt on her tongue. "I love being with you."

"So do I." He hesitated, as if he meant to say more. If he didn't say he loved her, it was all right. She knew it to be true, knew what lived in his heart. And that was enough.

Jacob caught her hand in his and guided her to his erect shaft. As Libby wrapped her fingers around his thickness, she felt the pulse of his heart thrumming there.

She never imagined he could be so soft there where he was rock hard. As she ran her fingers down the length of him to where curling hair tickled her hand, she was amazed at the trembling there. She found the drop of moisture at the rounded velvet tip of his erection and wondered at it.

If only he had planted this life inside her. If only this were his baby.

As if he understood, as if he could read her mind, Jacob laid his big hand on her huge belly.

"Take me inside you," he said quietly. "I want to love you, Elizabeth. I want there to be nothing but this love between us."

How could she ask for anything more? Libby had never had so much.

His erection swelled even more tightly against her palm. She gasped when she felt his hands at her waist, helping her move her awkward bulk over him. He sat against the wall. As Libby moved over him, she realized what he intended.

"I don't know how," she whispered, feeling foolish. She had been so forward with him, kissed him and lain with him and accepted him into her body as she had. But she knew nothing of love, nothing of this.

"Trust me."

His hot eager thickness nudged her inner thigh as she straddled him. Jacob's warm chuckle brushed against her throat, and when his mouth found hers, she kissed him back with everything she had.

"Wait." He caught her as she tried to take him inside.

Libby waited, her heart hammering in her chest, her body aching for completion. Jacob reached for a match, and soon light licked from the lamp on a shelf siding the bed.

She could see the hunger flicker on his face, not for physical release but for emotional ties. He smiled, and his whole face softened. Love lit his eyes like sunshine on clouds.

"I want to see you." His voice came raw with emotion. "I want to watch your face when I enter you."

Libby couldn't find one word to say. She shook with need as she felt the hard nudge of him against her. Jacob's big hands steadied her unbalanced weight as she straddled him, reaching with one hand to guide his heated thickness inside her.

"Look at me," he moaned softly.

She raised her eyes to his and felt, for the first time, the power of joining two lives, felt the power of making another.

Chapter Nineteen

Jacob opened his eyes in the webby dawn light in Eliz
beth's bed, and loved that she was the first thing he sa
That, and her smile.

"Stay here where it's warm," he whispered, brushi
one hand against the silk of her sleep-tousled hair. "
looks like another cold morning. I'll come get you wh
the cabin is warm enough."

"I should get up and help with the chores." She mov
up onto one elbow.

She looked soft, beautiful. "No. I want you to st
warm."

"Jacob, you are going to spoil me."

"So, what's wrong with that?" He brushed her foreh
with a kiss. "I want to take care of you. Relax. I may ev
make breakfast for you."

She smiled at his words. "You are so good to me, J
cob."

He rubbed one hand along the soft satin of her fac
unable to speak. She said his name with so much feelin
so much affection, his eyes smarted.

Last night's closeness hadn't faded with the cold hours of night. He was glad. He felt stronger as he knelt down before the cold hearth. He built a fire and watched the flames grow.

"Pa?"

Jacob glanced up the length of the ladder toward the pitch dark ceiling. A small button face blending with the shadows stared down at him. "It's too cold for you to be up. Slip back into bed."

"But I want to help feed Holly this morning."

Jacob smiled at his daughter who shared his passion for horses. "It's too cold for me this morning, let alone a girl as little as you."

"But I'm big!" Emma protested. "Pa? I wanna ask you something."

"You should get back in bed where it's warm," he said, but already she thudded down the ladder. Quick as a shadow, she hopped into the room.

"Can I crawl in with you?" She gazed up at him with eyes as wide as hope. "Granny always used to let me crawl in with her when Grandpa lit the stoves."

Jacob dropped to his knees. "You sure miss your granny, don't you?"

"I used to cry every night because she wasn't there to tuck me in and sing to me. But not anymore."

Emma slipped into his arms, and she felt like a small delicate bird against his size and his strength. Jacob hugged her more tightly, close to his heart.

He took her little hand in his. "How would you like to write Granny a letter? I'll help you."

"Can I tell her about my doll and my quilt?" Excitement shimmered in her voice. "Can I tell her abou Libby?"

Jacob's heart twisted. "Yes. You can tell her anything you want. But right now I want to get you warm and snug into bed. Should we ask Elizabeth if she'll let you craw in with her?"

"Yes!"

Emma bounced into his arms. Jacob lifted her up an she giggled with delight.

When he stepped into the room, Elizabeth stirred. Sh sat up in the dark, and he could see the white flannel o her nightgown shimmering in the faint light.

Elizabeth rolled over to smile up at them. "Well, loo who's going to cuddle up with me."

"I have cold feet," Emma warned with a bubbly giggl as Jacob stooped to lay his daughter on his side of the bee

"So do I." Elizabeth laughed, a warm throaty soun that seemed to fill up his heart. "Let me warm up thos cold feet of yours."

Everything would be all right. They were going to be family.

Libby stood in the kitchen and watched Jacob leave fc the livery, slumped against the bitterly cold wind. He heart sank knowing he was gone, even just for the day.

"Will you help me read the letter I wrote to Granny an Grandpa?" Emma gazed up from her place at the kitche table, the letter open before her.

"Again?" Libby asked.

Emma grinned. "Yeah. I wanna make sure it's ju right."

Jacob had worked over the letter with Emma whi

Libby had washed the breakfast dishes. Now she turned from sprinkling the clothes.

"I guess the ironing can wait. Some things are more important." Libby tugged out her chair at the table and settled her awkward weight into it.

"I wrote all about you in my letter. See?" Emma leaned close with the wrinkled parchment gripped tightly. "And I wrote these words all by myself."

"You did a wonderful job." Libby scanned the page, recognizing Emma's wobbly, unpracticed scrawl beside the black ink of Jacob's bold, intelligent handwriting.

Her throat tightened. After this baby came, they would have to face their relationship. She would know the true color of Jacob's heart.

"I can read most of it," Emma said.

Libby leaned closer, listening to the halting rhythm of Emma reading aloud. Emma told her grandparents she missed them and loved them, of missing her pony and riding in the forest with her grandpa. She wrote of the cozy log cabin and the curtains and rugs and the quilt Libby made. She even told of her new doll and her very own horse.

"That's a wonderful letter," Libby managed to say when the reading of it was done. "Your grandparents are going to be so proud of you for writing it."

"I hope so, 'cuz I hate having to go to Mrs. Holt's school." It was Emma's greatest burden, and the new term began in a week. "I wish I could just stay home with you."

"Your pa wants you to be educated, and I was never a schoolteacher."

"But you can read and write as good as Mrs. Holt."

Libby brushed the wispy curls from Emma's eyes. "No, I only manage. It's important to have a good education, even for a woman."

"That's what my granny says." Emma sighed. "I didn't tell her about the baby."

Libby laid her hand on the curve of her sizable stomach. Curiosity sparkled in Emma's blue eyes. "Do you want to feel the baby kick?"

"Oh, yes."

"Give me your hand." Libby placed the small fingers on her belly and cupped them beneath her own. Waited. "Feel that?"

"She's kicking." Emma stared up at her.

"So you think it's a girl?"

Emma nodded gravely. "I want a baby sister. That's the second reason why I wanted a mother."

"What was the first?"

"So Pa wouldn't be unhappy. Or me, either."

Libby's life slipped into a pattern. As the cold January days began to pass, her belly grew enormous, her movements awkward, her feet swollen and her back sore. Twice she was stuck in the rocking chair and had to wait until Emma came inside from playing in the snow to pull her out.

Each day, Jacob slipped from her side in the cold dark hours of the morning to warm the house. He feared she would catch cold in her condition and he would not let her up even to cook breakfast. Emma helped him in the kitchen, and when the cabin was comfortably toasty they ate his cooking at the small round table.

After Jacob left for town with Emma, Libby did the

morning work. Housecleaning on Monday and Tuesday. Washing on Wednesday. Mending on Thursday. Ironing on Friday. Baking on Saturday. After lunch, she drove Star to town and fetched Emma from school, then finished the day's work. While dinner cooked, she and Emma worked on her reading until Jacob returned from town.

Evenings were her favorite. Happy conversations at the table, punctuated by Emma's funny stories. Then Libby did the dishes while Jacob tended the stock. When the work was done she gathered up her sewing and settled down beside the fireplace while Jacob read aloud from one of his leather-bound books.

After he put Emma to bed, he came for her. With a grin he would help her from the rocker, bank the fire, and undress her in his room. He laid her down on his bed and made love to her despite the awkwardness of her huge belly, or just held her if she was too tired.

Libby feared she was living a dream. As February neared, she could feel her time approaching. Fearing this happiness might end, she cherished these days with Emma and Jacob, holding each moment close so this real home and real love would live forever in her heart.

Jacob lay in bed and listened to the wind scouring the side of the cabin. The cold, desolate howling seemed to reach right inside and tug out all that was troubling him. Elizabeth lay beside him, sleeping deeply.

He didn't know if he should be loving her like this so close to her time, but she enjoyed it despite her girth. In the darkness, Jacob didn't need to look at the obvious state of her pregnancy. He knew the birth would be coming soon.

He slipped from the bed, careful not to awaken Elizabeth. She slept so soundly she hardly stirred, a huge lump beneath the thick pile of blankets. They had propped her up with pillows so she could sleep on her side.

He tugged on his long johns and a pair of thick socks she had recently mended. Feeling his way in the darkness, Jacob closed the bedroom door and crossed the cool main room to the kitchen. He lit a lamp, and a pool of sepia light puddled on the table.

He found the letter and finally folded it open. His mother's hand, warm and sensible, filled every spot of the paper. She wrote how she worried for him and Emma alone in the wilderness. She talked of how her busy days were empty without her grandchild. She wondered when they might come home, even for a visit.

Jacob's heart tugged, and he put down the letter. Just by looking at her words he could sense how she ached for him. Mother had written him last year time and again, yet he had only sent one brief note to let her know they'd arrived safely in Montana Territory.

Jacob hid his face in his hands. He missed his home, the land he'd grown up on, the horses he helped to raise working alongside his father. He'd left, and he'd hardly looked back. He loved his parents, the farm, the sound of summer in the south meadows. He allowed himself to miss home for the first time in years.

Jacob found ink and paper and lit a lamp to write by. The sound of his words scratched loudly in the near silent room; the only other sounds were the wind outside and the tick of the clock.

He did not know how to tell Mother about Elizabeth, or her baby, or how he was living with hope. But he tried.

Then he wrote of his work, of the town, of how much Emma had grown and of her latest antics. He signed his name, promising to visit within the year.

But could he go home to the place where his heart lived?

As the blizzard built into a wicked fury, battering the north wall of the cabin, Jacob sat listening, until his hands were numb from the cold. Then he went back to his room, the ache in his leg grinding from the change in weather, and climbed into bed.

Elizabeth stirred. "Jacob?" Her thin and strained voice alarmed him.

"What is it? Do you want me to hold you?" He leaned over her, gently kissing her brow.

"Yes, my back really hurts. Would you mind rubbing it for me?"

His guts tightened. "Your back hurts?"

"I'm just stiff."

Reining in his fear, Jacob grabbed hold of her hem and hiked up the nightgown. Her back felt warm and tense beneath his hands. "Is this better?"

She sighed, relaxing a fraction.

"Your back was sore all day yesterday, wasn't it?"

"Yes." Libby fell silent, stiffened, and groaned into the pillow.

He could feel the contraction slip through her.

"Jacob?"

His hand stilled. "What?"

"I think something happened." Fear sharpened her voice. "I—I feel all wet. Am I bleeding?"

"No." He caught her hand before she could sit up in panic. "Lie still. It's probably just your water breaking."

"Oh, no. The baby's coming." Dismay sharpened her voice.

"It seems so." Jacob closed his eyes. "Let me go warm this cabin up and heat some water for you to wash with. Come lie on my side of the bed."

"But the straw needs to be changed and the tick thoroughly washed." Elizabeth's voice thickened and she gasped. "Oh, Jacob. This really hurts."

His hand trembled. "Just relax. When the pain has passed, come lie over here. I'll take care of you."

"I should help." She sat up.

Jacob stopped her. "No. You have no idea how exhausting this birth is going to be. Please rest while you can. Do it for me."

"I—"

"Please." He pressed her cool hand to his warm lips. "I will go stoke up the fire. Stay here."

Libby allowed him to lay her back into the pillows. "Your touch feels comforting, so solid and sure. I'm glad you're here. It makes me feel safe."

He eased her back into the bed and drew the covers up to her chin. His pulse drummed hard and fast as he reached to smooth back the hair from her face.

Grateful for the darkness, he didn't speak. He wanted to hide his fears from Elizabeth. He didn't want to remember another night and another woman in labor.

Libby dozed in and out of pain in her own room. Jacob heated the cabin so she would be warm. Then he made her a pot of coffee, rich and black.

Dawn grayed the edge of night, but made no dent in the angry storm. After hours of pain, Libby pulled herself from bed. A healthy fire crackled in the hearth, warming the chill from the main room. The large window by the door showed the sheet of gray-white snow like an impenetrable wall from sky to earth.

As a clinching pain gripped her entire abdomen, Libby pressed a hand to her stomach.

Jacob touched her elbow. "How are you doing?"

"Better now that the pain has passed." She breathed out slowly.

"You shouldn't be up." Jacob's worried gray eyes searched hers. "Labor can take a long time. You need to rest now so you're strong when you need to be."

"But I'd like a cup of coffee." Libby's heart twisted at the concern dark in his eyes. Concern for her. "I know babies can take a long time. I'll be bedridden soon enough."

He poured her a cup of coffee and set it on the table in front of her. She stirred in a spoonful of sugar and sipped slowly. Jacob's book lay closed nearby. She reached a finger to trace the spine of leather and the thick creamy pages.

Before she came here she had known nothing of sailing the furious sea, known little of the streets of London or the English countryside. Libby touched her enormous stomach. Her thoughts weighed on the baby to be born.

Jacob sat across the table with a cup of his own. Steam rose from the rim.

She studied his set face. "You're afraid."

He stared down into his cup. "Yes. I'm afraid the storm won't break in time. I can't fetch the doctor."

Libby reached out and caught his hand in hers. "Then

I'm glad I'm here with a man who has raised and bred horses all his life.''

Jacob's face twisted. ''You should be afraid to count on me. I haven't been much help to anyone in a long time.''

''Then think of what you can be to me.'' She smiled, softly like rain. ''I don't know anything about what's to come. I'm afraid.''

She should be. He tried to close his mind against the images sweeping through his brain. Since he was a boy younger than Emma was now, he'd witnessed the cycle of life. It was hard to miss living on a breeding farm. From mating to foaling, Jacob grew to manhood understanding it, seeing the brutal coupling and the complications of pregnancy and the amazing life that slipped into the world wet and wide-eyed and confused.

He had also seen stillbirths, foals unable to live, dams that died for too many reasons.

And then there was Mary. He hadn't been allowed to see her, hadn't been allowed at her bedside while she died giving birth to Emma. He'd been forced to wait in the parlor, his capable hands useless, listening to the frightening silence upstairs.

Fear tingled through his entire body. He tried not to show it as he looked at Elizabeth. He didn't want to frighten her. She sat so serene, only the anxiety dark in her eyes gave away her fears. The lamplight bathed her face with a soft glow, and her chin sat propped in one hand.

''Would you like me to read to you?'' he asked.

Gratitude shone in her eyes. ''Please, Jacob.''

He reached for the volume and tried to quiet the dark thoughts driving through his head like the winter snow.

Chapter Twenty

By the time day broke, Libby couldn't endure the pain. She allowed Jacob to guide her to bed and lay her down with a plump stack of pillows.

Sharp, gripping pain seized her insides, ripping down her back and her abdomen, streaking down her legs. She froze until the pain passed, relaxing into the pillows.

Never had her body felt so out of control. Pain ripped through her in predictable, rhythmic clinches. She felt unable to stop them, unable to control them. She wondered if this was normal. She feared it was not.

"I'm fine," she assured Jacob, even if it wasn't the truth. "You need to fix breakfast for you and Emma."

"I'll make pancakes." He reached out to brush tousled hair from her bangs. "You'll need to tie this back."

Libby closed her eyes, sighing. She had forgotten about her hair. She didn't want to move now.

"I'll plait it for you." He stood, finding her brush.

Libby concentrated on the comforting everyday task of brushing her hair and then separating the strands for Jacob. He sat on the bed behind her, silent and intent on his work. What was he thinking?

He wove strands of her hair back and forth, over and under, tugging lightly. His touch felt comforting. Yet he was so silent. She worried something could be wrong—and there was no way to fetch the doctor. The storm still raged.

Libby tried to keep her fears from taking root in her mind. A sensible woman knew babies were born all the time and mothers lived. Anyone could see she was healthy and the pregnancy trouble free. There was no need to worry.

Jacob tied the long end of her braid and plumped the pillows behind her. One look at his face told her of the fear he held so quietly inside. Lines drew down his mouth and eyes. His hand trembled when he snatched the brush from the quilt.

Libby touched the rings of that pattern, wondering about the woman who had given her life. Had she lain beneath this quilt, waiting for her baby to be born—Libby—worrying how it might end, staying silent about those unspoken, horrible fears?

"I'll be in the kitchen if you need me." Jacob wouldn't meet her gaze. He walked with an uneven gait, his shoulders stooped.

The snow pounded the cabin walls, grating against her nerves, and the soulless howl of the wind made her feel small and alone. She listened to Emma's voice in the kitchen asking about the baby, and she squeezed the tears from her eyes.

No matter how hard she had tried to ignore it, how hard she had refused to think of it, she loved this baby. She wanted this small life more than anything.

If she were lucky, maybe it would be all right.

* * *

There was no break in the pounding storm, and Jacob hung his head. He had hoped to have the doctor by now, the fairly capable man who would know how to do what he could not. He did not want to see Elizabeth's baby into the world—he had no experience with human babies. But Jacob knew he had little choice with the fierce battering of the howling wind and snow.

Emma insisted on staying on the bed with Elizabeth. The woman, pale with pain, tolerated the child's bright excitement with her gentle smile.

What if something went wrong?

Unable to think of it, he had to turn away.

"Pa?" Her need called him back. Emma sat against the wall, hugging the doll Elizabeth had so lovingly made her. Beth was dressed in a pretty nightgown for staying in bed all day. "How long does it take for the baby to be born?"

"I don't know," he answered quietly.

His heart twisted as Elizabeth brushed an unruly strand of hair from the girl's wide eyes. "Babies take as long as they need to," she said in that warm way of hers. "We might as well get used to it."

"I know how you're going to feed her," Emma said boldly, and Jacob headed toward the door.

Outside the room, he didn't bother to pretend. Fear drained him, and he felt inadequate to the task. He was no doctor. He wouldn't know what to do if something went wrong.

"Emma." He called out sharply. "Emma, come here."

She came with a flurry of flyaway, unbraided hair, bright yellow dress bobbing, her bare feet pounding the wood floor.

"I want you to stay in this room from now on." He

hated being cold and harsh, but it was for the best. What if something went wrong? He didn't want Emma exposed to it.

Of course, he should have thought of that earlier. She already loved Elizabeth. If Elizabeth died... *Stop it.* He couldn't bear thinking it.

"But I want to see the baby born." She looked up at him uncertainly.

"I said no. Elizabeth is going to be busy enough without a little girl to worry about."

Emma's face fell, but she said nothing. She walked stiffly toward the braided rug before the fire and sat down. She hugged her doll to her and stared into the flames. She sniffed once, but that was all.

Hell, he hadn't meant to be so harsh. His nerves felt frayed, at the edge of holding on. He leaned against the doorjamb. He was just so damn afraid. Women died in childbirth.

Jacob stepped into Elizabeth's room and closed the door.

Something was wrong. Libby was certain of it. Pain gripped her in an almost steady, unmerciful grip and still no baby, no sign of a baby. She felt as if one great claw gripped her insides and kept clamping and slicing. Sweat beaded on her brow and between her breasts and down her back. *This pain was never going to end.*

She clenched her teeth trying not to cry out, but pain forced a groan from her raw throat. Relief shivered through her when she saw a shadow in the doorway. Jacob eased back into the room with a fresh pan of water.

He sat down and wrung out a washcloth. Capable hands.

Dependable shoulders. The sight of him soothed her fears. Jacob wouldn't let anything happen to her. She felt stronger.

"Do you think it will be much longer now?" She had to ask.

He gave her the cool, wet cloth, and it felt so wonderful in her hand. She wiped her own face and neck, too weary to hold back the horrible moan when a fresh squeeze of pain clamped through her.

"I'll see." He lifted away the sheet and hiked up her nightgown. "I don't see a head yet."

Disappointment tore through her. She couldn't take much more of this. The day had passed. The storm still raged. There was only this horrible haze of pain. *Something had to be wrong.*

Jacob smoothed her nightgown over her calves, a furrow of concern dug deep into his forehead. *He was worried, too.*

A new wave of pain tore through her lower back, ready to split her in two.

"Jacob." She groped for his hand. She hated looking weak, crying out for him.

But his grip felt strong and comforting. "I've done everything I can, Elizabeth. We have to wait."

"I can't wait." She whined, and shame flooded her. Libby prided herself on being strong, stoic, unbreakable. But her self-control snapped with another agonizing contraction.

Jacob took the washcloth from her hand and wet it again, wrung out the excess, bathed her face. "Does this help?"

"No." Tears brimmed her eyes. "Oh, God. I hurt. think the baby is dead."

Jacob closed his eyes. Babies did die. "We can't think about that, Elizabeth. Here, hold my hand."

Tears ran helplessly down her face. He couldn't help her. He couldn't stop her pain. All he could do was to brush her tears away.

"Jacob!" Her hand clutched his and she sat up in bed "Jacob!" She screamed, and the sound tore through the small stillness of the room. Elizabeth flew into his arms pressing her face into the hollow of his throat, filling hand fuls of his shirt in her small fists.

Every instinct in his gut twisted hard. He rocked he gently, breaking a little. How he cared for her. He care for her so much he couldn't stand the thought of losin her, too.

"Lean back into the pillows," he whispered, but sh didn't hear him. He could feel the pain in her body, fee the way she trembled as the contraction bore through he She cried out, stifling a scream against his shirt collar.

"Hold me," she begged.

His throat tightened and he could find no words. H wasn't enough for her, this woman in his arms. He wasn brave enough, strong enough, able to save her from th horrible pain.

She screamed again, panting raggedly, and he closed h eyes, completely lost.

"Jacob. I—I can feel the baby." Excitement lightene the heavy pain in her voice. She gazed up at him wi wonder. "I can feel the baby move down."

Tears streamed across her face. As the lamplight washe over her, they sparkled like diamonds.

"Oh, Jacob, the baby is coming." Relief smiled in her eyes as she leaned back on her elbows, her face pinching as she bore down.

He didn't dare hope. Feeling broken, Jacob pulled up her nightgown and sat down at her feet. He saw the shadow of a baby's head like a rainbow at the end of a storm. Hope eased into his heart. He looked up over Elizabeth's knees, and he smiled at her.

Exhaustion rimmed her eyes, drew lines in her face and paled her complexion, but he'd never seen her more beautiful. She panted again, wincing as she tried to push the new life from her body.

Jacob could cup that head with his palm. He could feel Elizabeth's body bunch and push, stretching around the head that slipped out into his hand.

Two blue eyes stared up at him in complete amazement. Wonder washed over him and he laughed.

"It's a girl," Jacob choked. He laid a squirming tiny bit of life on her stomach, and Libby leaned just enough to see that the baby was alive.

Five of the tiniest, most perfectly shaped fingers waved in the air, and she caught that hand with hers. Pink and wet, the baby girl gripped her one finger with all five of hers, holding on so tightly Libby could feel her need.

All the love in the world bubbled out of her heart. More love than she ever imagined. Libby trembled with the wonder as Jacob wrapped the baby in a soft towel.

"Oh, Emma, come in." She saw the shadow of the girl standing in the doorway and she beckoned her forward. "Come see my new little baby."

Emma padded across the room, wary of her father, and came to stand beside the pillows. Together they gazed down at the little face, round like a full moon. Bright blue eyes stared toward the light above them, and Libby's heart broke in two.

"Now I have two little girls to love," she said quietly, reaching down to kiss that soft little forehead. Tiny fingers grabbed at her hair and she worked the strands free.

"She's grimy," Emma observed.

Libby couldn't tell what Jacob was thinking as he leaned forward.

"I need to clean off the baby," he said.

He sounded clinical and distant. Was he angry? Her heart squeezed as he lifted the little bundle from her arms. He didn't look at her. He didn't speak. Libby's heart ached as she watched him leave.

"What are you going to name her?" Emma eagerly sat on the bed.

"I don't know. I was hoping you might help me think of a name."

Emma's fingers squeezed hers. "Well, name her after who you love most."

"Then I will name her after my mother and after you." Old, unshed tears from a lifetime ago filled up Libby's throat. She knew now love could hurt, too.

Jacob held the tiny girl in his hands. He tried not to look at her. She was red and wrinkled and so small she could fit into both of his hands. Wet honey blond hair clung to her delicate head.

He carefully tested the water to make sure it wasn't too hot before he began to sponge off the baby. He tried to hold back his heart. She waved her fisted hands and threw back her arms in protest. Her old-woman face scrunched up and she cried.

He said nothing. He kept sponging her off, trying not to hear the need in her wails.

"Pa, she's *awful* loud." Emma padded to a stop beside him. Her brown head bobbed as she studied the newborn. "Libby said she needed you. Her stomach hurts again."

The afterbirth. Jacob laid down the washcloth and wrapped the baby in a soft towel. Emma trailed after him as he knelt down on the braided rung. Heat radiated from the healthy fire, and he laid down the baby a safe distance from the hearth.

"Stay here and watch her. Don't pick her up. Be careful with her." Jacob walked away, unwilling to witness the love shining like the sky in his daughter's eyes.

He felt so cold inside. So frozen.

Elizabeth smiled at him and lifted her head from the pillow. Damp tendrils clung in dark swatches to her forehead. "Is she all right?"

"Yes." He sat down on the chair and took her hand. "Looks like you need me to take care of this."

"If you don't mind." An apology shone in her eyes. "I'm sorry you had to do this for me. I know you didn't want to."

"That's not it." Jacob stood up and turned away, the pain in his old heart hurting too much. "Where do you keep your rags?"

Elizabeth blushed. "In the top left-hand drawer of the bureau," she answered quietly. "I've never had anyone take care of me before. Thank you for staying."

Jacob's throat filled, thickening with an emotion he

didn't want. "You don't have to thank me. I wouldn't leave you alone, Elizabeth."

Their gazes met, then locked across the small room. Jacob watched her face soften, watched tears fill her eyes. He didn't want her tears. He didn't want to love her. Fear still rocked him over the chance she'd taken. *What if she had died tonight?*

He rummaged through the drawer and found the soft muslin rags and clean underthings. "I'll take away the sheets and bring you in some water to wash with."

"I guess I am a mess," she answered shakily.

Jacob shrugged. "This is just a part of life, Elizabeth." He handed her the rags to tie for herself.

She gazed up at him. "Isn't she beautiful, Jacob?"

His throat closed. She was proud of her new daughter. She didn't mean to draw him closer, didn't mean to make him remember.

"Yes," he said, because it was what Elizabeth needed to hear. "You did a perfect job. You have a beautiful baby."

"Thank you." Tears winked in her eyes. "I've never been so happy."

Jacob turned away. "I need the sheets," he said quietly, remembering why he'd entered the room. "Emma is watching the baby. When you're washed up, I'll bring her back in to you."

"She sounds hungry," Elizabeth smiled at him.

Thin, tentative wails murmured through the walls. "Will you be all right?" he asked.

Weariness darkened her eyes, exhaustion lined her face, but she smiled. "I've never been better."

* * *

Oh, it felt like heaven to wrap little Charlotte Emma in the new gown. Libby smoothed the warm fabric over that tiny body. The bright yellow pattern was the same as the dress Emma wore.

"I'm glad I picked this out," she said now.

"So am I." Libby's smile warmed her from head to toe and all the way through. She never knew a smile could do that. "Look, we'll put on the red socks that match."

Emma snatched up the socks and presented them to her. She stared at the things, larger than necessary, and pulled them onto those tiny, perfect feet.

"Is her head going to stay like that?" Emma wanted to know.

"No." Libby smoothed her hand over the slightly coned shape. "Do you want to pick out a hat for her?"

The girl rummaged through the small knit caps and found one to match her socks. Bright red. Libby smiled at the color.

Jacob's boots sounded in the lean-to, and she felt the cool nip in the air as the pounding wind drove inside the house. The door slammed, shutting out the sound of the storm.

"How's Holly?" Emma called, not wanting to leave the baby.

"Shh," Libby reminded her. Emma covered her mouth, shrugged, then scampered off to talk to her father.

Leaving Libby alone with her own daughter. *Her daughter.* She studied her baby. Dressed and snug, Lottie now slept soundly after a small meal and a lot of comfort. Her eyes were screwed tight against the new sensation of light.

In all of her life, Libby had never imagined this. She touched the small moon face, so red and wrinkly. Lottie's skin felt as soft as a new kitten. She ran a loving finger gently across those chubby cheeks and little nose.

She felt his gaze and looked up.

Jacob stood at the table with a cup of coffee in one hand. His shirt was half-buttoned, showing the gray wool of his long johns beneath. Dark ebony hair scattered across his forehead and stubble clung to his jaw. She read the exhaustion shadowed beneath his eyes.

"You shouldn't be up. You need to stay in bed." Concern dug deep lines in his forehead.

Libby's heart sank. He seemed so distant. Even now he stood with the entire length of the room firmly between them.

"I feel fine. I don't want to lie down when there's so much to be done." Libby glanced down at her baby. "I've missed a whole day's worth of work. And think of the sheets I've soiled."

"I said I'd do the washing." Jacob's jaw worked, and he hung his head. Without saying more, he spooned sugar into the cup and stirred.

Libby looked away. She could feel his sorrow but didn't understand it. All of her dreams felt like sand in her throat.

What did you expect? She couldn't expect a man to love another man's child. Not even Jacob. Libby closed her eyes.

"Here. This is for you."

She looked up the solid length of him. His trousers were wrinkled. He bent down to set the full cup of coffee on the floor beside her.

She stared at the cup, filled to the rim. Tears burned at the back of her eyes. She knew he loved her. But was it enough?

Libby cleared the sadness from her throat. "Thank you, Jacob."

He only shrugged. "You missed supper. Are you hungry?"

Libby smiled. "I'm ravenous. It's a good thing I baked a whole pot of beans when I did. It will be easy for you to warm up." Her smile faded.

Jacob turned away. "I want you to stay right here. I don't want you to do anything more than rest."

Her heart twisted at the concern in his voice and at the love he tried to hide. He was afraid. Libby listened to his heavy, uneven footsteps limp from the room.

Who wasn't afraid of living? She touched a soft finger to Lottie's relaxed hand. There was so much to lose, so much to hurt, so much pain.

But look at what could happen. Libby traced those tiny pink perfect fingers. Love and joy and happiness. It all went hand in hand.

Chapter Twenty-One

Jacob leaned one shoulder against the wall and stared at the rumpled bed he felt too tired to change. The tick needed to be emptied and scrubbed clean. He closed his eyes. He didn't mind the work.

She could have died last night.

The unbearable bleakness gripped his heart. He'd made himself too vulnerable, damn it. Caring for her hadn't made him immune to pain, to the possibility of loss. To the darkness descending over him.

Closing off his heart, Jacob bent to the sheets and dropped them on the floor. He hauled the tick off the frame, the ropes creaking in protest. He would concentrate on work. That always made the darkness more bearable.

She was still there, in the middle of the front room, sipping her coffee, her wheat-ripe hair burnished liquid gold in the firelight. Her blue skirts swept the rug around her, and she turned her gaze from the sleeping baby to him.

He looked away. Emma hopped in with her Mother Goose book, chattering on, telling him how she was going to read to Lottie.

Jacob's heart pounded. Elizabeth had named the baby.

He felt numb. Somehow he managed to say something appropriate as he pushed the tick across the varnished puncheon floor. The mattress slid easily along the wood surface, and he skirted around the corners of the large rug where Elizabeth sat so quietly.

Go to her. She could make this better.

But he couldn't. Even looking at her emphasized what he could lose.

He reached the corner of the fireplace where the stone wall edged the kitchen, and he looked back. He saw them framed by the white-and-blue braid of the rug. Emma sat with the big book in her lap and searched through the pages for her favorite rhyme. The firelight glowed golden off the length of Elizabeth's braid. Between them lay the small, brightly clad baby.

He concentrated on doing what he could. Emptying the tick. Filling it. Putting the beans on to warm and boiling up another pot of coffee.

Libby smiled at the baby suckling at her breast. This was such a new sensation, one little Lottie had finally mastered. Nursing earnestly, she blinked up at Libby with her curious blue eyes.

Jacob stepped into the room and froze. His gaze fell to her exposed breast, embarrassment staining his face. He took one step back into the kitchen.

"It's all right," she told him. "You've seen more of me than this."

"Yes." He bowed his head, and she could not see what he might be thinking. "I was going to bank the fires. Will you be up much longer?"

''No.'' She could already feel Lottie's contentment and smiled down at her daughter. ''We're almost done here.''

She heard Jacob's uneven gait cross the wood floor. He hesitated by her side, then set something heavy down on the braided rug.

A cradle. A handmade, hand-carved cradle.

''She'll need something to sleep in,'' he said, uncertainty ringing in his voice.

''Jacob. It's beautiful.'' She stared at the cradle crafted from smoothly polished pine. Small raised flowers were carved into the wood. She wondered what his gift meant. ''This took so much time to make. You must have started it months ago.''

''Not that long. I've been working on it at the livery. With the storms, business is slow.''

He stood so close, yet felt so distant.

''This gift means a lot to me.'' Her whole heart squeezed.

He only shrugged.

Lottie began to doze, and Libby detached her from her breast. But before she could cover herself, Jacob knelt down beside her.

His hands covered hers. ''Let me.''

She sat still, her heart fluttering as light as air. Jacob's big fingers closed her dress front and buttoned the small round buttons.

''Can I hold her?''

She saw the loneliness in his eyes. ''Yes.''

Jacob gathered the baby from her arms, cradling the small, wobbly head in his huge hand. He rose, carrying Lottie.

He folded himself into the rocker, so close she could

reach out and touch him. He took such care with the baby. The small blanket had fallen away, revealing her bright yellow gown. Lottie slept, unaware of the big man who held her and the pain in his face.

"I was the first person to hold her," he said, his voice so tight it cracked.

"Yes."

"I walked away from Emma when she was as helpless as this." Unshed tears thickened his voice, and his shoulders slumped a bit. "I didn't even hold her. I just walked out the door and never came back, never came home until after the war."

"You didn't stay to see your Mary buried?" Libby asked into the silence.

"No."

Sadness hung in the air, weighted by Jacob's confession. The scouring wind outside howled, the clock ticked and measured the passing of each minute, but the stillness between them remained.

"I should have stayed, picked up the pieces of my life, been a good father to Emma." Jacob lifted the baby to his chest and tenderly laid her against him, sheltering her in the strong curve between his throat and shoulder. "Instead, I ran."

"You must have loved her very much." Libby rose from her chair and knelt down carefully before him.

"Yes. Both Mary and Emma." His throat worked. Pain lived on his face, ached in his eyes. "I left her with my mother because I couldn't be a good father to her. Do you understand? I didn't run away because I didn't want her."

Libby could feel the truth so painful in his eyes. "I know. You love Emma more than your life."

"I do." He waited. "I can't do this, Elizabeth. I can't give you what you want."

Libby laid her hand tenderly on Lottie's warm back. "What can't you give me, Jacob?"

"The love you deserve." He looked up and tears of grief filled his eyes. "This is just too much to lose. I can't do it. Go ahead and hate me for it."

Anyone could see his scarred heart. "I could never hate you, Jacob."

"I thought I could do it."

"I know." She touched his cheek, feeling the rough-smooth texture of his unshaven jaw. "Why don't we see what happens? You don't need to make a decision now."

He only nodded.

"Elizabeth?"

"Yes?"

"It isn't the baby." His voice broke. "I wanted you to know."

"I know." Tears burned in her eyes. Tears of sadness because she would never know another fine, gentle man like him. "Whatever happens, I love you."

Jacob swallowed hard, loneliness so dark in his eyes. "Hold me. I need you to hold me."

Libby set the baby down in her new cradle before he pulled her against his solid chest. She wanted him so much, yet today everything had changed. Except for the way she loved him.

Jacob tried. He really did. He stayed in the house with Elizabeth and did the chores so she could recover from the birth. The blizzard blew out midafternoon, and he fetched the doctor from town, just in case. Elizabeth and the baby were pronounced healthy. Nothing was wrong.

The next morning Elizabeth swore she was fine, and her color was good. He took Emma to school and came back near noon to check on her.

Every day she looked healthier. The tiny baby remained strong.

Sometimes, when he was working over the forge or exercising a horse, the fear would hit him with the thundering speed of a train. He never told Elizabeth how much he loved her, because he couldn't.

Damn it, he couldn't.

He could lose her. And then nothing, nothing could save him.

Libby watched Jacob's silence, felt his distance, saw the shadows in his eyes. He was friendly and polite, bringing in water before she could ask for it, keeping the wood stacked near the hearth, bringing groceries from town.

As she readied Emma for school in the morning and put breakfast on the table, she half expected Jacob to meet her gaze and confide in her. To tell her he needed some time to come to terms with the past. But he consistently avoided her, kept his eyes low, spoke only when necessary.

He'd shut her out of his heart completely. Libby felt hurt and amazed he could so easily erase what they'd shared together. How could he keep his heart so cold, his life so empty and not remember the tenderness of their lovemaking, turn his back on the soul-binding power of their love?

As she sat in the quiet cabin, nursing Lottie in the mornings after Emma and Jacob left, she did not know if he would change, if he could give his heart. And had it been only her, as it had from the beginning, she might stay, she might be able to give Jacob whatever it took to help him heal the bleakness in his heart.

But she wasn't alone. Not anymore.

"Jacob?" She pushed open the stable door. A pool of light gleamed in the darkness. Several horses turned to study her curiously. Star nickered.

He emerged from the farthest stall, pitchfork in hand. "Do you need me to carry in more wood for you?"

"No." Libby unwrapped her shawl, scattering snow to the board floor. No asking how she was. No smile. "You've stacked enough wood to see me through an entire blizzard."

"I just don't want you doing more than you have to." He sounded gruff. He turned and went back to his work.

He cared for her. Why else would he worry so about her health? Why else would he do the little chores that made her life so easy? Yet he might as well be standing in another town, the distance between them felt so great.

"I thought we could talk." She watched him freeze, his strong shoulders tighten, his head bow.

"There's nothing I want to talk about, Elizabeth. I'm busy here."

She'd never seen eyes as sad as his. "Jacob, you won't talk to me in the cabin."

"What do you mean? I was sitting at the table directly across from you."

"You didn't look as if you wanted to talk to me." Her heart twisted. She held her breath. Then, "Jacob, Emma needs another slate. There was an unexplained accident at Mrs. Holt's.''

"I'll see she gets a new one." His knuckles turned white as he tightened his hold on the pitchfork.

"I can't keep going on like this."

"I know." He kept pitching.

"Something has to change." She wanted to shake him out of this dreadful politeness. But she held back, uncertain. So uncertain. "I used to dream of a friendly marriage, not the cold silences of my aunt and uncle's marriage. I don't want this for Emma or for Lottie."

His throat worked. "Neither do I. Emma is miserable."

"And so am I." Libby's voice broke.

His gaze shuttered as he studied her. "I thought a friendly existence was enough, too. I was wrong. I can't love you the way you deserve, Elizabeth. I wish—" He stopped.

"Oh, Jacob." She ached to take him in her arms and hold him, give him the comfort he needed. A world of doubts held her back. Would he ever, truly need her? The distance between them felt like an ocean.

She took a breath, said what was on her mind. "You'll give me a reason why I should stay, why I should believe, won't you?"

His movements stilled. He set down his pitchfork. "No, Elizabeth," he said quietly. His cold gray eyes focused on hers, full of bleakness. "I never made you any promises."

"Promises?" Heart rending, she fisted her hands. Pain and anger swept over her fast, hard, blinding. "I didn't ask for promises. I want your heart. I want you to stop tolerating me. I want—"

"Tolerating you?" He winced. Stepped closer. "Don't

you know——'' He stopped. ''I don't have the heart for a real marriage. I thought——'' He stared down at his big empty hands.

''I'm asking for you to love me, Jacob. That's all.'' It wasn't so much. Yet it was everything.

Only the grayness in his eyes answered.

''I can't believe you. How can you let this die between us?''

He could stand there so still, so silent and her entire world was breaking. She knew what they'd shared together was merely a dream, too good to be true. *Fairy tales don't happen to you, Libby Hodges.* But she'd had a glimpse of happiness, of love and family and a deep abiding connection with Jacob that felt as wide as eternity. And she'd hoped——

It hadn't meant that to him. *She* hadn't meant that to him. He would never let go of his fears, of his past, and embrace this life and her love.

''Do something, Jacob. Is there anything I can do to help you?''

He lifted a shoulder in a one-sided shrug. ''Emma needs you. Please——''

''This isn't about Emma.'' Though her heart cracked at the thought of leaving the child. ''It's about your heart and what you won't give me. Some people have nothing, Jacob. No family, no home, no sunshine of a daughter waiting to fill up their lonely lives. Nothing, do you understand?''

''Yes.'' Eyes so deep, so filled with pain, met hers without excuse. His throat worked. ''But I could have lost you.''

"So that's why you're refusing to love me now? Why you're letting me leave?"

"You're leaving?" His face hardened. It was difficult to read what flickered in his eyes.

"Yes. As I see it, I have little choice." She had to go. She wouldn't spend her life begging for any man's love, endlessly hoping and waiting for something that might never happen. "I'll be moving back to town today." *Unless you would change your mind, your heart.*

Please, she silently prayed.

"I can't let you go." His voice broke. "You can stay here, I thought we were getting along well. I thought—"

"Being your housekeeper isn't enough." She stopped, tried to hold back the bright fire of anger popping in her chest. "I love you, Jacob."

She turned, tears smarting her eyes, and hurried toward the open stable doors.

"Elizabeth." His voice called her back. "You just can't leave with a new baby and no way to support yourself. Where would you go?"

Fury, blinding hot, bolted through her. Maybe leaving was the right thing. There was no hope for him, no chance he would ever give her his heart.

"That's what you're worried about? How I'll support myself?" She shoved her fisted hands in her cloak pockets. All her life she'd lived peaceably, never dreaming of harming another, but now she wanted to take the handle of that pitchfork and use it to smack some sense into him.

"It's a cruel world," he said reasonably. "You said yourself you can't work and take care of a baby at the same time."

"I'll be fine. I have savings. I can work." What she

didn't have was him. When the snows left and the stage ran again, she would head to her aunt in Chicago, to that home of cold silences. But she needn't stay there long. In time, she would be on her feet again, able to support both herself and Lottie. "Don't worry about me, Jacob Stone."

"But, I—" Emotion shadowed his eyes, and he looked for a second as if... But no, he stared down at the ground. "I could give you the shanty I keep out behind the livery. It's snug and sturdy. You could live there as long as you want."

"I'm staying with Maude. I spoke with her yesterday."

"It's decided then." He paused, then his shoulders slumped.

Why wouldn't he fight? Libby's heart had never hurt like this. And as angry as she was, she could plainly see he was hurting, too. She'd changed the rules. He'd been perfectly clear at the start stating what he could offer her and what he would not. *You will be my wife in name only. Not in my heart and not in my bed.* She was in his bed. Could she be in his heart, too?

She stepped closer and laid her hand on his arm, aware of his solid male strength and heat beneath the flannel of his shirt. A good man she loved with every bit of her heart. "I have Lottie now, Jacob. I can't be depending on a man who isn't my husband."

He covered her hand with his. "I'll keep Star in the livery for you. For free. Let me do this small thing if you won't accept anything else from me."

She hesitated, weighing his words, weighing what his gift of the mare had meant to him. Pride strengthened her. Anger sharpened her voice. "I want your love, Jacob.

Nothing else. You might as well keep the mare, keep her for Emma.''

His eyes winced. "I see."

She watched his fists clench, felt his pain filling the barn like a cold wind. She could not forget the power of loving him, could not erase the tides of her heart. Once, a safe home and a kind man sounded like paradise. Now, it was not enough for her or her daughter.

Libby forced herself to walk away, the most difficult steps she'd ever taken.

Jacob kept a tight rein on his heart. He could not allow himself to feel anything—no grief, no anger. It was better that way.

He loaded Elizabeth's few possessions, one small crate and two carpet bags, into the back of his sled, determined not to look at her. But her morning-soft voice, rich and drawing, tugged at him whenever he stepped into the cabin to haul out another satchel of her belongings.

''No, you can't go,'' Emma's high voice broke into tears, echoing in the kitchen.

Jacob staggered, as if an arrow had pierced his heart. If only he could keep Emma from being hurt, from knowing loss and grief. He didn't want his daughter hurt. He stopped, almost wondered if he could try. If maybe...

''I've already told your pa, Emma. You know that. He's loading the little sleigh for me right now.''

''*Nooo.*''

The tortured pain rang in her voice. He screwed shut his eyes. Grief washed over him like an ocean, cold and dark and suffocating. He couldn't let her go. He couldn't let her stay. And Emma—

"Make her stay, Pa!" Desperate words.

He looked down into her tear-filled eyes, at Mary's eyes, and his heart crumbled. The sheer impact of loving Elizabeth and now of losing her terrified him beyond his ability to endure. He had so much to lose and nothing, nothing terrified him more.

"It's Elizabeth's decision," he managed to reply.

"Pa!" Emma stomped her foot. "Pa, you can't let her go. She's going to be my mother now. I have a baby sister and everything."

"There'll be no argument." He cleared his throat and gazed into Elizabeth's eyes.

So clear, so deep and angry. "Have it your way, Jacob," she said. "Goodbye."

"No, Libby, you have to stay here with me!" Emma cried with all of her broken heart. "Pa, please, please, please make her stay!"

Elizabeth looked down, lifted her cloak from the wooden peg by the door and methodically slipped into the worn garment. "I'm sorry, Emma. Maybe you could walk me to the sleigh."

"No. You can't leave me." Emma's pain nearly broke him.

He swallowed hard and opened the door, tried hard to be different. For Emma. "Elizabeth, maybe you could wait and see. Maybe—"

"This is goodbye, Jacob," she whispered, her voice wobbling, then knelt to gather up her baby.

Stop her, his heart demanded. *Keep her from walking away.* He could reach out now and grab her back into the safety of his arms. Keep her here and keep trying—

Emma burst into tears and ran out the door after Elizabeth. He leaned against the door frame and watched the gentle love in her touch as she brushed away Emma's tears, then knelt to give her a goodbye hug.

Jacob stepped out onto the porch. Elizabeth granted him one last smile before climbing into the sleigh. Every feeling in his heart welled into his throat and he fought down those feelings. He could not risk changing his mind. He simply couldn't.

He watched her drive away, his heart shattering, Emma's grief as sad as the wind. Every step he took toward his little girl ached in his soul. She sat on the snow, crumpled and crying. Elizabeth's sleigh disappeared around the bend and was gone.

"You let her leave!" The accusation came sharp as a knife. "Pa, you have to go get her. You have to—"

Sobs tore up her throat, and he lifted little Emma from the frozen ground and into his arms, holding her tight, willing the pain from her heart. She was so delicate, so special. He wanted to protect her, save her from the same kind of grief.

Elizabeth could have died. It was all he could think about. And if he loved her again, there would be another baby, maybe another night of fear and death.

His heart squeezed. "Come inside, Emma."

"No!" She kicked and struggled, so full of pain.

He set her down and she raced into the cabin, her shoes striking the floor with a force that echoed through the suddenly empty rooms.

Jacob stood in the threshold, realization sweeping over him. His home was now a house again, his life merely an existence. Without Elizabeth, he was nothing.

A thud in Emma's room sent him into action. He

climbed the ladder to find her kneeling on the floor, tears staining her face, sobs racking her small body, shoving her beloved Beth doll into an opened satchel. All around her were Elizabeth's touches—the braided rug, the bright quilt, the rosebud ruffly curtains all made with a mother's loving hand.

"Emma, stop this." He knelt beside her, laid his big hand on her tiny shoulder.

Emma tilted up her face, tears raining down her cheeks. "I'm going to find Libby, Pa. I'm gonna go get her back."

"Precious, I don't think—"

"I love her," Emma sobbed, and he felt her heart breaking just as deeply as his own.

"I know, Emma." He closed his eyes, drawing her into his arms, holding her tight against his chest, this amazing blessing of a child. He felt her tears hot against his throat, staining his collar. And he held her until there were no more tears, only silence and the emptiness of a house—of a life—without Elizabeth.

Chapter Twenty-Two

Libby found help in her friends. Several of the women who lived in the boardinghouse offered to help out with Lottie. And Maude took the infant in her protective arms and cared for her daily so Libby could work.

Leah greeted her with a warm hug and an immediate offer of employment. There had been such a shortage of women in town who needed work, she hadn't found anyone to replace Libby.

It wasn't a bad life. Really. Working and caring for Lottie left Libby little time for dwelling on her loss, on her choices. She often wished, especially alone in her bed at night, that she had stayed, given Jacob more of a chance. She knew in her heart she couldn't fix what hurt inside him. Not even her love could do that.

She would look forward to her future with Lottie. The snows would soon melt and the stage would run again, and she would go on, without Jacob, no matter how much it hurt.

"Jacob, I told you no. Libby doesn't want it." Maude held the handful of gold coins in the palm of her hand.

He sighed. "She's got all she can do taking care of that baby. Let me do this for her. She doesn't need to know."

"Trust me, she knows. And she doesn't want such a trifling from you." Those wise eyes assessed him.

Jacob winced. "She won't accept anything else."

"She doesn't want you paying her rent." Maude laid the pile of gold on the top rail of the nearest board.

An appaloosa pony popped his head out of the stall and began lipping those eye-catching coins. Jacob rescued the gold. When he looked up, Maude was gone.

Elizabeth had refused even this small token from him. He felt so empty. Hurting for her at night, aching for her in the day, his life felt empty and bleak, she might as well have died the night she'd given birth. Lord knows his heart had.

And Emma... They tried to go on, the two of them, but nothing was the same without Elizabeth.

"Pa, I got a hole in my sock." Emma produced the offending article, a pretty red stocking Elizabeth had knitted while sitting in that empty chair before this very fire.

Jacob's gaze swiveled to the empty rocker, a physical reminder of everything he'd lost. "I guess we can see if the lady I pay to do our laundry can fix that hole for you."

"Libby could do it." So much hope in those eyes. So much sadness, too.

"No, Emma. Elizabeth doesn't belong with us." He said it, knowing it was a lie. Knowing the only reason she wasn't sitting in that chair, her knitting needles clacking above the snap and pop of the fire, was because of him.

He couldn't bury another wife. He couldn't lose another

future. He couldn't be responsible for another woman's death.

Emma sighed and walked off with the sock. He lifted his volume and stared at the title. *The Mill on the Floss.* Elizabeth would have enjoyed this book.

Just the thought of sharing a novel with her, read here before the cozy fire, filled him with loneliness, with loss. Not since he'd lost Mary had he felt so alone. For the first time in more years than he could count, he pined for the library in his father's home, the smell of something delicious baking in Mother's kitchen, the smell of bluegrass in spring.

Everything he'd held back, rushed over him like an avalanche, burying him with pieces of his old life, memories of joy he used to share there with his family and here in Elizabeth's arms. It all came together, became whole, his past and his present joined.

"Pa?" Emma walked toward him, dragging her feet. She used to skip and run before Elizabeth left. "I don't wanna go to school today."

Mrs. Holt was always Emma's biggest burden.

Jacob stood, stretched his aching leg. "I don't want to go to the livery today, either."

"You don't?" Confusion muddied Emma's big eyes.

He almost grinned. He was damn tired of burying himself in his work, in this wilderness, in his cabin without neighbors. Loneliness had a cure. And grief...well, maybe grief did, too. What was it Elizabeth had said? *Some people have nothing. No family, no home, no sunshine of a daughter waiting to fill up their lonely lives.*

He held out his hand and felt Emma wrap her small fingers around his, holding on. Need. It bound families, joined hearts and created life. Maybe it was all right to let himself need the love of his daughter. And more. He needed more.

"Let's go to Ellington's and pick out something just for you," he suggested. "Afterward I'll take you to dinner."

A small spark flickered in those sad eyes. "Can I have fried chicken? It's my favorite. Granny used to make it for me all the time."

"Sure." His throat ached.

He helped Emma into her wraps, bundling her well against the cold winds. She was precious. But the fact he could lose her didn't stop him from loving her. Life came with so many risks. Life, love, death. All had a season, a time and a place.

The world was so uncertain, nature sometimes cruel. But love, like a candle burning, could fill any darkness. Jacob gave Emma a little hug. He'd been so lonely without Elizabeth, living as if she no longer existed.

But she lived, and her love, like a candle, could help him find his way home.

"Pa, this isn't the diner," Emma pointed out. "This is a hotel."

"They serve fried chicken here, too." His heart rattled in his chest as he stared at the sign. Leah's hotel. Elizabeth worked here until the end of the week, when the stages started running again. Maude had told him so.

He took Emma by the hand and led her into the dining room. Neat, crisp, clean. And busy. Leah met them, surprise flashing across her wise face.

"Seat us in Elizabeth's section," he said quietly.

"Goody," Emma said as he settled her into a hard-backed chair. Then with wonder, "Pa, it's Libby."

Lord, she looked good. Like sunshine after a long winter. Bright. Shining. And slim. His gaze devoured her, tenderly remembering the shape of her shoulders, the curve of her neck, the way she dipped her chin. She wore a green calico dress and a white apron tied around her small waist. With her hair knotted at her nape, she looked more beautiful than when she'd first alighted from the stage, full of hope and dreams.

Then she turned, saw him. Surprise burned in her blue eyes, softened her dear face. She mouthed his name, Jacob.

Seeing the love in her eyes, feeling it answer in his heart, he had no choice, not anymore. He'd lost Mary, but he hadn't lost Elizabeth.

Life shone in her eyes, and the passion and affection she couldn't hide. She crossed the room, his heart stopped, his entire world stood still.

He didn't know what would happen in this life, but he needed the opportunity to love her completely, truly.

"Jacob. Emma." Love shimmered in her voice, even as she tried to hide it.

"Libby!"

Emma bounced off her chair and ran straight into Elizabeth's full skirts, wrapping both thin arms around the beloved woman's waist, holding on as if she never intended to let go.

"I'm so glad to see you, Emma." Elizabeth straightened away, lifting tentative fingers to brush the curls from Emma's happy eyes.

"You're looking well," Jacob managed to mumble. He

wanted to say so much more. He loved her. Deeply. Honestly. Without fear.

"Thank you." Elizabeth stiffened, set her chin. "What would you like for dinner? Fried chicken is the special today."

"That's what I want," Emma said happily.

"I knew you'd say that." Elizabeth smiled.

And knocked his heart off-kilter. "I'd like that, too."

"Chicken?" She lifted her brow.

No. You. But he managed to nod. "Maude mentioned you're leaving town at the end of the week."

Her eyes flashed, her chin lifted. "Yes. The stage is leaving and I'll be on it. I'm going to Chicago."

So much pride. Jacob's throat tightened. Did she want him? Was it too late? *You pushed her away, you damn fool. You tossed away the most precious of gifts. She isn't going to forgive you now.*

He couldn't leave without the question he had to ask her. But one look at her set face, her eyes flaring, made him hesitate.

"I'll be back with your meals," she said firmly, then flashed Emma a private smile.

"Pa, did you know Libby worked here?" Emma demanded.

His gaze swept across her button face, shining with love for the mother she'd chosen. His throat worked. "Yes, I knew. Why did you think I brought you here?"

"To get Libby?"

"To bring her home." The words felt so good, they filled his heart.

"Jacob Stone is still in the dining room waiting for you," Leah said, wiping her hands on a dish towel. "Did you want me to send him away?"

"No." Libby's heart ached. If only she didn't love him so much. "I want to see Emma one more time."

She carefully dried a dish and stacked it on the kitchen worktable.

"Then don't keep him waiting, honey. I'll finish up the dishes." Leah took the towel. "Go on, now."

With her heart held carefully, Libby pushed through the double kitchen doors and froze. Gentle sunshine filtered through the window, washing Jacob with lemony light. He looked so good, his shoulders just as dependable, his black hair a little longer, and the sound of his low rumbling voice melted her spine. He sat shoulder to shoulder with little Emma at the window, heads bowed together as they discussed the horses out on the street.

Her heart tugged. Father and daughter. They were so alike.

"Where's Lottie?" Emma asked, startling her from her thoughts.

Libby remembered to breathe. "My friend Maude is taking care of her while I work."

"Can I see her?" Such eager eyes.

Libby glanced at Jacob.

He stood. "Later, Emma. Right now I want to talk to Elizabeth."

"Jacob, no, I don't think there's anything more we have to say to one another." She took a step back. Love for him burned in her heart, true and pure and forever. But he didn't love her like that, he didn't—

"Elizabeth." He caught her hand. Tiny tendrils of sensation sizzled where he touched her. "This has been a hard month for me missing you."

She set her chin, pride fierce in her stance. "I'm leaving town."

"So am I." He paused, feeling awkward, hunting for the right words. "Maybe you could travel home with Emma and me."

No, that wasn't right. Her chin came up. Her hands fisted.

"I know I'm the one who changed, Jacob. I came here understanding we would begin as friends, but I thought in time we could have a good friendship. A real marriage. But you didn't want that, at least you don't want that with me. So why would I go to Kentucky with you?"

She wasn't angry; her voice rang warm and honest, gentle even when he'd hurt her. Her chin lifted, set firm with determination.

He looked into her eyes so gentle he could trust her with his life, with his future. He knew it was right, going home, bringing his life full circle, starting anew.

"You're a good man, Jacob. The best I've ever known. But I don't want you feeling as if you owe me something for loving you, for sharing a bed with you. You've given me more than any man, and it's enough. I don't need you anymore."

Like a gunshot to his heart, Jacob staggered. "I think you're lying."

"Think again." She headed toward the door with a swirl of green calico skirts, her head held high, her hands fisted. Too afraid to trust him, of being hurt again.

He followed her right out the door, down the steps and onto the icy street. "Elizabeth."

She whirled, faced him. The wind tugged at her skirts, teased wispy curls from her fashionable knot. Curls that brushed her face the way he ached to touch her. Unbidden, the image of loving in the dark, tender and soul-rending, flashed through his mind.

He dared to reach up and lay his palm against the soft curve of her jaw. "I could have lost you, Elizabeth. Something could have gone wrong during the birth."

"But it didn't."

"If something had gone wrong, I couldn't have saved you."

"Jacob, you already have."

It was true. She had saved him, too, made him whole, gave him a future. Looking into her honest blue eyes, he could see his own happiness, a new home on his Kentucky land, working long days beside his father, teaching two little girls to ride.

"Come live with me, Elizabeth. Let me show you I can be the man you need."

She dipped her chin. "Jacob, I'm not sure. You couldn't love me. I was only a friend to you, I—"

"You're wrong." In his heart, there was no more fear, only love. For her. For a future with her. "I love you and I'm not going to let you go."

"Jacob." Tears brimmed her eyes.

"I've been thinking about placing an advertisement for a wife," he said, taking her hand, holding it tight.

"An advertisement?" Her eyes widened, then she smiled. The busy street, the windy day, Emma watching from the window overhead melted away until there was only Elizabeth's smile, only her beautiful face.

"I'm looking for a real wife," he said. "Someone who

is kind, who has always wanted a daughter, who is strong enough to forgive me no matter what happens in this life.''

Hope as bright as dawn sparkled in her eyes. "What an amazing coincidence. I'm looking for a real husband. Someone to be a father to my daughter. Someone gentle enough to fill my whole life.''

Her skin felt soft, sweet with the memory of every time he'd loved her. Jacob felt renewed, like sunshine after winter. He felt strong, the way a new foal learns to run. Hope lived in his heart. They would marry, have more children.

"Come home with me, Elizabeth. Build a life with me. Build dreams with me.''

She stared up at him, forever shining in her eyes. "Only if you do me one favor.''

There was so much he wanted to give her, to share with her, to tell her about. The beautiful Kentucky hills, the scent of bluegrass, his mother's warm kitchen. "Anything.''

"Call me Libby.''

* * * * *

Coming in March 1998
from *New York Times* bestselling author

Jennifer Blake

**The truth means everything to Kane Benedict.
Telling it could destroy Regina Dalton's son.**

Down in Louisiana, family comes first—that's the rule
the Benedicts live by. So when a beautiful redhead starts
paying a little bit too much attention to his grandfather,
Kane decides to find out what the woman really wants.

But Regina's not about to tell Kane the truth—that she's
being blackmailed and the extortionist wants Kane's
grandfather's business…or that the life of her son is
now at stake.

Available where books are sold.

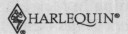

Not The Same Old Story!

Exciting, glamorous romance stories that take readers around the world.

Sparkling, fresh and tender love stories that bring you pure romance.

HARLEQUIN *Temptation*
Bold and adventurous— Temptation is strong women, bad boys, great sex!

Provocative and realistic stories that celebrate life and love.

HARLEQUIN
AMERICAN ROMANCE
Contemporary fairy tales—where anything is possible and where dreams come true.

HARLEQUIN
INTRIGUE
Heart-stopping, suspenseful adventures that combine the best of romance and mystery.

LOVE & LAUGHTER
Humorous and romantic stories that capture the lighter side of love.

DEBBIE MACOMBER

invites you to the

HEART OF TEXAS

Join Debbie Macomber as she brings you the lives
and loves of the folks in the ranching community
of Promise, Texas.

If you loved Midnight Sons—don't miss
Heart of Texas! A brand-new six-book series
from Debbie Macomber.

Available in February 1998
at your favorite retail store.

Heart of Texas by Debbie Macomber

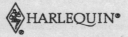

HARLEQUIN®

Available in March
from *New York Times* bestselling author

ELIZABETH LOWELL

Carlson Raven had no choice but to rescue Janna Morgan—
the beautiful, courageous woman who struggled against the
stormy sea. When he pulled her from the choppy waters and
revived her with the heat of his body, his yearning was as
unexpected as it was enduring.

But Carlson was as untamed and enigmatic as the sea he
loved. Would Janna be the woman to capture his wild and
lonely heart?

LOVE SONG FOR A RAVEN

Available in March 1998
wherever books are sold.

MIRA BOOKS **The Brightest Stars in Women's Fiction.™**

Welcome to *Love Inspired*™

**A brand-new series of contemporary
inspirational love stories.**

Join men and women as they learn valuable lessons
about facing the challenges of today's world and
about life, love and faith.

**Look for the following March 1998
Love Inspired™ titles:**

**CHILD OF HER HEART
by Irene Brand**

**A FATHER'S LOVE
by Cheryl Wolverton**

**WITH BABY IN MIND
by Arlene James**

Available in retail outlets in February 1998.

LIFT YOUR SPIRITS AND GLADDEN YOUR HEART
with *Love Inspired!*™

Steeple
Hill™

LI398

**Look for these titles—
available at your favorite retail outlet!**

**BORN IN THE USA: Love, marriage—
and the pursuit of family!**